Murder on Consignment

By Susan Furlong Bolliger

Martin Sisters Publishing

Published by

Martin Sisters Publishing, LLC

www. martinsisterspublishing. com

Copyright © 2013 Susan Furlong Bolliger

The unauthorized reproduction or distribution of this copyrighted work is illegal. Criminal copyright infringement, including infringement without by monetary gain, is investigated by the Federal Bureau of Investigation and is punishable by up to 5 (five) years in federal prison and a fine of $250,000.

Names, characters and incidents depicted in this book are products of the author's imagination or are used fictitiously. Any resemblance to actual events, locales, organizations, or persons, living or dead, is entirely coincidental and beyond the intent of the author or publisher.

No part of this book may be reproduced or transmitted in any form or by any means, electronic or mechanical, including photocopying, recording, or by any information storage and retrieval system, without permission in writing from the publisher.

All rights reserved. Published in the United States by
Martin Sisters Publishing, LLC, Kentucky.
ISBN: 978-1-62553-060-8
Mystery
Printed in the United States of America
Martin Sisters Publishing, LLC

DEDICATION

For my father-in-law, Gary (1935-2012) — who showed me the ultimate example of dignity and grace.

ACKNOWLEDGEMENTS

This book could not have been accomplished without the help and support of my husband and our children. I also had help from friend and editor extraordinaire, Sandra Haven, whose feedback and expertise is always greatly valued. A huge thank you also goes to the fine people at Martin Sisters Publishing who dedicate themselves to bringing quality books to readers everywhere.

Also, a special shout-out to my sister, Rebecca. Your entrepreneurial spirit and skills in crafting, refurbishing and 'up-cycling' trash into treasure, inspired Pippi and all her wonderful projects.

Most of all, thank you the readers that have encouraged me to continue this series. It's turning out to be an amazing adventure.

Chapter 1

I was never good at saying "no." I needed to work on that, because I just uttered two "yeses" in less than an hour. More than likely, one of those "yeses" was going to land me in a heap of trouble.

My current "yes" was to my cousin, Cherry Gallagher. Yup, that's her real name. My Aunt Maeve, and her husband, Chuck the-sixties-were-good-to-me-Gallagher, wanted their children's names to reflect their ... um ... let's just call it, earthiness. Anyway, I knew better than to tell Cherry I'd be her maid of honor, even if it was a bridal emergency. After all, it's not my fault that her sister, Willow, (see what I mean about the name thing) recently landed in trouble with the law and, therefore, couldn't perform her maidenly duties.

I'm not sure why I told Cherry "yes." Perhaps I was distracted by the garbage bag I was digging through with one hand as I held my cell with the other. Multi-tasking never was my strong suit. Who knows? Somehow that "yes" just tumbled out and now I was stuck listening to her babble about wedding details—most of which I tuned out. That was until she got to the part about the dress I was going to be wearing.

"Orange?" I croaked. I replaced the trash can's lid and sat down on the curb, giving our phone conversation my full attention.

"No, not just orange; pumpkin orange. What could be better for a fall wedding?" she said, sounding like a color-blind salesclerk.

"I can't wear orange."

"You have to," she whined. "We already have the dress. I don't have time to order another one."

I shook my head. Didn't Cherry realize a curvaceous, okay, plump redhead in a pumpkin-colored dress was going to suck the class right out of her wedding? Of course, knowing that side of the family, there wasn't going to be an overabundance of class anyway.

I squeezed my eyes shut and took a deep breath. At least the wedding wasn't for a couple of weeks; maybe I could lose a few pounds by then. "Fine," I relented. "But, you'll be sorry when I arrive looking like a giant squash in three inch heels."

"Great! And, don't worry about throwing me a bachelorette party."

"A bachelorette party?" *What had I gotten myself into?*

"Yeah, Willow already gave me one. That's the night she was arrested. It was the wildest party I've ever been to! I wish you…"

"Hey, Cherry, I hate to cut you off, but I'm working right now. We'll have to talk about this later. Bye!" I snapped my phone shut. I was being rude, but at the moment, I had more important things to think about…like the other "yes" which I'd uttered just moments before Cherry called.

Now that "yes" was completely out of my control. I mean, how could I have said no when Sean Panelli, my ex-boyfriend and a detective on the Naperville Police Department, called and asked if I could come to a murder scene and give my expert opinion? Besides, I would do anything for a second chance with Sean. I always regretted the way things ended between us and was dying for a reason to see him again.

Luckily, at the moment, I was close to home, rummaging through garbage cans in the Bridgewater neighborhood of Aurora. Sean said he wouldn't need me until the technicians had gone over the scene, which was probably a good thing. A quick sniff told me I better wrap up early and allow time for a shower before coming face to face with Sean. Although he was familiar with all the down sides of my career as a used merchandiser, it wouldn't due to have him smell me like this. Three cans ago, I had to dig past three day old Thai takeout to get to a great little blue and white vase which wasn't worth much as it was; but, after I wired it and paired it with a cute shade, it would make an awesome customized lamp. I'd be able to sell it for a nice profit at the Third Saturday Flea Market. I loved my job! I never tired of the thrill of turning a profit on someone else's junk.

On the drive to my apartment, I thought about Sean. His tone had been completely professional. He needed my "expert" opinion on something and was sending an officer to my house to escort me to a crime scene. That was a switch. During the few on and off years we dated, my interest in crimes was a source of contention between us. In fact, it was part of the reason we'd broken up.

Well, only part of the reason. The biggest reason was because I'd "sort-of" cheated on him with a steamy hot real estate developer last year, whose sexy body and bad boy reputation kept me in a hormonal tizzy for a couple of weeks. I never actually got physical with the man, which was a good thing as he turned out to be a deranged killer; but nonetheless, Sean couldn't get past the fact that I fell for the guy. "An emotional betrayal" I think he called it. Anyway, after our previous three years of sporadic dating, he dumped me and rebounded into the arms of Sarah Maloney.

I clenched the steering wheel. Sarah Maloney was every woman's nightmare. The type of woman you hoped your "honey" never crossed paths with--sexy, strong, beautiful, intelligent, successful, wealthy... I absolutely hated her. Especially since the word on the street was that they were still seeing each other. I wondered how serious it was. Or, maybe things between Sean and Ms. Maloney were on the rocks and that was the real reason he was calling.

The thought of it lightened my mood, and my step, as I parked my car and skipped up the rickety stairs saddling the side of my parent's garage where I lived in a converted one-room apartment. My mood dimmed a bit though, as I opened my door and caught sight of the mess I'd left behind earlier that morning. As usual, my cozy loft sported heaps of dirty clothing, dishes piled in the sink, and a collection of empty soda cans on the counter. I really needed to take time to clean up; but at the moment, I was in too big of a hurry.

Instead, I stripped my way from the door to the bathroom, leaving a fresh trail of dirty clothes, and ducked into the shower. After a few swipes of soap and spritz of my favorite cologne, I smelled better than new. I just needed to find something to wear.

What *did* one wear to a crime scene? I wanted to look professional, but attractive. After all, this might be the one and only chance to get Sean's attention and win back his affection. I picked through my closet trying to find an outfit that best exemplified unquestioned authority paired with smoldering sexiness.

After tearing through the piles on my floor and not quite finding what I needed, I resorted to the large plastic bins stacked around the sofa. Surely, my on-line auction stockpile would have something.

I lifted the lid on a half dozen plastic containers that contained last week's acquisitions—perfectly good clothing foraged from dumpsters or purchased for pennies on the dollar at garage sales—before spying a woman's navy blue blazer. Perfect! Lucky for me, I found this one just a couple weeks ago at a yard sale in Woodridge. It was just what I needed today.

I threw on my darkest pair of jeans, a crisp white T-shirt, and shrugged into the blazer. It was a wee bit tight, but as long as I didn't need to raise my arms above my shoulders, I'd be fine.

I had barely finished taming my red frizzes into a low pony, when I heard a knock on the door. I ran to open it, finding a petite, female, uniformed officer with her hand extended. "Phillipena O'Brien? I'm Officer Cheryl Wagoner. I'm here to drive you."

I shook her hand and suppressed a giggle. She looked like a twelve-year-old playing dress-up. I half expected her to hold out a trick-or-treat bag and beg for candy. Instead, she motioned for me to follow her down the steps where her car was waiting.

I hesitated. There was a little confusion on my part as I deliberated where to sit. I finally chose the back, figuring the front was for police only. I regretted the decision the instant I settled into the plastic-covered seat. The cage in front of me and the doors without handles made me feel like a trapped criminal. Talk about conspicuous. I wondered what the neighbors would think. I shrank down as low as I could; and then, sunk all the way down where I pretended to pick something off the floor mat as my mother passed by in her Mercedes.

I was too late though. Before I could get all the way upright, my phone started buzzing. I looked at the display and saw it was my mother. No doubt she wanted an immediate explanation for why I was in the back of a police car. I decided to let it go to voicemail. At the moment, I wasn't in the mood to deal with *that* issue. Little did I realize, my mother's intrusiveness would turn out to be the least of my problems.

Chapter 2

The short ride to downtown Naperville seemed to last for hours; but finally, the cruiser slowed as we rounded the corner onto Washington Street. Uniformed officers scurried everywhere. Murder didn't happen often in this neck of the woods, so when it did, it commanded a lot of attention.

Once I made my way through a crowd of bystanders and saw which building had been cordoned off, I realized why I was called. Apparently the murder occurred in a place I was familiar with—The Classy Closet. In fact, I had been there the day before with my friend Shep Jones, owner of the best resale shop in town, The Retro Metro. A little tremor of dread pricked at my conscious as I wondered what the real reason was for my presence today.

I followed Officer Wagoner under the yellow crime scene tape and walked into the store, not knowing what to expect. A dead body, blood splatters, a gruesome scene? As I took a few tentative steps forward, several cops glanced up from their tasks and stared at me curiously. What was left of my self-confidence suddenly drained from my body. I might as well have been walking into an international power summit at the United Nations Building; I was in way over my head.

Then Sean walked into the room.

"Hey, thanks for coming."

My knees weakened and warm sparks coursed through my body as he approached. "Good to see you, Sean," I said, reaching for a friendly hug.

He backed up, leaving my arms hanging mid-air. Embarrassed, I glanced around and quickly covered by pretending to adjust my hair-do. Another bad move. I heard a slight ripping sound as the fabric on my blazer strained with the stretch of my arms. It appeared I'd blown a seam as well as my dignity.

"Follow me," he said, his tone all-business, as he weaved through a myriad of displays.

It's weird what nerves could do to a person. There I was, following my "ex" to a murder scene when I found myself suddenly distracted by a sweet pair of designer sunglasses—black leopard frames with rhinestones. I had a pair just like them in my previous life. That would have been my six-figure salary days, when I could afford such luxuries. Now, I buy my shades from an out-of-the-way kiosk at Navy Pier. Just last summer I got a great pair of Ray Bans for only eleven ninety-nine. Well, they were actually *Ray Baks*, but...who would know?

"Are you coming?" It was Sean, looking a little peeved that I'd stopped to check out the glasses.

I reluctantly returned the glasses to the shelf and continued following him toward the back room. "You know, I was just here yesterday. I came by with Shep."

He stopped and looked at me. "I'm aware of that."

That uneasy feeling came back. Of course Sean already knew we were there; he'd checked through the receipts. The owner had accepted a wild offer I made to buy her out-of-season inventory. I'd scored a sweet deal and walked out with several bags of designer woman's wear. Shep found a few things too, but not as much as me. "Was it her, the owner" I asked, feeling a wave of sadness.

"Yes, Jane Reynolds. Did you know her well?"

"Not really. I didn't even know her name. I've been here a few times, but we never socialized or anything."

I glanced around, hoping not to see the body.

"She's at the coroner's," Sean said, as if reading my thoughts.

I rubbed at the goose bumps that popped up on my arms despite my long sleeves. A horrible image of someone I knew on a cold slab at the coroner's office was unshakable.

"You okay?"

I shrugged and tried to calm my emotions. "Yeah. It's just that she seemed like such a nice lady. Was it a robbery?" I looked around, wondering what would be so valuable in a second hand store. It wasn't the type of place one would normally consider a target for robbery. None of the stuff was especially valuable and in this business there wouldn't be much cash on hand.

"That's the thing; we don't think anything was stolen. We don't think robbery was the motive."

"What do you mean? You think it was personal?"

"We're not absolutely sure. It seems Reynolds came back to the store after hours to finish some office work and meet someone. Do you know anything about who she would have been meeting?" He was leaning against a display table, arms crossed in a sexy pose. I let my eyes roam for a second. He looked like he had been working out.

"No. Why would I know that?"

Sean didn't reply.

"Uh ... where was she found?" I asked, struggling to stay focused as another feeling of uneasiness crept over me. Something was up with Sean.

"Right over there." My eyes followed his finger to a spot by the door that separated the office from the rest of the store. "We think she must have come through the front and been heading back to her office. She was shot from the office. It seems the intruder entered through the back door and was standing by the office desk."

"What would the killer have been doing here in the first place?"

Sean ran his fingers through his hair causing it to stand on end. I took a moment to study him as he paced back and forth. He was wearing his hair longer than his usual standard issue cop-buzz. Something else was different, too. But, I couldn't place it.

"We don't know for sure," he continued. That's why we've called you."

"I don't get it."

"You and Shep were the last ones in the store yesterday. I thought maybe Jane might have mentioned something about who she was meeting later on."

I shook my head. "No, not that I can recall. We looked around for maybe a half-hour and I noticed she was taking her summer stuff off the racks, getting ready to change over the seasons. I made her an offer on the whole lot. I got a good deal."

"Did Shep find anything?"

My eyes slid over to corner hutch that he had been looking at the day before. It was set up with ladies' tea apparel: white gloves, hats, some gaudy jewelry and an antique tea set. The tea set was gone. My heart lurched.

"Pippi?"

"He was looking at a tea set that was in that hutch?"

"Did he purchase it?"

"No, she was asking too much for it. He passed."

"But it's not there now?"

I nodded. My mind racing with my own questions. "Maybe she moved it somewhere."

The corners of Sean's mouth tipped slightly upward. "Maybe so. Then what?"

"What do you mean?"

He sighed and shifted. "Then what happened?"

"Oh, she bagged my purchases and Shep and I left."

"Did you go straight home?"

I squinted his way. "What are you getting at, Sean?"

"I'm asking you if you went straight home."

"Yeah, I mean no. Well, we were heading down the street to grab a bite to eat, but Shep suddenly felt ill, so we parted ways. He said he was going to head home to rest. He's been sick a lot lately; probably some sort of hard-to-shake bug. It's really got him down."

"He didn't make plans to stop by here later?"

I searched my brain, trying to remember if Shep mentioned anything about returning. "I don't think so. Like I said, he wasn't feeling well."

He continued. "There's a tea set in the back wrapped up in a box. I want you to look at it and verify if it was the one in the hutch."

"Okay." I followed him into the office thinking this whole thing was seeming stranger by the minute.

"Jane only had one employee, her sister-in-law, Margie," he said as we made our way toward a large metal desk that was stacked with paperwork. "We interviewed her earlier and she can't think of anyone who would want to hurt Jane. I had Margie look over the store's inventory, but I'm not sure how reliable she was. You know, with being upset and all."

I nodded. "I'm sure this must be a shock to her."

"Yeah. Anyway, she said she didn't notice anything missing. After checking out this tea set, I want you to take a look. See if you see anything else out of place since yesterday."

"Okay, but Shep actually runs a business like this. He might have taken more notice of Jane's inventory and how her shop is set up. I'm sure he'd be a big help." I was testing the waters. Sean's attitude was making me nervous. I'd known him for a long time and could tell when he was onto something, or in this case, thought he was onto something. There was absolutely no way Shep was involved in Jane Reynold's murder. "In fact, maybe I'll just give him a quick call," I added, reaching into my bag for my cell.

I didn't even push the first number before his hand reached over and snapped my phone shut. "No need, we've already tried to contact him."

"Tried? What do you mean? Can't you reach him?"

He shrugged off my questions, pulling a box from under Jane's desk. The top of the box was marked with Shep's name. "Is this it?" Sean asked, opening it.

I set my purse down and gently lifted one of the green jadeite tea cups, the same design Shep admired the day before. I nodded slowly, the uneasy feeling in my stomach growing. "I know what you're getting at, but there's no way Shep had anything to do with murder. How could you even think that, Sean? We use to hang out together."

He turned his gaze away, his jaw muscles tight with tension. "Like I was saying, we need you to look around the scene and see if you notice anything else missing from her inventory." He started fidgeting with the hem of his suit, which I noticed was a designer label, definitely a step up from his usual sales rack pick. "Spend some time checking out the store and see what you come up with. Don't worry about disturbing anything; the crime techs are finished. Everything's been photographed and dusted."

I rolled my eyes around the room and nodded.

"By the way," he continued. "Do you know if Shep owns a gun?

"What! No, Shep doesn't own a gun!" At least I didn't think he did. I'd never thought to ask him.

Sean held up his hand. "Take an easy. I just thought maybe he kept one in his shop for security reasons." He turned and started walking away. "Let me know if you find anything. I'll have Officer Wagoner drive you back when you're done," he added over his shoulder.

I stared after him in disbelief. In all the years I'd known him, Sean had always put a high value on friendship. It wasn't like him to so easily doubt a friend, let alone suspect a friend of something as brutal as murder. One thing was for sure, more than just Sean's haircut and wardrobe had changed since I'd last seen him and I knew exactly who to blame ... Sarah Maloney.

As soon as he was out of sight, I dialed Shep's cell number. No matter what Sean said, I knew there was a perfectly logical explanation for all this. Getting Shep's voice mail, I hung up and dialed his business number at the Retro Metro. A diligent employee politely refused to divulge his whereabouts but promised to give him my message. For good measure, I redialed his private home number and left a message there, too.

A few moments later, I was still standing there, trying to decide what to do, when one of the officers approached and reiterated Sean's permission to move about freely. I obeyed, feeling a little conspicuous as I tiptoed through the store trying to look like I knew what I was doing. For the next half hour or so, I meandered around the racks and past displays of accessories and purses. The only thing that caught my eye was a couple of gorgeous designer handbags that were in perfect shape and priced ridiculously low. I must have missed them the day before. If only circumstances were different, I'd snatch these up and turn them around for a neat profit.

"Have you found something?" Officer Wagoner asked.

I replaced one of the purses I had in hand. "No, not really. I probably wouldn't be able to tell if something was missing. I'm not really familiar with her inventory."

"I understand. Just take your time. No hurry. I'll be ready when you are," she replied with a nod, her perky pony tail bouncing with her head. That, along with her tiny frame and petite voice, made me wonder how efficient she'd be as a street cop. Of course, I'd learned the hard way that looks could be deceiving. It was only last year that I had fallen for a sizzling hot guy who seemed quite normal until the day he held a gun to my head. Funny how easy it is to misjudge a person.

I sighed and roamed around for another twenty minutes before conceding defeat. "I'm ready to go now," I told Officer Wagoner. "I'm sorry but I didn't find anything. Just let me grab my bag. I left it in the office."

I made my way to the office and was about to shoulder my purse when I decided to take a quick look through some of the shopping bags lying around the desk. More than likely, these were full of recently received items for consignment.

The first couple I untied revealed a tangled mess of ladies clothing. A tag on the outside was marked Sokolov. Well, whoever Ms. Sokolov was, she'd not taken good care of packing her clothes. Usually, consigners get the best deal if they take the time to properly launder and prepare their clothing before trying to sell it. I pulled out and checked over a few items; they were wrinkled, but in good shape with expensive labels. Too bad she hadn't bothered to iron them. Fair or not, the wrinkles would probably depreciate their resale value.

Rummaging around, I found a couple of other boxes containing shoes, size eight, and all in nice condition. I took note of the quality, estimating that the cheapest pair would probably retail for two hundred bucks.

I had just started going through another bag when Officer Wagoner yelled, "Everything okay back here?"

"Yup. I'm ready," I replied, reclosing the bag and standing to leave. Before walking away though, my eyes slid back to the brown packaged box with the tea set. A bad feeling settled in the pit of my stomach.

Chapter 3

This time, on the ride home, I chose the front seat, which was enough of a thrill to momentarily shake any leftover uneasy feelings from the crime scene. After all, I hadn't sat in the front seat of a police cruiser since Community Hero Week in elementary school when my second grade class was invited to tour the police station. I'll never forget that field trip. My teacher must have assigned me to an errant parent chaperone, because somehow I escaped from my group and found my way into an open police cruiser. Having been one of those kids that had to touch everything, the first thing I did was hit the siren button. I can still recall how awesome the shrill screams of the siren sounded as they echoed off the concrete walls of the police parking garage.

"So you have a second-hand store, too?" Officer Wagoner asked, interrupting my thoughts.

"No, nothing like The Classy Closet, just a huge on-line store."

"An on-line store? Can you make money doing that?"

"I manage. I also have a regular booth at the Third Saturday Flea Market," I added.

"Cool. Sounds like fun."

I shrugged. "It's better than my old job, that's for sure."

"Oh, yeah? What was that?"

"I was an investment banker."

"Really?"

I let the surprise; no make that the shock, in her voice roll off me. I was used to getting that reaction from people when I told them about my past life. It was as if they just couldn't believe I'd traded the lucrative, respectable job of investment banking for my current career, which in my opinion, was still respectable, just not as lucrative. Or perhaps her analytical cop mind was secretly wondering if I became caught up in some sort of insider trading scam and was forced to leave my old career.

"Some of the guys were saying you broke a case last year," she said, changing the subject. "The Amanda Schmidt murder."

I sat up a little straighter. "Well...I wouldn't say that I broke the case. I...well...I did find the murder weapon."

"That's what I heard. Guess you used to date Panelli?" she prodded.

I sighed. "Yeah, used to."

"Panelli's a good cop. He's got a good reputation."

"I'm sure he does. He's dating a lawyer now, Sarah Maloney," I stated with a sideways glance.

"That's right," she replied, focused on the road.

I gave her the once over, wondering if I could trust her. "He seemed different today." I squirmed in my seat. "I mean, he's changed."

"Changed, huh? How's that?"

I struggled with my reply, wishing I hadn't brought up the subject. "I don't know. It probably sounds weird that I'm talking about it."

"No, not at all. I think I know what you're trying to say."

"You do?"

"I'll tell you something," she said. "It's just woman to woman though, you can't repeat it 'cause it could get me into trouble, know what I'm saying?"

"Yes, sure." I was hanging on her every word.

"I think Sarah Maloney is a little strange."

"Strange? Sarah Maloney? She's one of the most respected attorneys in town. She's gorgeous, smart and probably rich."

She squinted my way for a second. "You sound like the president of her fan club or something."

"No. Not at all. I can see why he would fall for her, that's all."

We were pulling into the alley behind my apartment. Wagoner put the gear in park and turned toward me. "She calls him a lot, like maybe fifteen times a day. At least that's what I hear. I also see her at the precinct all the time."

"She *is* a criminal defense lawyer."

"No, she's not always there on business. She's checking up on Panelli. It's starting to cause trouble, too. Everyone's getting sick of it."

"Really?" I was trying to keep the delight out of my voice.

"Really. So, if you think he's changed, that's probably the reason. Sarah Maloney is driving him crazy," she added with a mischievous little wink.

I did a double take, not sure if I heard her correctly. I hoped I had. I'd like nothing more than to have a second chance with Sean.

*

Inside my apartment, I tore off the too-tight blazer, kicked my way through a few laundry piles and flopped on the sofa. What I needed was a nap. However, I no sooner began to close my eyes when my cell rang. I scrambled to retrieve the phone from the blazer's pocket, but shouldn't have bothered—it was Cherry.

"You hung up on me earlier. That's no way for a maid of honor to act."

"Sorry. But technically I'm just a fill-in."

"Uh, huh. Well, I didn't get a chance to tell you about your fitting."

"Fitting?"

"Yes, in case the dress needs to be altered. You'll need to go in today."

"I can't. It'll have to wait a couple of days."

She muttered something I couldn't quite understand. "You'll have to go today. The wedding's in less than two weeks."

"All right, fine. It'll have to be tomorrow, though." I was using my spare hand to open my kitchen cupboard. I rummaged past packages of chocolate cookies, a bottle of wine, a couple boxes of macaroni and cheese, and some miniature candy bars, finally settling on the cookies.

"Are you *really* going to go tomorrow?"

"Sure. No problem." I popped a cookie in my mouth and reached back in for the wine bottle. "What size is Willow? Maybe I won't need to have it altered."

"She's a six."

A *six*! I shoved the cookies aside. "I'll go first thing in the morning."

"Good. It's at Brenda's Bridal Boutique. Call me if there's any problem."

A problem, I thought, hanging up. *A problem? Well, let's see… I didn't want to be in this stupid wedding, I looked horrible in orange, and there's no way I'm going to be able to squeeze my behind into a size six dress.*

I popped the cork and rifled through the cabinet for a clean glass. Finding a stadium cup tucked in the back, I filled it to the brim and snatched the cookies off the counter. I knew I shouldn't, but my stress level was on overdrive.

Settling on the sofa, I crunched my way through half the bag and surfed channels until I found a Matlock rerun. Well…at least something good had come of the day. Munchies, Merlot, and Matlock—the three M's; a magic combination almost as good as the three S's—Sugar, Shopping, and Sex. Not that I'd hit on all three of the S's in a long time.

*

The next morning, I awoke to someone pounding on my door. I reluctantly rolled off the sofa, brushed off some cookie crumbs, maneuvered around a couple stacks of boxes, and reached the door just as the bellowing started, "Phillipena, answer this door!"

I braced myself before opening. "Hi, Mom."

As usual, my mother was impeccably dressed in a light grey pinstriped suit unbuttoned to reveal a cobalt blue blouse and her signature pearls. I had to hand it to her: she knew how to set off her best features—her intense blue eyes and her knockout figure. I didn't inherit her talent for fashion or her figure.

"I'm here to take you to the bridal shop," she said, offering a small hug before breezing by me. "Your Aunt Maeve called last night. She said Cherry was in a tizzy, worried you weren't going to get your fitting. She doesn't think you're taking your bridesmaid responsibilities seriously."

I watched as mom circled my apartment, her heels clicking against the wood planks. She seemed to be checking out my current acquisitions. "Have you been busy, dear?" she asked.

"Not really," I admitted. "Curbside acquisitions are down. Probably due to the economy, people just aren't discarding like they used to. On the plus side, consignment stores are being bombarded with merchandise and in response are reducing the mark-up on resale items."

Even to me, that spiel sounded like something out of the mouth of the current Chairman of the Federal Reserve. For some reason, I always felt like I needed to glamorize my profession, especially to my mother. Although she always says she's proud of me, I know that both she and Dad wished I would get a normal, respectable job. Something like my old position at Global Financial Trading, Inc. Back then I drove a Lexus and wore expensive suits. I dined at five-star restaurants and shopped the Mag Mile. I had a brownstone apartment two blocks from Wrigley that made even the most expensive furniture store showroom look like a candidate for a HGTV makeover. Although, what I had the most of was stress—major stress accompanied by high blood pressure and an extra twenty pounds around the hips. Hard telling where I'd be today if I hadn't decided to leave the corporate world and pursue a career in used merchandising.

Unlike me, my mother could easily handle the pressure of a successful, demanding career. Not only did she raise us five girls, she obtained her real estate broker license, opened shop and climbed to the top. Everyone knew Maureen O'Brien—her face was plastered on real estate signs all over the city.

Of course, she had lots of help from my father. My mother and father were like Yin and Yang: two opposites which fit together and formed one great team. Mom was the breadwinner, while Dad, more of the quiet, intellectual type, tended to the everyday tasks of running a family. When he wasn't working as a part-time librarian at Community Union library, he was busy making dinner, washing clothes, and doing the grocery shopping. My father was one of the original "Mr. Moms"—and he was good at it.

"I presume you're going to put on some makeup and change into something decent before we go." Mom was browsing through a bag of clothing I'd bought at rock bottom prices from a garage sale in an upscale Lisle neighborhood. "Hey, there are some nice pieces in here," she said, holding up a scoop-necked blouse.

"Do you want that?"

"Oh thanks, dear. But it's really not my color." She stuffed it back into the bag and crossed over to my personal closet. "You go get cleaned up and I'll find something for you to wear. I have a showing at one o'clock, but maybe we can squeeze in lunch after the fitting. Go on…get moving!"

I obeyed and scurried into the bathroom. I rinsed, brushed, and swiped on some makeup as quickly as I could, all the while wondering what my mother was going to come up with for me to wear. My wardrobe was limited.

"Mom! What are you doing?" I hit panic mode when I saw her rummaging through the plastic bins stacked on kitchen counter. "That's stuff I'm getting ready to list!"

"I know, but the only things I found in your closet were jeans and T-shirts. Oh … look at this!"

She'd pulled out a pretty floral skirt and a coordinating button-down blouse.

"This is perfect, don't you think? It looks like your size, too," she said, obviously proud of her efforts.

"I can't wear that blouse." I pointed to the tags that dangled from the lapel. "I have to sell it NWT."

"NWT?"

"New with tags. It's worth more that way."

"Where are the scissors?"

"What?" I watched as she carried the blouse across the room to my coffee table, where I package boxes for shipping, and found a pair of scissors. With a swift sinister snip, she removed the tag and depreciated twenty-five percent of the garment's resale value.

My jaw dropped. "Mom! That's going to cost me about ten bucks!"

"Oh, relax. I said I'd buy lunch, didn't I? Now put this on and let's get going. Time's wasting."

Chapter 4

As soon as I walked into Brenda's Bridal Shop, I was glad my mom had dared to snip. This was definitely not a jeans and T-shirt type of place. "Is Cherry paying for the dress or am I?" I asked, looking around and feeling a huge price tag coming on. "Don't worry. Chuck and Maeve are covering the cost," she said, directing me to the front desk where a girl who looked eerily like Cinderella, or maybe it was Brendarella, was waiting for us with a frozen smile on her face. Suddenly it occurred to me that this whole shop was like a royal ball waiting on the fairy tale princess to appear. The walls were painted three shades of pink which coordinated with the pink rugs on the floor and heavy pink drapes cinched with golden tassels. Everywhere I looked there seemed to be something sparkly: sparkly purses, sparkly shoes, and sparkly veils. There was even a display of sparkly rhinestone-studded tiaras nestled on a table covered in pink satin. Adding to the effect, a dozen mannequins attired in long, puffed-sleeved, pastel-colored gowns seemed to hover over the floor as if they were suddenly frozen mid-dance. I kept my ears peeled for the trumpeters as Mom introduced us and our mission to the clerk.

"I can certainly help you with that, Mrs. O'Brien," the clerk was saying to Mom. "Let me get the dress and have the seamstress measure her for the adjustments." Brendarella was giving me a disapproving up and down look so I threw back my shoulders and sucked it in. Somewhere I'd heard that good posture took off an instant ten pounds.

I continued to keep my gut sucked in as I strolled around and pretended to study the displays with interest. I had some fun with a couple of tiaras before moving on to the display of little squishy silicone breasts inserts that promised to make any bride go from a B to a double D in seconds. I wasn't all that interested in the displays, though; what I was really doing was avoiding too much contact with my mother. I knew that while we were actually *in* a bridal shop, any conversation between us could only be focused on one thing—my impending marriage or lack thereof. It bothered Mom that, except for my sister "the sister," I was the only O'Brien girl that wasn't happily married and busy adding little twigs to the O'Brien family tree.

Luckily I didn't have to avoid her for too long, as Brenda soon returned, followed by a stout woman carrying a cushion of pins and wearing a measuring tape around her neck like a doctor's stethoscope.

In Brenda's hand was the ugliest dress I had ever seen.

"Oh my!" I heard my mother exclaim. "Is *that* the dress?"

Brenda answered with a slight raise of her brow and a nod toward the back of the store. "There's a fitting room right around the corner."

I followed as Brenda directed me down a long hall of curtained doors, shoved me and the pumpkin-colored atrocity into the room and ripped a heavy pink curtain across a wooden rod. "Let me know if you have any problems," she said.

After a long spell of shimmying, pulling, shimmying, and more pulling, I managed to get the ugly thing over my hips. Sweat was dripping from my brow and my hair was frizzed around my face like a halo when I finally emerged from the dressing room.

"What took you so long?" Mom asked, spinning me around. "You're not zipped." She began yanking with all her might. "Suck it in," she ordered.

"I can't. Stop!" My arms flailed like a ragdoll as she viciously worked the zipper.

"Well, come on then," she sighed, giving up the effort. "They're waiting for us down the hall."

I felt like an orange wrapped mummy. The dress was so tight around my thighs I could barely walk. Mom kept one hand on my elbow as I shuffled like a shackled inmate down a long hall of pink curtained chambers. We finally worked our way into a mirrored room where a skinny little twenty-something was perched on a carpeted block with a white sequined train flowing behind her. The seamstress was pinning up extra material while an entourage of blissful supporters stood by gushing with compliments.

"I'll be with you in a second," the seamstress said as my pumpkin-colored reflection slid into the mirror next to the soon-to-be Mrs. Happiness and her fifteen thousand dollar wedding gown. I heard a few gasps and giggles from the bride-to-be's posse, confirming what I already knew—this dress was a joke.

I ignored the girls and struck a few poses in the mirror trying to keep an open mind about the dress. It was a strapless design with a figure-hugging bodice and a large double ruffle around the bust line. The ruffle was ugly, but it did serve to cover the rolls of fat that spilled from my armpits. "What do you think, Mom?"

"Uh...well...," she sputtered. A first for Mom, usually she could find something diplomatic to say about everything.

The seamstress helped the bride off the block and moved over to me. "Let's see," she said, pinching and pulling at the fabric. Then wielding her measuring tape, she worked every angle of my body with dogged determination. "I think what we'll need to do is take some material from the hem and sew in a panel in the back. The dress will be a little shorter than intended, but it should work."

We all tried hard not to stare at the two inch, flesh-colored gap protruding from the back of the dress.

"I'll make a few more measurements and see what I can do," the seamstress offered.

Brenda poked her head into the room and addressed the seamstress, "Doris, you're eleven o'clock fitting is here."

"Send her in. I'm just finishing here," Doris answered, making a couple quick notes. I wished her luck and turned to leave. I'd almost shuffled my way back to the dressing room hallway when in walked Sarah Maloney. We stopped face to face, regarding one another with shocked interest. She looked like an angel adorned in the most beautiful wedding gown I'd ever seen; I, on the other hand, was looking like a rotting veggie.

Of course, I recognized her instantly, but I think she was a little baffled by me. We'd only run into each other a couple of times when I was still dating Sean. She studied me for a moment, looking me up and down. Then, with a twinkle in her eye and a smile tugging at her lips she moved aside to let me pass. "Excuse me, Phillipena," she said, arrogance tinting her tone.

My gap of protruding flesh in mind, I immediately turned away from her and started shuffling backwards down the hall. Mom, oblivious to whole scene, was still asking Doris questions. "Are you sure you'll be able to add enough material to make the dress fit?" Then, "Is it too late to order a couple of sizes up? I'd be happy to pay for express shipping."

Appalled, I tried to shuffle faster. Unfortunately, that wasn't so easy with chiffon-bound thighs. With a sharp rip of fabric, I fell flat on my bootie. After catching my breath, I struggled on the ground for a moment. The dress was so tight, I couldn't bend my legs enough to get back up. Finally, in a last ditch effort, I rolled over on my stomach, dug in my toes, and did a little push-up. By walking my hands back to my feet, I was able to form an inverted "V" with my body. Then, with one final hoist, I was upright. I turned and scurried the best I could down the hall; Sarah's laughter following me all the way.

I changed in record time and was waiting by the car when mom finally came out of the shop. "Phillipena, what in the world is going on with you? I'm so embarrassed. Not to mention the dress. Who knows if they'll be able to fix it now?

You tore the side seam. Then, you just left it waded up on the floor of the…"

I held up my hand. "I know. I'm sorry, okay? Let's just get out of here."

We rode in silence for a few blocks before she asked me, "Who was that woman in the bridal gown, anyway? Do you know her?"

"She's Sean's new girlfriend…or fiancé, I guess. Sarah Maloney."

"Oh, I see," she said. "I thought you were over him."

"Well, I'm not, okay? Let's drop it." My voice was shaky and tears were threatening to spill. I shifted in my seat, turning my face away and pretended to study the passing scene out my window.

She sighed, "Can I treat you to some lunch? Wong's Stir Fry is just down the road. I know how you love stir fry."

Ugh. I used to eat there all the time with *him*. Of course, there really wasn't any place I hadn't been with him. In the three plus years we dated, Sean and I practically ate our way through all of Naperville and several of the nearby burbs. "No thanks, Mom. I'm really not up to it. Besides, I've got a lot of work I should be doing."

Her posture stiffened slightly. I knew she wasn't going to let the issue drop. "I understand," she started, paused, and then had to add, "but let's talk about this. Tell me what's going on with you. I've noticed that you haven't been dating at all these days. If you've been holding out for Sean, well…you can let that go now. Obviously, he's serious about this girl or she wouldn't be trying on wedding gowns."

I groaned. "Please, Mom, please! I don't want to talk about it."

"I'm just saying it's not healthy, that's all. You should be moving on by now. Do you remember when your sister broke up with that boy from DePaul, what was his name…?"

I sighed. "Bobby Nolan."

"Yes, that's right. Bobby Nolan. Anyway, Anne was completely heartbroken. She was so sure she'd never find anyone else and look at her now. She's found a wonderful husband, lives in a great neighborhood, and is already expecting ... *blah* ... *blah* ... *blah*."

I tuned her out, my mind veering off on its own path. That would be the path to destruction, or more specifically self-destruction. I was working myself into a terrible funk allowing my thoughts to dwell on my ex's pending nuptials and my own lonely, pathetic existence.

"Phillipena, are you listening to me?" I snapped back to attention. "I was saying that you should join that singles group at church. I'm sure there are a lot of nice men there."

Thank goodness we were pulling into the driveway. "That's a great idea, Mom. I'll look into it," I promised as I hopped out and headed immediately for the hedges that separated my parents' yard from the back alley and the entrance to my above-garage apartment.

"I'll let you know when the final fitting is scheduled," she yelled after me. "And don't forget to call the church!"

*

I immediately peeled off my shopping outfit, planning to wash and return it to my resale stockpile as soon as possible. After throwing on my most comfy stretch pants and a favorite hoodie, I went directly to the fridge and stopped. There, stuck with a magnet was the note I hung the previous day, CHECK YOUR EMOTIONS. It was to remind me to stop and think about my emotional state before opening the fridge. I got the idea the other day while I was standing in the checkout line at ValueMart, stocking up on chocolate and soda. One of the magazines boasted the headline—*No More Emotional Food Binges*. The article suggested posting verbal reminders to help keep unbalanced eating in check. I thought it was a great idea. I posted little reminders everywhere, even in the bathroom where just last week, I downed an entire bag of chocolate chip cookies while soaking in a hot bath.

I paused and checked my emotions; *Damn, I hate that Sarah Maloney!* But, was eating a thousand calories going to help me feel better? I thought about how great she looked in her wedding gown and how horrible I looked in the pumpkin-colored disaster. I drew in a deep breath. No, I didn't need the extra calories.

I opened the fridge and, with all the self-control I could muster, moved past the left-over pizza, past the soda and chocolate pudding cups, and extracted a low-fat yogurt. Proud of myself, I took my healthy food choice to the computer and settled in for a couple hours of work. I had been lazy the last couple of weeks and didn't have my usual amount of items listed on-line. I also noticed several people hadn't paid their invoices and I was a little behind packaging and mailing. I really needed to ramp up my efforts. Besides, busy-work would help keep my mind off Sean.

Since school had started, I focused on kid's clothes. I cleared a large spot in the middle of the room and pulled out a half dozen plastic bins marked "Fall-Kids." After an hour of sorting by size, I was able to put together fifteen lots of brand name clothes. I carefully arranged and photographed each lot before bagging them into separate, numbered bags. Then, after grabbing another yogurt, I downloaded the photos, typed descriptions and listed them on-line. I was a day behind this week. Usually, I preferred to do seven-day listings ending on Sunday afternoon. That way, the end-of-auction bidding would occur when most people were off work and in front of their computers. However, looking at my on-line bank account balance, I needed to get some things moving now.

After finishing my listings, I moved to packaging. The living area of my apartment served as shipping and handling. At any one time, there were enough boxes, strapping tape, and sharpies between my sofa and television to supply an entire UPS store.

I flipped on the television, printed off a couple dozen address labels, double checked my mailing list, and went to work wrapping, stuffing, and taping. A couple of infomercials later, I had a stack of tidy boxes ready to be shipped, not to mention the order number for an *Abomizer*, a neat little contraption that was guaranteed to whittle my flabby abs into sculpted six pack in just five days. Which would be a good thing to order, since in a little over a week, I was going to be paraded in front of two hundred wedding guests while wearing a veggie-colored bridesmaid dress.

I checked my cell phone for any new voice mails. None. I dialed Shep's number and left another message. This time, I let my annoyance come through the phone. I'm sure he was just at home trying to recover from whatever bug he had, or maybe he decided to take an impromptu vacation; but still, I was one of his best friends. What would it take to return my call? I needed to warn him that Sean was looking for him.

The thought of which made me angry again. How could Sean ever suspect Shep of anything criminal, let alone something to do with murder? Here's a guy that ran away from an abusive situation as a teen, grew up on the streets with nothing, turned his life around and was now owner of the Retro Metro, one of the hottest consignment shops in the city. Shep also used his success to help wayward kids. He hired dozens of runaways, paid them well and helped them get the counseling they needed to turn their lives around. He was an all-around good guy. There's no way he would ever hurt anyone. I simple had to figure a way to convince Sean of Shep's innocence. It was time to find out more about Jane Reynolds.

If I'd learned anything as a used merchandiser, it was that people's cast-outs spoke volumes about their personal lives. For example, go through the garbage of a young family and you'll find out-grown clothing, used up toys, and other remnants indicative of a growing family. A garbage with lots of take-out bags and Styrofoam Starbucks cups usually belonged to a young single person; and, the dumpsters on the college campus...well, needless to say, those kids aren't spending *all* their time studying. Point being, if you want to know something about someone, go through their garbage.

Chapter 5

I felt a bit uneasy as I pulled into the parking lot of The Classy Closet. For a second, I considered abandoning my mission, but I knew if I wanted to get to the bottom of things I needed to find out more about Jane Reynolds.

As if on cue, the sun dipped low on the horizon, casting long shadows across the pavement as I eased my car next to the security fence that surrounded the dumpster. Using my station wagon as a step stool, I clambered up the windshield and made my way to the top of the car. I cringed when I heard a few metallic popping sounds under my feet, but I didn't let it deter me. By stretching onto my tip-toes, I was able to get a firm enough grasp to hoist my upper body onto the top-edge of the fence. I teetered there for a moment, catching my breath, before swinging my legs up and over.

I landed with a thud on the other side, my palms acquiring a few splinters from the maneuver. Looking up, I was proud of my ninja-like prowess until I realized I hadn't planned for a way out. Lucky for me there were several wooden pallets stacked next to the dumpster. I'd have to use them to fabricate a makeshift ladder. No problem.

The sky was growing dark; I'd needed to work quickly. I surveyed the giant container. The left lid was open with stacks of folded cardboard boxes protruding from its depths.

By utilizing a couple of the pallets, I was up and into the dumpster in no time at all. At first glance I saw the usual: empty boxes, waded up plastic bags, broken hangers, shredded papers, and…oh…a beautiful black sequined purse. The dainty shoulder strap was broken, but heck, I could just take the strap off. It'd make a great little clutch. Wow, what a find!

Momentarily forgetting my mission, I began rooting around for more resalable treasures. In the corner, I found a partially opened box. Peering inside I was surprised to see several hardcover books. Weird. Jane didn't sell books, just clothing and accessories. What were these doing here?

Turning the box on its side, I saw the word Sokolov—the same as marked on the bags in Jane's office. I wondered if I'd been wrong about the bags being brought in by a consigner; Jane probably picked up these items at an estate sale. A lot of consigners shop estate sales. I even go to them every once in a while, but only when I'm desperate—it gives me the heebies to buy dead people's stuff.

I thought about it for a moment. Jane, the owner, probably hit an estate sale and purchased a large lot of clothing and accessories. This box must have been mixed in with the lot by mistake. So, instead of trying to return these books, she disposed of them.

I began going through the box, shining my light on each spine. The books were in good shape, leather bound, and written in a foreign language. I could tell they were somewhat valuable. I could definitely make a good profit selling them online.

On the other hand, maybe this was the connection I'd been looking for. Was there some sort of tie between the Sokolov estate and Jane Reynolds' murder? I remembered that the clothing bags in Jane's office were disheveled, as if someone had packed them in a hurry. I was rethinking that now. Could it have been that someone was searching through them? If so, what would be so valuable—valuable enough to kill for—in a bag of used clothing? Perhaps this was the type of connection Sean was hoping I'd make.

I flipped open my cell. Darn, no reception. Well, maybe I could run the box over to the precinct.

I was trying to figure out how to get the books out of the dumpster when the sirens started. They seemed to be coming from everywhere. North, south, east…then there were lights. I looked through the top of the dumpster and could see the darkening sky lit up in red and blue.

"Police. Don't move!" I dropped the box and straightened up, raising my hands above my head. A giant strobe light flooded through the slats of the fence creating tiny dissecting lines that danced throughout the dumpster.

"Don't shoot," I tried to yell, but my voice came out in a dry whisper. I could feel all the blood draining down to my feet, making my ears whiz and my head spin. I kept my hands up even though they felt like two concrete blocks.

Then, I heard the scraping of steel on steel as the cops popped the chain that locked and secured the fence around the dumpster. The gate swung open with a shattering thud, followed by the sound of a dozen footsteps.

"Don't move," the deep voice ordered again. Little did he know, I was too scared to move.

I heard something scraping the concrete outside and then a clanking noise on the side of the dumpster. They must have been using something to climb up.

I stood ram-rod still, my eyes squeezed shut, trying to figure out how I was going to explain being inside this dumpster.

"What are you doing here?" I immediately recognized the squeaky little voice. I flipped open my eyes and saw Officer Wagoner staring at me over the barrel of her gun. "Hold it guys. I know this woman," she said, holstering her gun and waving off the officers that must have been positioned and ready outside the dumpster.

Officer Wagoner reached down and offered her hand. Reluctantly, I allowed her to pull me out. Once outside, I attempted to explain to her why I was in the dumpster, but she told me to keep quiet and wait inside her cruiser. I was still there a half hour later when Sean arrived. He leaned in so we were face to face. "Pippi?" he said, his voice low and his eyes searching for an explanation.

"Uh, hi Sean. I tried to call you earlier. I just couldn't get any reception from inside the...." I let my voice trail off, glancing over his shoulder to where the other officers were gathered. They all wore smirks, except Wagoner who was regarding me with concern or pity. I wasn't sure which.

"Hey guys, leave us alone for a minute, will you?" Sean said, grabbing my arm and pulling me out of the cruiser.

I stood with my back up against the cop car as he paced in front of me. I started to explain, "I found a box of old books in the dumpster. I think it's from an estate sale..."

He stopped and placed his hands with a thud on either side of me, trapping me against the car. I stiffened. Usually, I would love to be trapped against a hard surface with Sean leaning in close, but tonight he was scaring me.

"Unbelievable." His voice was low and husky, his face just inches from mine. "You haven't changed a bit. What made you think you should come over here and break into their garbage dumpster? You're trespassing!"

He was so close, I could actually feel his body heat. I was struggling emotionally somewhere between fear, lust, and anger.

"Wait a minute. I was tying—"

"Trying to do what? Play detective? Don't you remember what happened last time you did that?"

I thought for a minute. Sure, I behaved a little stupidly last time I got involved in a police investigation, but that was different. It wasn't like I was going to get killed digging around in a garbage can. I do that all the time. Of course, not in the middle of the night at a known crime scene. Not usually accompanied by a half-dozen armed officers, either.

I put my hand on his chest and gently backed him up, trying to keep the situation calm. "What do you expect me to do? You're the one who brought me into this case in the first place.

Then you practically accused Shep of being somehow involved."

"Look," he snarled, grabbing a hold of my shoulders. "I don't want you getting hurt. A woman was just killed here. What were you thinking coming here alone, in the dark?"

My eyes roamed his face. His eyes were wild, his skin flushed, his hair tussled. I could feel the intensity of his emotion and a rush of heat crept over me as I struggled not to lean into him. Whatever I was feeling was wrong. He was getting married. It was over between us.

I searched for something to say to squelch the heat rising in me: admit an error, change the subject, anything. "Okay. You're right. I do need to be more careful. I did find something interesting, though. There was this box of books from an estate sale, marked Sokolov. I think there could be a connection."

There, I'd got it out. I felt a speck of pride as I waited for his reply. Certainly he'd be pleased with my discovery.

He began rubbing his temples.

"So," I continued. "When your guys get the books could you have them look around for a black sequined purse? It's damaged a bit, but—"

"This is why it didn't work out with us," he practically shouted. "You can't stay out of things."

"What!" Suddenly the temperature in my hot head matched the heat in my lower extremities. Surprising how I could go from intense desire to downright ticked-off. "It didn't work out with us because you never could commit to any sort of serious relationship. Although you don't have that problem *now*, do you?" It was my turn to get in his face. I began jamming my finger into his chest to emphasize every word. "You and Sarah deserve each other. And you want to know who hasn't changed? You. You're still a jerk."

I started toward my car. "Where are you going?" he called after me.

"I'm leaving." I turned and shot him a daring look. "Unless you're planning to arrest me." I glanced over to the other cops.

They were each pretending to be wrapped up in some sort of task, but I knew they were hanging on every word. Well, I didn't care.

I dramatically held out my wrists. "Well?" I taunted in my loudest voice.

He looked down, not responding. So, I turned and walked away.

Thinking back on it later, I wished I wouldn't have been so dramatic. Had I just been just a little nicer, maybe he would have let me retrieve the books. They were fair game since they were in the dumpster anyway, even if behind a locked fence. If I'd really gotten on his good side maybe I could have even talked him into picking up that black sequined purse with the broken strap. I just hated to see a repairable discard go to waste.

Chapter 6

The next morning, I grabbed a bagel and twisted the top off a soda. Not much of a coffee drinker, I preferred to derive my daily caffeine fix from soda with its sugar kicker. Wearing my best jeans—or at least the only pair I could get buttoned—and a practically new fleece hoodie, I loaded the back of my station wagon with boxes to ship later in the afternoon. My first stop, however, was going to be the Retro Metro, where I hoped to find my elusive friend, Shep.

Ogden Avenue was packed with morning commuters, so it was almost nine when I finally made it to Westmont. A few more turns and I was pulling into the lot of the Retro Metro. I glanced at the brick-fronted warehouse which housed three stories of consignment heaven. Shep had a knack, that's for sure. Only he could convert a nuts and bolts warehouse into the best consignment shop in the tri-state area.

Although they weren't officially opened for business until ten, I knew that several employees would be in setting up displays and sorting through merchandise. I rapped on the door for a couple of minutes before anyone came to answer.

"We're not open yet," a young guy announced through the closed door.

"I know. I'm here to talk to Shep. I'm a friend," I yelled back.

The door opened a crack. I caught a glimpse of a kid with a plethora of piercings and a swatch of fuzz on his chin.

"Shep's not here," he said.

"When is he coming back?"

The kid shrugged and started to shut the door. I moved my foot in front of the frame and leaned in trying to wedge my body in the opening. "Hey, is Pauline here?"

"She's busy," he said, pushing harder on the door, which was cutting off circulation in my leg. I pushed back, but he was proving to be strong for such a scrawny guy.

"Hey, Owen. What are you doing? Let her in," a female voice came from behind.

Owen let go of the door and I tumbled into the room.

"Pippi! How are you?"

I righted myself and greeted Pauline, Shep's right-hand gal. We'd come to know each other well over the past year. "Hey, fine. I shot a menacing look at Owen; but he wasn't making eye contact.

"What brings you to the Retro Metro?" she asked.

"I've been trying to reach Shep. Do you know where he is?"

She glanced uneasily at Owen. "Why don't you go back and help the guys with that new load of boxes," she told him. "I'll be back in a minute."

After the door-warrior departed, Pauline motioned for me to follow her. We moved into a retro-eighties style room that instantly transported me back thirty years. "What a great room," I commented, parking myself on a pink and black director's chair. A faux zebra-striped rug stretched under my feet.

"Yeah, Shep wanted to get this finished before ... well... it used to be a fifties-style dinette. He worked hard to collect all these items."

"Wow," I said glancing around. Shep had a knack for decorating. He never seemed to run out of ideas. The whole warehouse was divided into several different rooms, each showcasing a different era of style and décor. The eighties room was done so well it made we want to break out a white sweatband and don some fuzzy pink legwarmers.

"So you're looking for Shep?" Pauline interrupted before I could get too far into the eighties groove.

I turned my focus away from a framed Ferris Bueller movie bill and back to her. "Yeah, so where is he? I've been trying to call him for a couple of days. He's not returning my messages."

"I'm sorry you've been worried. He's fine. He's taking some time off to visit with his parents."

"His parents? He hasn't spoken to them in…what…twenty years?"

Pauline shrugged. "Well, I guess they've reconciled."

I eyed her curiously. Shep's parents kicked him out of the house when he was just a teen. I'd never heard him say anything about wanting to reconnect with them. "Reconciled? Are you serious? Come on, Pauline. What's up?"

She glanced downward and squinted at the zebra rug. Bending down, she made a production of removing several pieces of lint that had gathered on the black stripes. "Nothing's up. He's just taking some time off. He'll be back in a couple of weeks," she continued to pick as she spoke.

Her aloofness bothered me, but I sensed I was going to get her to tell me what was really going on. "Well then, I guess I'll let you get back to work. If, by chance, you talk to him, please tell him to give me a call. It's important," I emphasized. "Someone we know was murdered and the cops want to question Shep," I added, watching for a reaction. A weird feeling settled over me when she didn't seem surprised by the news. "Does Shep already know about the murder, Pauline? Is that why he's taken off? Is he in some sort of trouble?" I was working hard to keep my voice steady.

She stood and glanced at her watch. I took it as a dismissal and also stood, but still maintaining eye contact. She shifted her stance and looked away. "I've said all I can say, Pippi. I'm sorry. I'll tell Shep you were here. I'm sure he'll be calling you soon. Now, I've got to get back to work, but if you want, you could go through some of the stuff out back. We've been sorting through a couple of lots from estate sales and there's some things we can't use."

"Sure, thanks," I muttered as she turned and started for another part of the store.

Not knowing what else to do, I headed for the Retro Metro's dumpster which, lucky for me, turned out to be a virtual smorgasbord of resalable goodies. Unbelievable what Shep was throwing away these days. I guess his clientele base had moved a little more upscale. Good for me, because my clientele (the Third Saturday Flea Market crowd) wasn't so hard to please. They were going to jump all over the corner shelf unit I was trying to cram under my passenger seat. Not to mention the CD rack, wooden stepstool, and miscellaneous kitsch I'd found buried throughout the dumpster—my personal favorite being a framed cross-stitch sampler that said: *Funny, I don't remember being absentminded.* What a hoot! I'd probably sell it to someone's grandma for five bucks.

I was struggling to fit my acquisitions in between the packages I still needed to ship when I looked up and saw Sean. He was across the lot, leaning against his car, watching me. I shoved the sampler between some boxes, slammed my back hatch, and crossed the lot with clenched fists.

As I approached, he held up the sequined purse I'd left behind the night before. "Peace offering," he said, smiling as if last night's fight never happened. That's the thing with guys; they could turn it on and off. Not me, I carried a grudge.

"Thanks," I said, snatching my purse before he could change his mind. "What are you doing here?"

"I'm still looking for Shep. Heard from him?"

"No, but I just talked to Pauline and she said he's taking some time off or something."

"Really? Did he mentioned this vacation to you before?"

We stood, staring at each other.

"Why are you so stuck on this Shep thing? You can't possibly think he had something to do with Jane's murder."

"I'm not sure what to think. I have to say it seems strange we can't track him down." I started to protest, but he cut in, "There's another possibility, too."

"What?"

"He could have witnessed something. We have Jane's phone records and they show that Shep called later that day. Since the teapot was wrapped, I'm assuming he changed his mind about buying it and was going to come back and pick it up."

"And, you think he came by last night and witnessed something and now he's in danger?"

"It's hard to tell. It could be anything. I'm going to talk to his employees now."

I glanced over my shoulder at the Retro Metro. "Good luck. I just tried to get something out of Pauline, but she was pretty tight-lipped."

"There's something else," he started as I turned to leave. I faced him again, noticing his eyes were darting about nervously. "I want to explain… I mean, I feel bad you found out about me getting married. I should have told you the other day…I just…" His voice faded to a whisper.

A thousand ugly retorts popped into my head, but I managed to keep them to myself. "What do you want me to say? Congratulations?"

"No…I mean, yes. Thanks. I just…well, I wanted to clear the air. Like I said, I felt bad because I didn't really tell you the other day when we were at the crime scene. I didn't know *how* to tell you. Then I saw you last night at The Classy Closet, and well…you know how that went. By the way, Sarah said she ran into you at the bridal shop. Why were you at the bridal shop?"

"Why do you care?" I shot back.

He shrugged. "Just wondered. Are you serious about someone?"

My mind raced. Would he feel jealous if I said yes? Maybe I should make up a fake fiancé and see how he reacted. Then I reconsidered. "No, I'm not dating anyone. I haven't since…" I let my words drop. "My cousin, Cherry Gallagher, is getting married a week from Saturday. I'm her maid of honor."

He smiled. "Well, congratulations to Cherry." He seemed happy. Was I sensing relief in his voice?

"When's your big date?" I asked.

"June."

"Good for you. Hope you'll be happy." My voice sounded false, even to me.

I turned to leave, but he gripped my arm and wheeled me around. "Pippi, I'm sorry." He paused, searching my face.

"Don't be. I'm happy for you, really."

"Really?" he asked, moving in closer. His eyes were half-mast, his lips slightly parted. His breath was coming in short shallow rasps. I was feeling that old familiar tingling I'd always felt right before the onset of a passionate kiss.

We teetered there, suspended in lustful confusion for a few seconds before I decided to make a move. I leaned in, closed my eyes and parted my lips, ready for the familiar warmth I had missed for so long, but all I felt was cold air.

My eyes snapped open. He'd backed up and was regarding me with what…confusion, fear, amusement?

Then, I did something I'd never done before. I slapped him. I'd seen Scarlett do it to Rhett and Sally do it to Harry. Heck, I'd seen it done a thousand times on trashy daytime talk shows, but I had never done it. Quite honestly, I shouldn't have waited for so long…it felt great.

I spun on my heel and walked away. I was fed up with Sean and all his hormonal superiority.

Chapter 7

I peeled out of the lot, tires squealing, and junk rattling from every corner of the Volvo. I could hear the sound of glass breaking as I screeched around the corner. Probably the cross-stitch sampler, but I didn't care.

I drove straight to the nearest fast food drive-through. Thank goodness, they had switched over from the breakfast menu; I don't know what I would have done without a double layered hamburger to calm my slap-happy soul. I went to retrieve a couple of bills from my wallet and found them wrapped in a tidy little note reminding me to check my emotions. Well, to heck with my emotions; I was beyond that. I needed a good, old fashioned, high calorie binge. So, just for good measure, I coughed up a couple of more bills and added a chocolate shake and small fries.

Sufficiently carb-loaded and stuffed with saturated fat, I was feeling better by the time I reached the post office. After shipping my packages, I made my way back to my apartment to unload my car.

Exhausted after hauling all my new acquisitions up the steps, I went straight to the kitchen, tore down yet another one of those bothersome "check your emotions" signs, and pulled a soda out of the fridge. I settled in front of my computer, twisted the cap, and let the cool fluid clear my mind. What was going on with Shep? Was he on the run because he'd witnessed a brutal murder? I couldn't just wait around for Sean to figure it out, I needed to find a few of my own answers.

I hesitated for a second, my fingers hovering over the keyboard. Where to start? The only thing that I'd garnered from the crime scene was that Jane had recently purchased a large lot of items from an estate sale. The books I found in the garbage were obviously part of that sale, discarded by Jane as she sorted through items. Remembering the marking on the outside of the box I saw in the dumpster, I typed Sokolov into the search engine. Sitting back, I took another sip from my soda as I studied the options on the screen: Sokolov the famous Russian pianist; some law firm in Philly; a Wiki reference to popular Russian surnames... I refined my search by cross-referencing Sokolov and Chicago. All I got was a listing of names. Lots of Sokolovs in the area.

I went to the *Tribune* online and accessed the obituary listings. I typed in the name Sokolov and found two references. One was archived May 8th, three years ago. The other was a more recent entry—three weeks ago on the 24th of September. I clicked on it and read the blurb.

Calina A. Sokolov, age 47, of Ukrainian Village, died at home on September 23th after a long battle with illness. She is survived by one son, Alex Sokolov, of Kirillov, Russia. Funeral arrangements are pending.

Not much of a death notice. I scanned the obituaries for the following week, but found nothing more on Ms. Sokolov. Then I searched white pages on-line for her residence and found she'd lived just off West Superior Avenue, downtown near the Ukrainian Village. I jotted down the address, crossed referenced a telephone number, and started formulating my strategy. I was half way through my second soda when I finalized my plan. All I needed was a little luck and a great outfit.

I dialed the number.

"Hello," a deep, slightly accented, male voice responded.

"Good afternoon," I replied, in my haughtiest tone. "This is Prudence Overton from Tolmey's Auction Gallery. May I speak to Calina, please?"

There was a slight hesitation from the other end. "May I ask what you want to speak to her about?"

Smart guy. "I'm sorry, it's confidential."

Another hesitation. I held firm on my end, not offering any more information.

"I'm her son. I'm sorry to tell you this, but my mother has passed away. Is there something I could help you with?"

"Passed away! Oh, no...I'm so sorry." I began really pouring it on. I could tell this guy was sharp, I needed to be convincing. "I knew she was ill, but I thought ... I'm sorry. You must be Alex. She told me about you."

"She did?"

"Yes. Well, she mentioned you a few times. She seemed proud of you." I hesitated a minute before adding, "Would it be possible to meet with you in person, Mr. Sokolov? There's something of great importance that we need to discuss...much too important for over the phone."

"Uh...I'm not..."

"I can come to your mother's place first thing in the morning, if that'll be convenient. Let's say nine o'clock?"

"Well, I guess that would be alright."

"Fine. I'll see you at nine." I disconnected before he could change his mind. Then, I quickly dialed Shep's number again, but there was still no answer.

I spent another hour or more searching for information online before hitting my resale clothing stockpile in search of the perfect get-up. It wasn't easy, but by bed-time, I felt confident I'd pieced together something that made me look like an antiquarian book dealer ...something understated, modest and business-like.

*

Eager to execute my plan, I awoke early the next morning, grabbed a quick bowl of cereal and went right to work transforming myself into Prudence Overton.

The night before, I assembled the most bookish outfit I could dig out of my storage bins: a long brown, wool blend skirt; a high-collar, button-down blouse with a ruffle; and the same navy blazer I wore to the crime scene a couple days earlier. There was still a tiny rip in the armpit of the blazer, but surely, no one would notice that.

Everything worked great except the skirt; it was way too long. No problem. Having always been on the short side, I was an expert at length adjustments. I grabbed a roll of packing tape from my coffee table and went to work. A few minutes later, the skirt looked like it was tailored for my body.

With my outfit perfected, I turned my focus to the rest of me. I studied my reflection in the mirror for a few minutes before deciding on a conservative French twist and minimal makeup. Taming my red curls into a twist took a half-bottle of goop and some major stamina, but the efforts were worth it; the new-do transformed me from frizz queen to sleek professional. A pair of round, silver Windsor-framed glasses that I used once when I attended a costume party, completed the look.

I stepped back and gave my reflection a thumbs up. I looked just like someone named Prudence Overton should look.

After several trips around the block, I found a parking space on West Erie and started hoofing it north towards Calina's address. No easy feat, since Prudence had chosen three-inch heels to wear with her wool-blend skirt.

Downtown, with the breezes off the lake, was always slightly cooler than the burbs, but today it felt particularly chilly. I cursed my wardrobe choice. My feet were killing me and a cold wind was blowing up my skirt—my butt cheeks were actually shivering.

Nonetheless, I persevered on my quest. Crossing over Hoyne Avenue, I made my way around some city workers who were working on the water main. As I passed, they stopped and gave me their full attention. One even broke loose with a high-pitched whistle.

I was a taken aback; I never drew that type of attention from construction workers. Actually, I couldn't help but notice a lot of men were turning to give me a second glance. Geez, guys must really go for the smart, nerdy type. Who knew? Smiling inwardly, I gave them a little extra wiggle as I continued down the walk. Being Prudence was turning out to be fun.

I reached Calina's address just as the bells of St. Volodymyre began to chime. I eyed her place, quite surprised by what I saw. Nestled on a tree-lined street, her classically designed, red brick three-story home boasted a large front porch and an oh-so-beautiful garden tucked behind a black iron fence. In a neighborhood where multi-family housing and small cottages reflected its proud working-class roots, a red brick beauty like hers would be worth a fortune. Of course, it was humble in comparison to the million dollar mansions down the street in the Wicker Park neighborhood; but still I couldn't help but wonder how she could afford such a place. I shrugged. Maybe she'd had a great job.

I pushed my glasses back on the bridge of my nose and ascended the front steps. The door swung open before I knocked.

"Ms. Overton?"

The first thing I thought when I saw Alex Sokolov was Sasquatch on steroids. The man was huge and very, very furry. Dark shocks of hair sprung out from every angle of his head, outdone only by the black, bristly uni-brow that seemed to spring to life as he spoke.

He held the door open and invited me in. I smiled politely and inched past him unable to avoid noticing the large tuft of hair that peeked through the top of his button-down shirt. Thankfully, he was wearing loafers; hairy toes grossed me out.

Once inside, he motioned me to one of the only two chairs left in the place. I got right down to business. "Thank you for agreeing to see me today, Mr. Sokolov. Again, I'm sorry about your mother."

Despite all the fur, his smile was warm and genuine. His age was difficult to determine, but I guessed him to be in his late twenties. "Thank you. However, I'm sorry to say that my mother and I weren't all that close. I was raised in Russia by my grandparents. When they died, she brought me to the states, but well...it was a difficult transition for me as a young teen and I was quite hard to handle. So, she sent me to a boarding school on the East Coast where I finished my schooling before returning to Russia. We really only bothered to keep in contact on the holidays and such. So you see, her passing seems almost like the death of a stranger."

How sad, I thought. While my mom drove me nuts sometimes, if anything ever happened to her, I would be devastated.

An awkward silence fell over us. Alex cleared his throat and quickly changed the subject as if embarrassed that he revealed so much personal history. "So, you're from Tolmey's Auction Gallery?" he asked.

"Yes," I perked up, ready to relay my pre-planned spiel. "I'm actually associated with the antiquarian book division of Tolmey's. Your mother contacted us a while back in hopes of auctioning a valuable book. I was assigned to assist in the assessment of the volume. When I called yesterday, I was hoping to let her know that I had ascertained a number for her...and it's quite extraordinary."

Thank goodness I had taken the time to memorize a few of the terms on the *Glossary for Book Collector's* website; I sounded quite official.

"I don't understand what you mean. What type of number?"

"The value of the book," I answered, as if he had just asked the dumbest question in the world. I paused, letting the tension build. "Of course, your mother was very protective of the volume and I was only allowed to see it for a few moments, but if upon further inspection and authentication, it proves to be in the same condition as when I first assessed it, she...or you as her heir, should be able to procure around two thousand at auction." I uncrossed and re-crossed my legs, letting the dollar amount hang in the air. "Would you like for Tolmey's to continue to handle the auctioning of the book, Mr. Sokolov?"

"I don't...what was the title of the book?" he asked, his accent becoming more distinguished as his frustration grew.

"It was a Tolstoy's preprint edition of Anna Karenina. There were hand-made notes on the pages," I answered, matter-of-factly, even though I had made it up in the wee hours the night before. I held my breath. What I knew about Russian literature would fit on the end of Mikhail Baryshnikov's pinky.

"I'm sorry, Ms. Overton. I'm afraid I don't have that book or any volumes anymore. You see, I've had all but a few things of my mother's estate liquidated. All that's left is what you see here—just a few things I need for the duration of my stay, which won't be long. So, all the books are gone. I would have no idea of where to even start looking for this valuable volume."

"Well, that's easy. Who handled the estate auction?"

"Uh...A to Z Estate Sales."

"You could call them and request a record of sales. Maybe they have a listing of who purchased the books. If you could track down the purchaser, you might be able to get the books back."

He shrugged. "Maybe, but that seems like a lot of trouble for two thousand dollars; and besides, I don't know how much longer I'll be in town."

Did I hear him right? A lot of trouble? Was two thousand dollars chump change to this guy? "Did I say two thousand? It could be more. Much, much more."

He shrugged. I started feeling like my visit with Mr. Sokolov was wearing thin. He reinforced this by glancing at his wrist, which sported an expensive gold watch. "I'm curious, Mr. Sokolov. Your mother seemed to have such a fine collection of books. What was it that she did for a living? Was she a writer, perhaps?"

He gave me a look that screamed mind your own business lady. "No, she wasn't a writer. She just appreciated the finer things in life." He stood, silently announcing the end of our visit.

We exchanged a couple of pleasantries while he showed me to the door. As I stepped out onto the porch, I glanced over my shoulder and caught him staring at my backside. When he looked up and saw that I had noticed his little indiscretion, his face broke into a mischievous grin—he didn't even bother to look embarrassed. I shot him a murderous look and descended the porch steps with my chin held high. That guy was nothing but a spoiled, perverted, hairy brat. No wonder his own mother didn't want to be around him.

My heels had only clicked a few feet down the walk before I stopped and turned around. I couldn't put my finger on it, but something wasn't quite right at the Sokolov home. For starters, how did Calina Sokolov afford such an elaborate lifestyle? Russian mob, maybe? I shuddered. With his Wookie-like attributes, Alex Sokolov could easily be a mobster. Just looking at him, I knew how it had all gone down: *Alex Sokolov, known amongst the other Russian gangsters as "Scary-Hairy", realized something incriminating had been sold off with his mother's estate. Probably a weapon used in a mob murder, or maybe his loan shark book, or…whatever. He somehow found out it was sold and tracked it down to The Classy Closet. Poor Jane stumbled across him as he broke in to retrieve it and Alex eliminated her. It should be a case easy to solve based on forensics alone. A guy like that would have left thousands of hairs at the scene…*

I snapped back to reality. I was jumping to conclusions—a very bad habit of mine. What I needed was proof.

I glanced back at Calina's house, double checking to make sure I wasn't being watched, before approaching the house next door. My knock was answered by spry-looking, old lady.

"I already have a church," she squawked, shutting the door in my face. I knocked again.

"I don't need anything, I'm busy." She started to close the door again, but failed when it hit my foot, which was wedged between the door and the frame. I could hear the Price is Right playing in the background. The showcase showdown was just getting under way. No wonder she was so anxious to get rid of me. My mind raced; I needed a good cover story if I was going to compete with the popular game show.

I assumed an authoritative posture. "I'm Prudence Overton with Liberty Insurance. We're conducting an investigation on the death of your neighbor Calina Sokolov. I'd like to ask you a few questions, if I may."

I stared directly into her milky-blue eyes, daring her to defy an official investigator.

"What type of questions?" she snapped.

"Official questions. Your cooperation is imperative, Mrs...."

"You're an investigator and you don't know my name?"

Good question. This old bat was a sharp one.

"Actually, we're just in the initial phase of questioning; we're canvassing the neighborhood." I glanced back to Calina's house. All seemed quiet. I removed a steno pad and pen from my purse. "This won't take much of your time. I just have a few questions...please." I turned off the authority and turned on beggar mode.

She gave me a scrutinizing once over before standing aside and waving me into her living room. She motioned to a floral-upholstered chair as she picked up the remote and turned down the volume on the television.

I glanced around. Her house was a study in contrast compared to Calina's home. The combination of dark woodwork and poor lighting made me feel instantly depressed. Adding to the dark mood, a large wooden image of the Russian Madonna stared at me from the fireplace mantel. I squirmed under her watch. It wasn't easy being a liar.

"Well, what are your questions?" She slouched into a light blue recliner, adjusting a couple of pillows behind the small of her back and pulling a hand-crocheted afghan around her legs. I'm not sure why she needed the afghan; it must have been close to a hundred degrees in the room.

I opened my pad. "What is your name?" I asked, pen poised in air.

"Yelena Stanislav. What do you want to know about Calina?"

"Did you know her well?" I asked.

"Well enough."

"Were you on friendly terms?"

"We were neighbors, weren't we?"

I sighed. This lady was all about patience and understanding. "Had Mrs. Sokolov been ill for a long time?"

"Yes. Cancer. I would take her some *yushka* about once a week. It was her favorite."

I adjusted my glasses. The word cancer always made me squirm. "That was kind of you, Mrs. Stansilove," I managed to say.

"That's Stanislav. Get it right," she hissed. She turned to check on the showcase showdown. The first contestant was making a bid of sixteen thousand five hundred. Way too low, I thought.

"Stanislav, sorry. My firm is making inquiries into Mrs. Sokolov's finances. Do you know where she worked?"

"She didn't work." She was fingering the remote, getting ready to turn up the volume again.

I looked at her over the rim of my glasses. "There is some question as to how she made a living. You see, if she falsified information on her tax papers, she may not be entitled to a full payout. Or if she was involved in some sort of illegal behavior...."

"Illegal behavior? Calina?"

"Yes, well...you know... like maybe the Russian mob."

She sat upright, making some sort of weird noise that sounded like a mixture of air letting out of a tire and a cat's hiss. I watched tiny droplets spray from her mouth, glad that I was positioned far enough away to be safe from the spittle-splash.

"Mobster?" her voice crackled with what I took to be laughter. "Why do all you people think every Russian is a mobster? Calina earned her money honestly. She was a... what do you say? Kept woman."

That's not what I expected to hear. "A kept woman?"

Mrs. Stanislav raised a wrinkled hand in my direction as if to emphasize her next point. "Such a beautiful woman. Too young for cancer. And where was *he* when she died? Nowhere. Not even descent enough to be with her in the last moments. She died all alone."

"Her son wasn't here?"

"No, her lover. But, her son? That no good...," Mrs. Stanislav paused. I could see her working her tongue inside her mouth, adjusting her dentures. They must have been slipping. "Her son is a spoiled brat. Calina was a weak mother. She could never say 'no' to him. He never wanted for nothing."

"I see," I said, thinking that what Calina really should have given him was about fifty electrolysis sessions. "Do you know who her, her, um...?"

"It's no secret. Calina talked about him all the time. An Irishman, James Farrell. They'd been together for years."

My heart thudded with excitement. Golly gee, a solid clue. I jotted it down enthusiastically.

I heard the sharp dinging of bells. Mrs. Stanislav turned up the volume just as the showcase winner was announced. I was right; sixteen five was way too low.

She sat grinning at the boob tube, her cloudy eyes round with excitement and her jaw working frantically back and forth. I thanked her and quietly excused myself, nodding guiltily to the Madonna as I showed myself out.

Chapter 8

"*That* James Farrell?" I was talking to myself as I typed on the keyboard. It had only really taken two clicks to get a full biography on Calina's lover.

I thought the name sounded familiar. James Farrell the hot dog king. Of course! I ate at JimDogs all the time. Best deal in town. My personal favorite was the Junior J-dog combo meal with a CubbyPup and a frosty mug of root beer.

What a story James Farrell had. The product of a large, poor south-side Irish family, James Farrell had worked hard and built his hot dog dynasty from the ground up. No rich daddy, no fancy business degree, no government grants, just a determined spirit, hard work, and innovation—that innovation being his version of the hot dog bun. As the story goes, young James spent days in his mother's kitchen, experimenting with her bread recipes, until he created what, in my opinion, was the best hot dog bun in the whole world. Light…flakey…buttery…my mouth was watering just thinking about it. He took his products and hit the streets, peddling his cart from one street corner to the next. His reputation grew quickly as everyone started talking about James's Dogs which was eventually shortened to JimDogs. Soon, he had enough revenue to move his pups to a permanent JimDogs residence, which he opened right here in Naperville. Since then, the business had grown with franchises in twelve states. The guy was the quintessential American rags-to-riches story.

And now I had discovered that he was also the keeper of a Russian mistress. Not so good, considering he was married with a grown son.

All very interesting, but how could there possibly be any connection between JimDogs and Jane's murder? I had no idea. My previous excitement began to fizzle. I thought I'd stumbled upon some case-breaking evidence, but there was no way to connect James Farrell with these murders. What motive would he have? The guy was worth millions; he'd probably never set foot in a consignment shop. Unless...maybe he was mixed up with the Russian mob somehow. I watched enough mobster television shows to know that businessmen get mixed up with the mob all the time. So, maybe my first theory was correct. I could see how easily it could happen: *A young James Farrell had the best hot dog bun in the city, but couldn't start up his business without capital. Desperate, he turned to a two-bit mobster for quick cash. As he grew his business, the mobster was always there to take his share. Poor James was forever indebted to the boss; he'd sold his soul to the mob and they took care of him. They even gave him a beautiful Russian woman, or no ... maybe Calina was the mob boss's daughter ... yeah ... that really tied James into a life of crime. And now that Calina was gone, he wanted to sever his ties with the family, but they had some sort of hold on him...maybe proof of some illegal activity, or who knows? Whatever the crucial link was, proof of it was mistakenly sold off in Calina's estate and James had to get it back. Murder could come easily to a man who was that desperate...*

I smiled to myself; proud that I'd put it all together so quickly. All I needed was a little proof. If I could just find a *wee* piece of evidence to support my theory, I could prove Shep wasn't involved in any of this.

I sat back and carefully considered my options before deciding to follow up on my one other lead—A to Z Estate Sales. I typed their name into the search engine prompt and printed out directions. On the way out, I smeared peanut butter on a piece of white bread and folded it in half for a lunch to go. As a final thought, I grabbed the round-framed glasses again and tucked them away in my bag; Prudence may be needed again on this mission.

I barely made it down my steps when Mom appeared from around the hedge. Pretending not to see her, I made a mad scramble for my car.

"Phillipena!"

I cringed. I wasn't overly fond of my name, especially when my mother yelled it out like that. No matter how it was said, it had a weird sound to it. I had my dad to blame. When I was born as the fifth girl in the O'Brien family, he gave up on waiting for a male namesake and stuck me with some strange feminism of his name. Then, in the third grade, Phillipena became Pippi when the teacher read to us about another precocious red-headed character, Pippi Longstocking.

"What in the world! Stop right there!" Mom was running across the yard at break-neck speed.

I obeyed, turning around to face her.

She descended upon me like ants on melted ice cream. "What in the world are you wearing?" she asked, punctuating her question with an open-jaw, eye-popping expression.

I backed up a little. "What am I wearing?" I reiterated, looking down at my wardrobe choice. It seemed fine to me. "A wool skirt, button-down blouse, and navy blazer." I brushed some dust off the back elbow of the blazer. "I admit, this blazer's a little dusty. It's the color; it seems to attract dirt. And there's a tiny rip in—"

"Turn around."

I backed up a little more. Was she going to spank me for my wardrobe choice?

"Turn around right this instant!"

I pivoted, slowly, squeezing my eyes shut.

"That's obscene!" she screeched.

I opened my eyes and faced her. "Obscene?"

"Your skirt." She grabbed my shoulders and spun me back around. "What's this?" she asked, pulling and tugging at my backside. "Oh, no. Did you try to tape the hem of this skirt?"

"Yes, why?" I was twisting my head like an inebriated owl, trying to see what she was fiddling with.

"The tape is tangled in the skirt's liner and stuck to your waist band in the back. You're completely exposed back here. Look at these holes! You need to get some better panties. Well, at least I caught you before you got out the door. How embarrassing if someone else had seen you this way."

I shriveled, thinking about how many people I previously mooned: the construction workers; Alex the Sasquatch Man; all the people on the street. "Yeah, that would have been really embarrassing," I replied thinking there was no need to embarrass the both of us.

"Where are you going?" she asked.

"Uh…well, I have an appointment in Ridgewood."

"With whom?" My mother's grammar was impeccable.

"I have an appointment with an estate auctioneer. Why?" It was natural to be suspicious when my mom inquired about my whereabouts.

"Why? Because you're wearing makeup and you've actually styled your hair." She gave me an approving once-over. "I thought maybe you had a date."

"A date?"

"Didn't you follow my advice and call about the singles club at church?"

"Well, I haven't actually had—"

"What will you do at Cherry's wedding without a date? You'll be bored to death."

Hmm. I hadn't thought about that. Another good reason to get a hold of Shep. He'd always come through when I needed a male stand-in. "I'm working on it."

"Fine. Just remember to stop by the house when you get back. I picked up the dress today and you'll need to try it on again, just in case Doris needs to make any more alterations. The wedding's just a week away, you know?"

I grimaced. "I know. Here, take this," I said, handing her my peanut butter sandwich. "I won't need it." Just thinking about that skin-tight chiffon atrocity was ruining my appetite.

*

Thirty minutes later, I walked through the door of A to Z Estate Sales, and came face to face with Chuck Norris. Well, not the actual Chuck Norris, but someone that looked just like him.

"Can I help you?" he asked.

I stood speechless—my slack-jaw mouth unable to produce an intelligible syllable. I had a huge crush on Chuck ever since I was in junior high. Even now, I'll stay up until all hours of the night just so I can watch him strut his stuff on late night infomercials.

"Miss?" Chuck was waiting for my reply.

I stuck out a wobbly hand. "I'm Prud…no, I mean…I'm Pippi O'Brien." The eyes of the ranger were upon me. I couldn't lie. "I need to speak to the manager."

"That's me." He grasped my hand and gave it a firm shake. "I'm Charlie."

"No way," I said, before I could stop myself. "Does anyone ever call you Chuck?"

"Yeah, I get that all the time. What can I do for you?" He seemed in a rush. "I need to find out about an estate sale that your company handled for Calina Sokolov. Do you recall the name?"

He tilted his head back and studied me through furrowed brows. "Yes, why?"

I took a deep breath and continued, "Did you keep records of who purchased books from that estate sale?"

"We always keep records of sales, but they're confidential." He smiled and winked. Strange, I'd never seen the *real* Chuck wink.

"I think there may be a connection between that estate sale and a recent murder."

"Murder?" Chuck suddenly looked nervous.

"It's just a hunch. But if you could simply verify if you sold items from the Sokolov estate to Jane Reynolds or perhaps to her business, The Classy Closet, it would be a huge help to me."

"Why, are you a cop?"

I chuckled. "No, I'm not a cop. Although, I am sort of working as a consultant for the police."

"Sort of working?"

"Well, not officially, I guess." I hesitated and shifted a little. "Actually, it's just a personal thing. Can you help me out? Please?"

He moved over to his desk and fingered a manila file. Even from where I was standing, I could see the name Sokolov written on it with black sharpie.

"That's the Sokolov file," I stated, practically salivating.

"Yes, it is." He kept a firm grip as he leaned back on his desk and smiled like a sly cat.

Like an idiot, I reached for it. He snatched it away. "You gotta be kidding," he laughed, "I don't know what's going on, but these names are worth at least a thousand bucks."

"A thousand bucks!"

"Yeah, that's what the other lady paid."

"A lady? What lady? What was her name?" I took a deep breath. I half expected him to blurt out the name Farrell.

"She didn't give me her name. Just said she had an interest in antiques and wanted a chance to approach the consigners who bought from this particular estate. There were only a few buyers, so I didn't think it was a big deal." Chuck had folded his arms and was leaning back on his desk, the file crunched up in his muscular biceps.

I narrowed my eyes at him. "So you just let her copy down the information without even knowing her name?"

"Hey, she paid me a thousand bucks," he stared at me expectantly. Did this guy actually think I looked like someone who could pull a thousand dollars out of my purse?

"Would you consider letting me look at it without paying any money?"

"No."

I dug around in my bag. "Fourteen dollars?" I asked.

He tilted back his head and let out a hearty laugh before moving around his desk and throwing the file into a drawer. This guy was definitely no Chuck Norris. Chuck's morals would never be for sale— just his exercise machines.

I paused, considering my options.

"Well, lady. What's it going to be?"

"Fine. I'll leave," I said. "But, could you at least tell me what she looked like?"

"Sure. That type of information would be worth oh…fourteen dollars." He held out his hand. I reluctantly handed over the money and waited expectantly.

"She wore a long coat, a hat and dark glasses." He smiled mischievously. I wanted to scream.

"Young, old?" I pressed.

"Middle-aged, maybe. Maybe older, maybe younger."

"How about hair: blonde, brunette…?"

He shrugged and pointed mockingly toward his head. "Like I said, she was wearing a hat."

I slammed the front door on my way out. I couldn't believe I paid fourteen dollars for nothing.

Chapter 9

I left A to Z Estate Sales with my tail between my legs and fourteen dollars poorer. The latter really ticked me off. I was a woman used to getting what I paid for, and that guy ripped me off. Although, it might have been money well spent, if what I just learned could help to clear Shep's involvement in all this.

After a little deliberation, I decided to give Sean a call. Funny how my fingers automatically remembered his number even though I hadn't dialed it for over a year.

I could barely hear his voice mail message over the nervous thudding of my heart, but at the beep, I cleared my throat and started in, "Hi Sean. This is Pippi. I'm just leaving a place called A to Z Estate Sales in Ridgewood and I think you might want to check it out. The sleazebag that runs the place calls himself Charlie. You can't miss him…he looks just like Chuck Norris. Don't let his looks fool you … he's nothing like the real Chuck—he's a slime ball. Anyway, he's got this file that lists the consigners that shopped at the Sokolov estate auction. That's S…o…k…o…l…o…v. Remember? I got that name off the box I saw in the dumpster at The Classy Closet. I definitely think there's a connection between Sokolov and Jane's murder. There has to be. I mean, you're on the wrong track with Shep. I think a guy named James Ferrell might be involved somehow. You see, I stopped by Calina Sokolov's home and spoke to her neighbor who told me Calina was involved with James Ferrell. That's Ferrell as in JimDogs. Anyway, the big thing is that Charlie here at A to Z said a lady paid him a thousand bucks for the info in the Sokolov file. So, there's got to be some sort of connection. You should get a warrant for A to Z Estate

Sales right away so you can get that file and a description of the woman who paid to see it. Oh, and while you're searching the place, see if your guys find fourteen dollars in crumpled bills: two fives and four ones. That's my money ... that guy Charlie practically stole it from me." I paused, trying to think of anything I may have left out. "Ok, then. Bye, and um ... well, sorry about slapping you."

I felt regret the instant I disconnected. What was wrong with me? Not only had I apologized for a perfectly legitimate and well deserved face slap, I pretty much sounded like a babbling idiot.

I shrugged it off. The important thing was that I turned over the information to Sean. With that done, I decided to let it go and get back to my own work.

*

In warmer weather, I usually spent Thursday afternoons hitting early garage sales, but since October wasn't a big month for sales, I thought I'd run by a couple of my favorite consignment shops instead. I actually scored big at the Thrifty Kids shop. The owner was anxious to unload a bunch of unsold summer clothes which I practically stole for five bucks a bag. Nice stuff, too. Mostly brand names. Luckily for me, she took a check, since ol' Chuck had taken my last bit of cash.

Although I definitely needed exercise, carrying my latest acquisitions up all twenty-two steps leading to my above-garage apartment was exhausting. My glutes were starting to burn as I headed out for trip number four and found my mother on the top step. She was holding the two remaining bags. "Looks like you've been busy. I'm glad. I always say work is the best therapy."

I knew she was referring to my troubles with Sean, but I didn't really want to go into it again. "Look, Mom, thanks for helping, but I've got a lot to do."

She patted my shoulder and smiled. "Sure, dear. I just came to see if you wanted to eat dinner with us. Your dad's been cooking all day."

"Really? Sounds good," I backtracked without hesitation, my rumbling stomach prompting me to trudge down the steps behind her. My mood softened as I ducked around the hedge, and crossed the backyard toward the warm glow of kitchen lights cast against the increasingly darkening evening. My nose began twitching as soon as I opened the back door—Mulligan stew, my dad's specialty. Paired with hard rolls and cold Guinness, it was the ultimate comfort food.

"There you are," my father said, pulling a sheet of oatmeal cookies from the oven. "Your mother asked me to make something special for dinner. She said she needed an incentive to get you over here to try on the dress for your cousin's wedding."

I shot my mother a look. I should have known she had an ulterior motive for inviting me to dinner.

I was just about to pop a piece of hot cookie into my mouth when she grabbed me. "Dress first, then food. Come with me."

I followed her into the family room. She pointed to the dress which was draped over the sofa. The television was tuned into the six o'clock news and the weather girl was promising lower temperatures and a possibility of rain for the next couple of days.

Mom sighed. "I certainly hope Cherry has good weather for the wedding. It's risky planning an outdoor event this time of year. Are you excited for the wedding, dear? All your sisters are going to be there, you know."

"I can hardly wait," I said with a sigh, attempting to squirm out of my jeans. "I wouldn't worry about the weather. The only thing that's going to ruin this wedding is me in this dress."

Mom was stooped down, holding the dress open. I rested one hand on her shoulder as I stepped into it. Amazingly, she pulled it over my hips with no problem.

"That Doris is a miracle worker," she said, zipping and buttoning my back side. "You can't even tell this was altered."

I looked down at my front side, which from my angle, resembled one of the off-color relief maps I would have colored in grade school. I always preferred using my orange crayon for the foothills and mountains. Much brighter and more imaginative than the boring old brown my classmates always chose.

"Run up and take a look in my bathroom mirror. It looks so much better," she said, pointing to the staircase.

I'd only made it to the second step, when I heard something that made me stop and run back into the family room. "Did you hear that?" I asked, grabbing the remote and turning up the volume on the news program. The anchor was relaying a breaking story. She was standing in front of the Retro Metro.

I'm reporting live from a popular home décor shop in Westmont, where, less than thirty minutes ago, a 911 call was placed indicating a murder had occurred. Investigative teams are on the scene now, but the police are offering no comments. We'll keep our viewers informed as new details develop...

Her words faded from my perception. All I could think of was Shep. I ran back through the house and through the kitchen. Ignoring Mom and Dad's questions, I grabbed a coat off one of the hooks by the door and threw on my tennis shoes. I ran double time up my apartment steps, retrieved my keys, and within minutes was speeding down the road toward the Retro Metro.

I was about two miles from home, when my cell rang. I almost crashed trying to retrieve it.

"Pippi, it's Shep."

"Shep! Where are you? I was watching the news and they said—"

"I know. That's why I'm calling. It wasn't me. I'm at Saint Edward's Hospital. Can you come over? I need to talk to you."

"St. Edwards? What's going on? Are you hurt?"

"No, that's not why I'm here. Can you come now? I'm on the fourth floor."

"I'm on my way."

He disconnected, leaving me with a thousand unanswered questions.

I zoomed another block, checked my mirrors, and flipped a u-turn picking up speed as I made my way toward the hospital.

I grabbed my cell again just as I was turning onto Ogden.

He answered on the first ring. "Sean. It's Pippi. I'm on my way to St. Edwards Hospital. Shep called. He's there. On the news they said there was a murder at the Retro. What do you know about it?"

"Nothing. I hadn't heard about it. That's out of my jurisdiction, but I'll make some calls and see what I can find out. Was Shep hurt or something?" he asked.

"I don't know." My mind raced. What was he doing at the hospital? "He didn't say why he's there. Actually, he was kind of vague about the whole thing. He just said he needed to talk to me." I didn't care. He was alive. That's all that mattered.

I hung up with Sean as I pulled into a space on the North Parking Deck of the hospital. Ignoring the little white sign that marked my spot for Dr. R. Patel, I hurriedly locked my door and headed for the walkway leading to the main building.

The elevator doors opened a few feet from the fourth floor care station. An efficient-looking nurse, dressed in orange and black scrubs with miniature jack-o-lanterns, pointed the way to Shep's room.

As I entered, an older couple stood and walked out. They didn't bother to introduce themselves, but I knew who they were. I also knew if they were there, something bad was going on.

"Hey doll, come over here," Shep beckoned from his bed.

I hesitated, taken back by his appearance. I'd just seen him a couple of days ago, but today his normally coffee and cream complexion was a sickly, milky color; his eyes dull; his lips dry and cracked.

I slowly approached and took his outstretched hand. His fingertips felt ice cold against my skin.

"What...," I started, my voice catching in my throat.

"I know you've been trying to reach me and I should have called earlier. I just didn't know how to tell you."

"Tell me what?" Although I already knew.

He smiled, a small painful-looking smile. "I've been sick for a while, but I was trying to keep it from you. Don't worry, though. This is just a temporary setback. I'm going to beat this thing."

I swallowed hard and nodded my head as tears spilled down my cheeks. "What's wrong?"

"Cancer. It spread before I recognized the symptoms. Now it's pretty far along."

"I knew you'd been sick here and there. I thought you were having trouble shaking a virus. We were just out together the other day."

"I know. It's the effects of the chemo. I have good days and bad days. The last couple of days have been bad. Real bad."

I started shivering even though the room was stifling hot. My lips twitched, but for some reason they wouldn't form any words.

Shep continued, filling the silence. "Those were my parents. We've reconciled. Can you believe it? How many years has it been? Twenty at least."

I was trembling now. "You'll beat this. I know—" My words were choked out by a sob that broke loose and then turned to full-on cry fest. He pulled me close, patting my back, comforting me. Which made me feel horrible. I should be the one comforting him, but I couldn't help myself.

He let me carry on for a while before getting tough. "Okay. That's enough now. It's going to be alright. Really."

"I'm sorry. You're right. You're going to beat this," I said again, this time with more conviction. I sat up, grabbed some tissue from his bed stand and started blowing and wiping. Each time I got my face dry, new tears would start again.

"You're a good friend, Pippi. You've always been here for me. I'm going to need you now, doll. I'm going to need you to help me with something important."

I nodded. "Sure, anything."

"It's about what happened at the Retro this evening. You saw it on the news?" he asked.

"Yes. Who—"

"It's Pauline. Her boyfriend found her. He called me right after he dialed 911."

"Oh, no. I'm so sorry, Shep." My words sounded empty, even to me. The truth was, I was so numb about Shep I could hardly feel anything for Pauline. I knew her. I liked her. But I was already full of sorrow; there wasn't any room left in me to grieve for her. The news of her death seemed to hover over me without sinking into my conscious.

"I want you to keep an eye on the investigation. Make sure the cops don't push it aside."

I stared at him, unable to answer.

His eyes darkened. "I asked her to stay late this evening. I asked her get some paperwork done for me. It was my fault that she was there, Pippi. It's my fault. She didn't deserve to die. She was young, good, healthy..." His voice trailed off with an echo of gurgling. He hacked a few times.

"Her boyfriend found her?" I asked, trying to keep my mind clear and stay on task.

"He didn't do it. I know the kid," Shep said, squelching any accusations I might make. "He found her ... body...you just have to trust me on this. The cops are wasting time on him."

I waited for a minute, caressing his hand and giving him a chance to regain his breath. The silence was punctuated with the beeping and whirring of machines.

"It should have been me," he finally continued. "I'm sick anyway. What a waste and just ...." He shook his head as if trying to shake off the horror of it all. "She was a runaway. That's why I think the police won't put enough effort into finding her killer. She was really into the drug scene at one time; but, her past doesn't have anything to do with this. She was getting her life back together. Taking classes and everything. She wanted to major in business. She was only twenty years old." I watched as he reached for his water bottle.

His hand wobbled as he drank. Water dribbled out the side of his dry lips. I grabbed a tissue to blot it for him, glad to feel of help. "I want you to promise me that you'll do everything you can to make sure the police find the person who did this. Don't let them give up."

"I will," I promised.

Shep grabbed my hand and squeezed lightly. "I know you will."

We grew silent again. For a second, I thought he'd fallen asleep.

Suddenly, his eyes popped open. "Now I need to ask you something really serious," he said, a slow smile creeping over his face. "What are you wearing?"

I stopped and looked down. I forgot I was still wearing Cherry's gawd-awful bridesmaid dress.

I laughed. Then laughed some more. Soon I was rolling with almost hysteric laughter. From bawling to laughing. My emotions were shot.

"This," I said, taking off my coat and twirling around, "is a dress I have to wear in front of two hundred people next Saturday for my cousin's wedding. What do you think?" I struck a couple of poses, just to give him the full affect.

"Whew ... that's ugly—really ugly."

I laughed and sat back down on the edge of his bed. "Isn't it? Even I think it's horrible and you know I'm no fashion diva."

He offered a weak smile in response. "Wish I could help you out with that, hon."

I shook my head. Tears were starting again.

Thankfully a nurse came in to change his IV. As she entered, I caught a glimpse of his parents hovering outside the door.

"I think I should go and let you rest," I said, laying my head down on his shoulder for another hug.

"I'm counting on you," he whispered in my ear.

I nodded and gave him a quick peck on the cheek before moving out of the way for the nurse.

I left the hospital thinking how quickly life can change. Here I was, so stressed out over this stupid dress when two people had lost their lives and my best friend was fighting for his.

Chapter 10

When I reached home, I found Sean's car parked in my drive. He was sitting on my bottom step, waiting. I sat next to him, shivering in the cool autumn night air.

He wrapped his arm around me. "It was Pauline," he said softly. "She was shot to death at the Retro Metro. I'm sorry, Pippi."

"I know. Shep told me. I just ... I saw her yesterday."

Sean turned me until I was facing him. "Why's Shep at the hospital?"

"He's sick. It doesn't look good. Cancer." The words caught in my throat.

Sean searched my face, but remained silent.

"He feels like it should have been him instead of Pauline. I left you a message earlier, but it might not have made too much sense. Sean, I think Jane and Pauline's murders are connected and that they're tied to James Farrell somehow. You can check the gun ballistics, right? See if they match."

"Pippi, I don't think—"

"I don't care if you agree with me or not. Just promise me that you'll check into what I'm saying. I told Shep I'd make sure Pauline's killer was brought to justice. He seems to think the police won't put much effort into investigating her murder because she's a reformed addict."

There was a long pause. To my surprise, he didn't argue. Instead, he leaned in, kissed my forehead lightly, and raised my face to his. "The Westmont PD is handling Pauline's murder, but I'm in contact with the lead investigator. Plus, I've already starting checking into A to Z Estate Sales. If there's a connection to James Farrell, I'll find it. In the meantime, promise you'll be careful," he said. Then he stood and left.

*

I set my alarm earlier than usual. I needed to get up and get busy first thing. Not only to keep my mind off Shep but to keep my business going. I needed to increase my cash flow, especially if I was going to be tied up looking into things for Shep.

My first task, after my usual morning routine, was to turn my attention to packaging a few extra on-line sales. These would be my late payers—the people I had to invoice two or three times before getting a payment. If only everyone could just be an instant payer.

After packaging, I hurried and rushed through my on-line account and responded to questions about auction items. I was sailing through my responses too, until I opened a question from *FrugilMom5*, who was bidding on a lot of kid's clothes. She wanted me to measure every item from pit to pit and crotch to hem. Ugh!

My finger hovered over my mouse, as I briefly considered committing email homicide. I would have just loved to click her request into the cyberspace graveyard; but I was a professional, and who knew, she might end up being my high bidder.

So, after a half-hour of tedious measuring, and a couple bowls of cereal, I had satisfied my daily work quota and was ready to get down to the business of checking into Pauline's murder.

I packed a soda to go, grabbed the packages I needed to ship, and headed out the door for the Retro Metro.

After leaving the post office, I called Shep at the hospital so that he could arrange for someone to let me in the store. It was closed for the week so the employees could have time off to attend Pauline's funeral. I didn't want to think about it, but wondered if perhaps the Retro would never reopen, especially since Shep was so ill.

Pessimistic thoughts plagued me the entire drive until I pulled into the parking lot about a half-hour later. I immediately recognized Owen as soon as I saw his unforgettable piercings. Today, he seemed nervous, fumbling with the key a few times before successfully opening the door. Of course, a murdered co-worker would make anyone nervous. I felt sorry for the kid.

As soon as I walked in, it hit me that Pauline was actually gone. In the face of my sorrow for Shep, I hadn't been able to grasp her death; but, it was right here, just a few days ago, that I had seen her last. Now she was gone and I was trying to find out the truth about her murder.

Owen hovered wide-eyed just inside the entrance. His arms were crossed tightly around his chest, as if he was trying to hold himself together.

"Were you here yesterday during store hours?" I asked him.

"Yeah. I was here until we closed at five. Pauline was staying to work on some stuff for Shep. She wasn't going to stay too long because she was going to go out with her boyfriend."

"Tanner's his name, right?"

"Yeah. He's a nice guy. He hangs around here a lot. They were serious, I think."

I made my way toward Shep's office. "Was she in here?" I asked, although I needn't have. I already knew. The room had a forbidden feeling. Almost like death was still hanging in the air.

He nodded, keeping his distance. I tried to imagine what he was feeling. I wondered how he was going to be able to come back to work after losing his friend in such a horrible way.

I skimmed over the room, not looking too hard. I really didn't want to see any signs of her brutal murder. Instead, I mulled over what Owen told me. It was almost as if the murderer had timed his visit to find Pauline alone. Why? To kill her or for something else? How did he know she'd be alone in the office?

"Owen, did you have a lot of customers yesterday?"

He shrugged. "Yeah. We were busy, I guess."

"Anyone who stood out? You know, someone who was maybe dressed weirdly or seemed to act suspicious."

"No," he said, but I sensed a slight hesitation in his reply.

"How did you know Pauline had a date last night?"

He paused and shrugged again. "I don't know."

"This is important, Owen. How did you know? Did she mention it while you were working?"

He squinted, obviously trying hard to remember. "I think she told me right before we got ready to close down for the day." His eyes widened. "Yeah, that's when she told me. I remember, she had just got off the phone with Shep and she told me to take care of the cash register receipts before I left. She said she'd be staying late to do some work in the office. She'd wanted to get it done because Tanner was going to pick her up around six or something."

I stood and walked to where he was standing and looked him directly in the face. "Were there customers around when she told you that?"

"Sure, I guess."

I put a hand on his shoulder. "Really think about it, Owen. I need to know who was in here and what they looked like."

"Maybe three or four people. One was a couple. They were young. I think they were moving in together or something and were looking for furniture. They were really into each other. They got real cozy on that couch over there." He pointed to great leather sofa about twenty feet away. It was the centerpiece of a modern display featuring clean-lined furniture and lots of black accents.

He continued, "Then there was a woman shopping for stuff. She seemed mostly interested in books."

"Books?" That caught my attention.

"Yeah, she hung out by the book cases. I asked her once if I could help her find a particular book, but she said she was just looking around."

"What did she look like?" I wondered if perhaps she was the same woman that visited Chuck at A to Z Estate Sales.

"I don't really remember. Just normal, I guess. She was older."

"Older like me, or older like your mother?"

He shot me a strange look. Certainly I looked much younger than his mother. Didn't I?

"I don't know," he said after a moment. "I can't remember. I'm not sure I even looked at her."

I tried not to appear as discouraged as I felt. "How about the other person, woman or man?"

"Him, I remember. He looked like a big spender. I was trying hard to make a sale with him."

My antennae shot up. "What made you think he was a big spender?"

Owen perked up. "His shoes. Actually, everything about him. He seemed, I don't know … like he had money."

James Farrell had money. "Old or young? Dark hair, short, tall, fat …."

"Um, older, but not too old. I'm not sure about the hair. He was wearing a hat and had the collar of his coat turned up. He wasn't too tall. In good shape. Dark eyes, maybe."

I bet JimDog was of average height. He was probably fit, too. "Did you see what he drove?"

"No. But I'm sure it was nice."

"Probably," I agreed, wondering what James Farrell drove. "Had Pauline been to any estate auctions lately?"

"We do those all the time. Why?"

"Do you keep records?"

"Yup," he answered, moving to the office doorway and pointing toward a three-drawer file cabinet. "Bottom drawer. Unless it's not filed yet; then it would be somewhere on Shep's desk. We file the receipts and then enter the items on a spread-sheet on the computer. The receipts aren't really detailed. Just the amount of the purchase and a general description of what was bought. We don't put everything on the spread-sheet, either. There's not enough time. Sometimes we bring in a whole truck of stuff from those sales."

I pulled out another drawer. "No problem. I just need some general information." I'd found the drawer with files and started leafing through, eager to find one marked Sokolov. There wasn't any.

"What exactly are you looking for?" Owen asked.

"An inventory for a sale from the Sokolov estate."

"That sounds familiar. I think we did buy from that estate."

"Where would the receipt be?"

"In the file cabinet, probably."

I sighed. If the killer was trying to cover his tracks, it would only make sense that he had removed the receipt. I started rummaging through a few piles on the desk, just in case it hadn't made its way to the file cabinet.

"Have you received any unusual books lately? Books in a different language?"

He shrugged. "We get tons of those. Oh, you know Pauline did find something in a book yesterday morning."

My head snapped up. "What?"

"An envelope."

"An envelope? What was in it?"

"I don't know. I didn't ask. We were busy."

"You didn't see her open it?"

"No, but I'm sure she did. We're always finding things like that in books or inside sofa cushions. If it's something valuable, we try to find the owner."

"Did Pauline try to find the owner?"

"I don't know. I didn't think much about it."

Owen was starting to get upset. "You think it has something to do with her death?"

"I don't know. Maybe. Can you remember what book she found it in?"

His eyes grew wide. "I don't know. There were so many."

"Okay. Don't worry about it." I tried to calm the panic rising in his voice.

"Were you here when the police looked around?"

"Yeah, Shep called and asked me to come down and answer their questions."

I looked around. "So, did they take anything for evidence?"

"Just Shep's laptop. They said they would have it back to us by early next week."

My eyes immediately moved to the empty spot on Shep's desk. So much for my powers of observation; I hadn't even noticed his laptop was missing.

I restacked a few of the paperwork piles I'd shuffled through. The Sokolov receipt wasn't on the desk and there was no sign of the mysterious envelop Pauline had found. "Did you happen to notice if the cops took any envelopes or papers of any sort?" I asked in vain. I already knew whoever murdered Pauline was after that envelope, and it was long gone.

I opened my cell and found it was too low on charge to make a call, so I picked up the phone on Shep's desk and dialed Sean. He answered on the first ring.

"Sean, this is Pippi. Can you find out if the Westmont police found an envelope or a bill of sale from A to Z at the scene of Pauline's murder?"

I glanced up as Owen motioned that he was going to be in the next room.

"Why?" Sean asked.

"Well, a kid that works here said that Pauline found an envelope in one of the books they bought from an estate sale. I can't find it here. I also can't find a receipt for a purchase that they possibly made at A to Z Estate Sales for the Sokolov estate. I thought maybe the cops took it for evidence."

Silence.

I took a couple of deep breaths. "Sean? Could you check into it for me? Please."

"Sure," he sighed. I was testing his patience.

"Did you happen to find out anything at A to Z sales?" I asked, pushing it a little further.

"I sent a couple of guys over there, but they didn't get much."

"Really?"

"Yeah. Charlie denied that a woman paid him a thousand dollars for the Sokolov file."

"Chuck said that? He's lying. Does he have security cameras in the place? Maybe you could review the tapes and see if the lady is on video."

"Nope, no security cameras. Just a hard-wired alarm system."

Sean's answers were so short and curt, I wondered if maybe he wasn't alone. "Did they search the place?"

"You know no judge would give us a warrant based on assumptions."

What he meant was my assumptions. I bit my tongue.

The line grew silent. In the background, I could hear a female voice. I had assumed correctly. He wasn't alone; he was with Sarah. Great. "Well, guess I'll go. I've got a lot to do," I said curtly.

I hung up and took a second to collect myself before setting out to search for Owen. I found him restocking bags under the cash register.

"Hey, Owen. I'm leaving now. Do you want to walk out with me?" He readily agreed. Neither one of us wanted to be alone in the Retro Metro.

I felt overwhelmed with sadness as I watched Owen lock the doors. The Retro Metro had always been my retreat from the world. Now, after Pauline's death and Shep's illness, it would never be the same.

I stopped off at a gas station, filled my tank and grabbed a quick snack, before heading back toward the suburb of Lisle. Taking Seventy-Fifth Street, I worked my way west until I found the Farrell's' main residence on Hobson Road.

My eyes were easily distracted by the scenery as I struggled to find the correct house number. I didn't often venture to this pocket of the Lisle. It was like a whole different world—white fenced acreage, large horse barns, and opulent residences with guarded gates.

Then I saw James Farrell's house. Wow! Nestled on probably four acres of land, at the end of a windy, tree-lined drive, was a stately stone English manor which could easily be ten thousand square feet of living space. The house was situated on a small rise with manicured gardens and an impressive matching stone stable and a white-fenced pasture. Everything about the property said civilized taste and abundant wealth. Hotdogs had definitely been good to James Farrell.

Despite strange looks from the gate guard, I lingered across the road for a few minutes, admiring the grand home and trying to get a feel for the family that lived there. What type of secrets were the Ferrells keeping; and were their secrets dark enough to kill for?

I pulled away from the curb and drove on, my mind racing with even more questions. I knew James Farrell was an adulterer; could he be a murderer, too? Who was the rich-looking woman that paid Chuck a thousand dollars to look at the Sokolov estate file, one of the Farrell women or just someone hired by James Farrell? What was in the envelope Pauline found? Perhaps, most importantly, how was I going to get close enough to James Farrell to find the answers to my questions? What I needed was a connection and if my instincts were correct, I knew just where to start.

Chapter 11

The St. Benedict campus is usually an orderly place; today it was pure chaos. People were everywhere and the circular drive in front of the main building was jammed with cars. For a lack of a better spot, I parked my Volvo down the road in front of the gates to the campus cemetery. With its black iron fencing and the bare tree branches stretching against the cold sky, the cemetery's menacing appearance seemed to match my own dark mood.

The sky was darkly threatening rain and the cold October wind was blowing in from the northwest, causing the last few dangling leaves to swirl to the ground. I hoofed it toward the monastery's entrance, weaving in and out of people, trying to reach the front steps.

I made my way through the front doors, waved to Sister Eileen who was working the front desk, bypassed the elevator and took the old marble steps to the second floor. My sister's office was just down the hall past the chapel's entrance. I gave a little polite knock before cracking open the door. "Mary Frances?" I called out.

"Pippi!" My sister squealed and jumped up from her desk, sending her chair on wheels flying across the room. She engulfed me in a giant bear hug, her dangling cross earrings flashing and her shoulder length hair smelling a lot like coconuts.

"What's going on downstairs?" I asked after we settled into chairs. She offered me a bottled water from a dorm-size fridge in the corner of her office. Her desk was cluttered with scraps of paper and yellow post-its.

"Oh, that's Sister Veronica's family and friends. After Vespers, there's going to be a jubilee celebration." My sister beamed as she spoke. "Can you imagine celebrating fifty years of service? What a joyful occasion!"

"That is wonderful," I reiterated, trying to match her enthusiasm. The truth was I couldn't imagine fifty years of anything, let alone celibacy. Obviously, consistency wasn't my strong point. I couldn't even keep a job, a boyfriend, a diet routine, not to mention a balance in my checking account.

"What are you working on?" I asked, trying to be polite. I hadn't visited for a while and felt like a jerk for popping in to ask a favor.

Mary Frances shoved a pile of papers out of the way and leaned forward on her desk. "Our monthly newsletter. I must keep the public informed, you know?" She leaned back in her chair and regarded me seriously. "What brings you here, Sis? I haven't seen you for a while. Everything okay at home?"

"Everything's fine," I reassured her. "Yeah, we haven't got together for a while, have we? Sorry, guess I've just—"

"Oh, it's not your fault. I've been busy, too," she said, waving off my apology. "Time flies, doesn't it? Thank goodness for on-line social networking, or I would have lost touch with everyone by now." One of Mary Frances's duties, and probably the most suited to her vivacious personality, was to serve as a public liaison for the convent. She coordinated special masses, prayer intentions, a monthly newsletter on monastery life, and several outreach ministries. She'd even ventured into social media and knew more about the popular sites than most teenagers. I often envied my sister. She always seems so happy. Which seemed strange to me, considering there was no hope of marriage, kids, or for that matter, sex in her future.

"I actually came by to ask a favor," I said.

She sat forward again. "Sure, of course. What's up?" She fiddled with a pen, twirling it between her fingers like a baton before finally tucking it behind her ear. Her auburn hair, loose and layered, fell attractively against her bare face, making her look much younger than her thirty-something years. Today, she was wearing khakis and a Mt. Carmel hooded sweatshirt.

"Do you remember that game we used to play when we were kids? The Six Degrees of Kevin Bacon?"

"Oh my, I haven't thought of Kevin Bacon in years. I had a poster of him from *Footloose* over my bed. I used to be a pro at the Six Degree game. Let's see, Harrison Ford, he was one of my favorites, especially in *Indiana Jones*. Well, Harrison was in *Working Girl* with Sigourney Weaver who was in *Aliens* with Bill Paxt—"

I threw up my hands. "Stop!" I laughed. "I was actually hoping we could play it with James Farrell instead of Kevin Bacon."

"James Farrell? As in JimDogs?"

"Yup. That's the one."

"The Farrells are big donors to our convent," she commented.

I had hoped as much. They didn't live far from St. Benedict, and Farrell was, after all, an Irish Catholic name. My sister continued, "Why do you want to know about James Farrell?"

"Oh, come on, Sis. How many degrees?"

"You're not messing around in police business again, are you?" My sister had a way of cutting to the chase.

"No. I'm just checking into something for a friend."

"What do you think the Farrells have done?"

"There's been a couple of murders. Their name keeps coming up." I stood, shoved my hands into my pocket, and moved toward a small window above the heat register. Outside people were collected in small groups and milling around the fountain. "I need to find out some things. Things I can only find out if I get close to the family. I was hoping you could help me."

"I doubt the Farrells would be involved in murder, Pippi. They're a well-respected family. What would be their motive?"

"I don't know. That's what I need to find out." I held up my hand before she could get started again. "For the record, I'm doing this for my friend, Shep. A girl at his shop was murdered. Shep's sick, Mary Frances. Really sick. He asked me to do this."

She took a deep breath but didn't respond. Instead, she sat silently for a minute, seemingly contemplating her next move. Or, maybe praying, I wasn't sure.

"Two," she finally said, with a wicked little grin.

"Two?"

"Two degrees. I'm only two degrees away from James Farrell. I'm currently spearheading a garage sale to benefit the Daily Transitional House for Women and serving on the committee with me is Patricia Farrell, wife of James Farrell. So, there you have it, two degrees. Can you top that?"

I crossed the room and hugged her. "That's great! Can you introduce us?"

"Better than that. Welcome to the committee, Sis. Hope you're ready to roll up your sleeves and do some serious work. The homeless women of our community are counting on you. All the volunteers are meeting at two o'clock tomorrow at the Farrell's residence. We're going to discuss plans for the sale over tea."

I hugged her again, practically gushing with joy. "You're not going to mention this to Mom and Dad, right?" I asked with trepidation, almost afraid to test my luck.

"Not unless you're putting yourself in danger, which you won't be, right?"

"Right."

She stood, glancing at the wall clock. "I need to change for Vespers."

"No problem. Guess I'll see you tomorrow," I said, following her to the door.

"One good thing about this," she added. "We'll get to spend some more time together." She squeezed my arm.

We hugged one more time before I started the trek back to my car. As I walked, an idea struck me. If Owen had noticed the 'book lady' and the 'rich man' in the Retro the day Pauline was killed, maybe these same shoppers were at The Classy Closet the day Jane was killed. A long shot, but it was worth checking into.

*

The next afternoon, as I began to get ready for the tea at the Farrell's, I couldn't help but wonder if it was just fate that Mary Frances knew Patricia Farrell or divine intervention. Whichever it was, I'd caught a huge break. All I needed now was something perfect to wear.

What *did* one wear to tea? An image of white gloves and parasols popped into my mind; but that was so Victorian. What I really needed was something classy. I could just imagine a table full of well-coiffed socialites wearing navy wool trousers, coordinating sweater sets, and strands of pearls. Boy, would my mother fit in there. Problem was, I was more of the jean and sweatshirt type.

I tore through my closet and then moved to my on-line auction bins. Nothing. Why hadn't I thought of this before? I really only had a half-hour to pull something together. I always was a procrastinator. I should have listened to Mrs. Beeman, my fifth grade teacher. What was it she always said? *Don't put off for tomorrow what you can do today.* Well, I obviously didn't heed her advice because, over the years, my personal motto had evolved to: *Put it off today, so you can freak about it tomorrow.*

I continued to rip through bins of clothes creating another disaster on top of the disaster I already had. Even with all my efforts, all I came up with was a funky blue and brown polyester scarf printed with tiny white flowers.

Then it dawned on me; my Prudence Overton outfit might work. I scurried across my apartment and threw open a closet where I kept a stackable washer and dryer. There it was, waded up on the floor. I shook it out and sniffed the fabric. Not too bad, except for a few wrinkles, it would do.

Checking the clock, I wiggled out of my sweats and back into the long wool skirt and high-buttoned blouse, double checking to make sure my behind was completely covered this time. I did a mental chuckle thinking of the reaction my bare bottom would cause at a ladies' tea.

I retrieved the black pumps from under the coffee table and slipped into them on my way to the bathroom. My hair actually didn't look too bad. The humidity must have been low, because usually by that time of day I looked like a frizz queen. I pulled my locks into a jeweled clip and covered a zit that was emerging on my chin. A quick smudge of lip-gloss and I was ready to go.

I leaned into the mirror for one final inspection and decided that I needed a little something extra. Hmm...what?

Looking at the clock, I cursed again. I needed to hit the road. As it was, I was going to be fashionably late. In a last ditch effort, I grabbed the flower-printed scarf off the back of the sofa and slipped it around my neck. I nodded one more time at my reflection. The scarf added that little extra *something*. Now I was ready.

Thankfully, traffic was moving right along. I was only ten minutes behind schedule when I finally reached the Farrell's.

The gate guard, a round-faced, pot-bellied man with a gray handle-bar moustache, gave me a nasty once-over, checked his list three times and radioed the house for verification before pushing the button which allowed the iron gates to swing open for my admittance. I shot him my best indignant look as I jammed my Volvo into gear and peeled out; my tires squealing sharply as they burned asphalt and sent a plume of rubber fumes into the air.

As soon as I neared the house, I spied Mary Frances waiting for me in the driveway. She was standing against the bumper of her 1970's baby blue Volkswagen bug and waving cheerfully in my direction.

I parked and went to join her. We walked together toward a large stone porch covered in pots of bright yellow and orange chrysanthemums.

"You look good. I've never seen that scarf before. Is it new?" she asked, looping her arm in mine. She looked very "sisterly" in a dark gray skirt, light blue blouse, and dark navy cardigan. A small gold cross was pinned on her lapel. Her head was bare. My sister rarely wore a head-piece.

"Sort of." I adjusted the knot of the scarf so it was in the front.

"Well, it's very unique. Isn't this home lovely?" she added, as we approached a large ornate door.

"Very." I felt my nerves kick up inside me.

Mary Frances must have noticed. She squeezed my arm and offered some reassurance. "No need to be nervous. Mrs. Farrell is a gracious person. You're going to love her."

I had my doubts about that, but I put on my best social smile and headed for the front door. A pinched-faced, middle-aged woman answered the bell. I immediately offered my hand. "Hi, Mrs. Farrell. Phillipena O'Brien."

Next to me, my sister stiffened and jabbed me with her elbow. Ms. Pinch-face let my hand hang like a wind-starved flag and turned on her heels. "Follow me," she said with a sigh, "the others are in the conservatory."

"That's the maid," Mary Francis whispered as we made our way over a vast expanse of marble floor. My pumps, which were a half-size to big, caused me to slip a few times, making nasty little black skid-marks on the floor. The maid turned and eyed the marks disapprovingly. I continued along more carefully, wishing I'd remembered to stuff the toes of my shoes with tissue.

Entering the conservatory was like walking through the wardrobe in C.S. Lewis' *The Lion, the Witch, and the Wardrobe*; old world marble and mahogany opulence gave way to a light and airy botanical paradise. I gazed about, holding my breath as I took in the scene before me. I felt like a fish inside a beautifully done aquarium. Several huge pots held exotic-looking plants, which seemed to grow all the way to the twenty-foot glass ceiling, providing a lush green canopy of shade. Behind the high-pitched murmuring of the guest, I could hear the faint sound of babbling water and the tiny chirps of birds. I even caught a glimpse of a tiny yellow finch as it darted about the overhead branches.

Walls of glass provided stunning views of pristine gardens, green rolling acreage, and the large stone stable at the back of the property. Scattered about the room, several well-dressed women stood in small groups holding champagne flutes and dainty plates. Their conversation was punctuated with tiny giggles and exaggerated gestures with diamond-studded hands.

Five small round tables were arranged in the middle of the room, each draped with a simple white cloth and low arrangement of blue asters. My eyes roamed to the sidebar where I could see several platters of goodies and a row of flutes filled with a sparkling, amber-colored liquid. This was my type of tea party.

"Sister, you're here." A willowy, dark-haired-woman lightly embraced my sister, air-kissing each of her cheeks. I was taken aback by her appearance. Her shoulder length hair was cut to perfectly accent strong cheekbones, dark round eyes, and full pouty lips. She was beautiful! I couldn't help but wonder why, with a woman like Patricia Farrell, James would have an affair.

She shook my hand graciously as Mary Frances introduced us. I noticed Patricia's eyes lingered on my scarf for a few extra seconds. It must have made a good decision in wearing it; I noticed her pouty lips turning slightly upward as she studied it.

"Excuse me, everyone," Patricia said, turning away from us and tapping on her champagne flute to command the room's attention. "Sister's here. We can get started now. Please find a seat."

She ushered us right past the refreshment bar and toward one of the little round tables. I managed to grab some champagne as we passed, but that was it. I guess the goodies would have to wait.

"I thought you two would enjoy sitting with my daughter-in-law, Morgan," Patricia said.

A thin, blonde girl rose to greet us. Her handshake jingled from the collection of gold bangles on her wrist.

We barely had time to introduce ourselves before Patricia started the meeting. Having moved to the front of the room, she was holding a clip-board and pen in her hand. "It's my pleasure, ladies, to serve once again as the chairwoman of St. Joan's garage sale. As you know, we've partnered with the St. Benedict Convent to raise money for the Woman's Transitional Day Center. This charity event is very dear to my heart and I'm proud to say that last year we were able to raise over ten thousand dollars with this sale alone."

Everyone clapped. Well, if you could call it that. It was more like tapping. I tried to mimic Morgan's rim-rod straight posture and the way she lightly tapped her fingers against the palm of her left hand. These girls would not fit in at a Sox game. Although, judging from my first impression, Morgan probably wasn't a huge baseball fan.

Patricia raised her hand and the tapping instantly stopped. "I have an announcement," she said, pausing and letting her eyes roam the room for effect. "I'm happy to report that James and I will be matching the amount of funds raised at this year's sale." That garnered another round of tapping, even more enthusiastic than the last. Whispers of amazement broke out among the guests.

"Please, please," Patricia's hand was up again, modestly waving away the compliments. "Remember this is for a good cause. Think how many women we will help with our efforts this year. The Woman's Day Center is counting on us. Let's just make this the best sale ever!"

I joined in with my own palm tapping and glanced over at Morgan who was regarding me curiously while munching happily on a tiny cream cheese-filled tart. "Want one," she asked, sliding her plate toward me.

I scooped one up and popped it in my mouth, smiling while I chewed. Hmm, maybe I had misjudged this prissy blond with perfect highlights. She *was* sharing nicely.

"So, you're married to Patricia's son?" I asked, attempting to break the ice.

"Yes, James Junior; we all call him J.J. Two years now," she replied smiling and giving a little wave with her left hand so I could see the proof—a rock that was surely worth more than three years of my average income. "He was just promoted to CFO of JimDog Corporation," she stated proudly.

I'll bet he was.

"We're living here now, but we'll be building a home in Schaumburg." She glanced around and lowered her voice as if sharing a secret. "I hear they have great schools and, well …. J.J. and I want to start a family soon." Her golden bob bounced around her face as she spoke. I squinted at her scalp, looking for a few dark roots. None. She must spend a fortune on her hair.

"Oh, that's wonderful," Mary Frances chimed in, "I'm sure you'll have a beautiful family."

I smiled and nodded. About what, I'm not sure. Beside our mutual appreciation for cream cheese tarts, I was finding very little in common with this twenty-something girl. I'd dealt with her type before. Namely in college, where MRS ranked right up there with BA and MA. It always amazed me how much time some women put into grooming themselves for a chance at a lofty marriage--the right clothes, the right attitude, the right social appearances, all so they could meet Mr. Rich and be set for life. I was always too independent to buy into that crap. I spent my college years developing my own career. Although, maybe I needed to rethink that plan, I thought, glancing down at my outfit and then back at Morgan who was rooting through a designer bag that would bring enough money on-line to pay my rent for three months.

Deflated, I turned my focus back to Patricia who was going from table to table passing out committee assignments and schedules. Mary Frances and Morgan continued to chat away.

I watched Patricia carefully as she mingled with the attendees. Was she the well-dressed woman that paid a thousand dollars for the Sokolov file? Was she driving around town, murdering second-hand dealers, and checking them off her list? She didn't strike me as the murdering type, but who knew? Maybe she hired out her dirty deeds?

Morgan, attempting to draw me back into the conversation, tapped my arm politely. "Cool scarf," she said, pointing to my neck. "I think I had one of those once." She sipped her champagne and then added with a sweet smile, "You must have really enjoyed being a Daisy Scout."

Mary Frances honed in on the scarf and snickered.

Morgan, on the other hand, was regarding me with a little more interest. "What was your troop number? We were 2511. Didn't you just love summer camp? I went all the way through high school in the scouts. I loved...."

Blah, blah, blah ... I drowned her out and fingered my scarf. Daisies? That was the grade school version of Girl Scouts, which I'd tried once, but they kicked me out when I ate all the profits for the troop cookie sale.

Actually, forget the Daisy scarf. What I really needed to do was get away from Morgan the airhead and find some connections between the Farrells and the recent murders. Somewhere in this house was proof that one of the Farrells was a cold-blooded killer. If I found it, I would be one step closer to fulfilling my promise to Shep. Plus, as an extra bonus, I could prove to Sean that I was right about the Farrell connection.

If only I could figure out a way to do some sneaking around. "Excuse me, Morgan," I said, interrupting a recantation of her favorite scout service project. I leaned over and whispered discretely in her ear, "Where's the ladies room?"

She smiled and pointed. "There's a powder room right off the front foyer, to your left. Do you need me to show you?"

"Oh, no. I think I saw it on the way in." I slid my chair back and slipped out quietly. Once I was in the hallway, I considered my options. I could hear the clinking of dishes coming from my far left, where I assumed the maid was slaving away in the kitchen. The rest of the house seemed relatively quiet. JimDog was more than likely at the corporate office, working hard. That left JimDog Jr. who must be at work also; after all, he needed to keep his nose to the grindstone if he was going to pay for that new house in Schaumberg.

Sure the coast was clear, I made my way toward the foyer, but instead of turning into the powder room, I snuck through a magnificent pair of oak-paneled doors. I'd guessed correctly. I was standing in JimDog's den.

Chapter 12

I shut the doors quietly behind me, headed straight for a king-size mahogany desk and began searching. Four drawers later, I had nothing but the usual office type stuff. The only thing I learned was that this family had racked up more debt than the federal government. In fact, they should have named their first-born Chase instead of James Junior.

Next, I got down on all fours and examined under the desk. Everyone knew the really incriminating stuff was usually taped to the underside of the desk. Nothing. I stood and rechecked the desk drawers for a secret compartment before moving to the file cabinet, which turned out to be nothing but a storage place for family photos and newspaper clippings. Interesting, I'm sure, but I didn't have time to go through them in detail and a quick scan didn't reveal anything unusual.

Mindful of time, I sighed and took one last glance around the room. There had to be something ... there had to be ... of course! There's always a safe hidden behind a picture.

I moved to a wall of pictures and started checking behind frames. I stopped, realizing it would need to be a sizeable picture to hide the safe. There was only one of those in the room—a four by three oil painting of JimDog standing outside his first franchise, holding one of his famous dogs and wearing a cheesy grin. Not my idea of good art, but hey.

I ran my fingers carefully along the back perimeter of the frame and found what I was looking for, hinges. I pulled on the picture, which swung away from the wall like a door, and presto—a safe. I stared at the digital number board for a second and even punched a few of the numbers, but I knew there was no way I could crack the code. I also knew, just as sure as I was standing there, that inside that safe was the envelope Pauline found. It had to be there. James killed her for it, hadn't he? It would only make sense he'd store it away in this safe.

Frustrated, I repositioned the painting and turned to leave. That's when I noticed it—a book that looked a lot like the ones I saw in the dumpster at The Classy Closet.

I dashed across the room and took a quick look. It was a huge, leather bound book; the only one like it on the entire shelf. A number one on the bottom of the spine indicated that it was the first in a series, but I didn't see another volume. *Huh? That's strange.*

I was about to pluck it from the shelf and take a closer look when I heard a noise outside the room. I quickly turned away and tiptoed to the door, pressing my ear against the wood.

"Mr. Farrell, you're home." It was the maid talking.

"Yes, I left some papers in my den." JimDog's voice sounded deeper than I expected.

Oh no! How was I going to explain this? I looked around for a hiding place. None. Not even a closet. Could I get to the window, open it, and squeeze my big behind through in time? I didn't think so.

"Mrs. Farrell is in the conservatory with the ladies. They're discussing the sale," the maid informed him.

"Oh, that's right. I forgot that meeting was this afternoon. Well, no problem. I'll just get my papers and get out of the way."

The door started to open. I did the only thing I could think of at the time.

"Call the cops!" JimDog shouted. "There's a dead woman in here!"

I kept my eyes closed and focused on staying limp as JimDog continued yelling. Lying with my left ear against the floor, I could hear the click-clacking of high-heeled women resounding through the floor-boards; the noise resembled a herd of buffalo running over the prairie.

High-pitched voices descended upon the room. Panic had broken out among the tea ladies. "Someone call 911! Is she dead?"

Then out of the chaos came a clear voice of authority. "Excuse me. Let me in, please." It was Mary Frances. She flipped me over and began patting my cheeks. I tried not to giggle.

"She's alright," Mary Frances assured everyone. "She's passed out, that's all. She'll be fine in a minute."

"Someone, go get a cool cloth," Patricia ordered. I let my eyelids flutter open. She was hovering above, taking charge of the situation. "And, someone help me get her to the sofa," she added.

I tried to maintain my dazed look and limp body as JimDog scooped me off the floor. He hauled me into a formal looking room and placed me on chintz-covered couch. The click-clacking group of ladies followed on his heels. They were all abuzz with excitement. Probably wasn't often that someone passed out at one of their functions.

I let Mary Frances put the cool cloth on my forehead before fully opening my eyes. I sat up slowly and heaved a dramatic sigh. "What happened?" I asked, looking about me innocently.

"I think you passed out," Mary Frances said. There was a hint of sarcasm in her voice. After all, she'd seen me pull this shenanigan many a time when we were kids.

"Are you feeling better?" Patricia inquired, still looking concerned. Morgan was standing next to her with an extra cloth.

"Who are you and what were you doing in my office?" I looked over to where JimDog stood, his dark features scrutinizing me. The look on his face definitely wasn't one of concern.

"James!" Patricia admonished. "This is Phillipena. She's Mary Frances's sister."

JimDog's eyes darted angrily from Mary Frances and then back to me. His territory had been invaded, and I don't think nepotism with the Godly was high on his list of plausible excuses.

"I'm sorry," I said in my weakest voice. "I started to feel ill and was making my way to the restroom. I must have made a wrong turn. I think maybe I was having an allergic reaction to something I ate."

Mary Frances joined in my charade. "Oh my goodness, were there nut products in any of the food?" she asked, implying that I had a nut allergy. She knew darn well that I didn't have any food allergies. In fact, food and I were completely compatible.

Patricia wheeled around to the maid. "Anna?"

The maid sheepishly spoke up, "I did use crushed pecans in the tart shells."

"Oh, I'm so sorry," Patricia moved closer and was poking at my skin. "Do you have a rash? Trouble breathing? Maybe we should take her to the hospital?"

"No, no ...," I waved off her concern, sat up, and put my feet on the ground. "I'm much better now. Just embarrassed. I'm so sorry to have caused all this trouble." I stood up and shot a quick glance toward JimDog. I couldn't tell if he was buying my act or not. He mumbled something under his breath and moved in the direction of his den. He probably wanted to check things over. I needed to scram.

I turned to Mrs. Farrell and assured her once again that I was feeling better, thanked her for her hospitality, and made a hasty retreat for the door. Mary Frances was right behind me.

Once outside, she grabbed my arm and pulled me aside. "Stellar performance, Sis," she said.

"Thanks for covering for me. That was a great bit about the nut allergy."

"Just don't put me in that situation again. I don't like being dishonest."

"Well, I'll have you know that it was worth it," I said, smiling. "I found something."

"You did? What?"

"A book."

"A book?" Mary Frances seemed frustrated.

"A book that suspiciously looks like the ones that were at the Retro Metro and The Classy Closet. It's a connection."

"Okay. If you say so." She didn't sound as enthusiastic as I felt. "I'll see you Monday morning, right? We'll have to start sorting and marking items for the sale. Come by the parish hall by nine o'clock. We're the first shift; nine until one."

I glanced once more at the house as we hugged good-bye. I had one of those creepy feelings I was being watched. JimDog was tied into all this. I was sure of it. My gut feeling was that he was the male shopper Owen saw inside the Retro Metro the day Pauline was killed. All I needed to do was get Owen to make a positive identification and I'd have my proof. I'd track him down first thing in the morning. For now, I was going to take a spin by The Classy Closet to see if I could find Jane's sister-in-law, Margie.

*

The next day, Owen stood next to me, hair matted on one side, smelling slightly stale, and looking more shaggy than usual. I wondered how he was holding up after Pauline's death.

He rubbed the stubble on his chin as he squinted at the pictures I brought. I'd copied a few online photos of both James and Patricia at various black tie events; the other one was a picture I found of James Junior from a recent copy of *Chicago's Young Entrepreneurs Magazine*.

While he looked at the pictures, I checked out his place. Other than some annoying pop music blasting from his stereo, Owen's apartment was pretty nice. Surprisingly, for being such a shaggy looking dude, he seemed to know how to clean house.

"Nope, it wasn't any of these people," he finally answered.

"What? You didn't see any of these people in the Retro on the day Pauline was killed?" I couldn't believe my ears.

"No. Sorry." He handed over the photos, just to have me shove them back at him.

"Look again, please."

"It wasn't them," he insisted.

I didn't know what to say. I'd been so sure. Although, once I thought about it, Owen not being able to make a positive ID didn't really prove anything. They could have been wearing disguises. I would have, if I were casing a place and planning a murder.

I got some quick directions to Tanner's place before leaving Owen's apartment. Luckily, Tanner lived nearby in Downer's Grove.

On the drive over, I thought about the case. After leaving the Farrell's yesterday, I stopped by The Classy Closet and talked to Margie. Unfortunately, she didn't remember any shoppers that fit the description Owen had given me. She was, however, surprised to hear I'd found the box of books in the garbage. She swore that Jane found a buyer for the books and was preparing to ship them. So either that deal fell through and Jane pitched the books, or, more than likely, the murderer tossed the books into the garbage to cover their tracks. I wondered what could possibly be in the envelope that would warrant murder.

My head spun with possibilities. Maybe a birth certificate showing JimDog as the father of Alex Sokolov. Did Patricia know about Alex? If so, it could be embarrassing, especially to a society queen like Patricia Farrell. Maybe she was the murderer. But would an illegitimate child be embarrassing enough to commit murder? I doubted it, but then again, after my last case, I had learned never to underestimate what motivated the high society types or what they'd stoop to in order to protect themselves. The one that pointed a gun at my head last year was a good example.

I also knew the two biggest motives for murder were money and love. With that said, there was one Farrell I hadn't considered yet, James Junior. He was next in line for the hot dog dynasty. What would happen if another heir, like Alex the

Hairy One, showed up and staked claim to the family fortune? Did J.J. know about Alex? I needed to find out.

A half hour later, I pulled in front of the junky looking two-bedroom house that, according to Owen, Tanner rented with four other guys. The small black top driveway was jammed with clunkers, the lawn cluttered with ten-speeds, and the front porch featured a raggedy, lopsided couch and a fully racked weight-lifting bench. I wasn't sure how anyone could manage not to go nuts with five people in a two-bedroom house; but college-age guys could probably survive easily in such substandard conditions. Kind of like pigs packed in an overcrowded pen. It didn't really matter how messy things got, just as long as there was enough slop to go around.

I stepped over a skateboard and rapped on the door. A stocky, dark-haired kid appeared. He was wearing baggy sweats and a stained white tank.

"Hi. Is Tanner around?"

He looked me up and down. Probably trying to decide how I knew Tanner. Finally, he shrugged and replied, "He's usually around. Want to come in and check?"

I thought for a second. "Actually, can you go check and send him out here?" The house looked toxic.

A couple minutes later, a guy wearing a black and white skull and cross-bones sweatshirt scuffled out of the house. A shock of black hair peeked out from under the hood. "Yeah?" he asked, approaching me with dark look.

I introduced myself and shook his hand.

"I already talked to the cops. I told them everything I know." He started to turn away.

"Shep asked me to look into this," I blurted trying to keep his attention. "He also told me that there's no way you had anything to do with Pauline's death."

He turned back and faced me straight on. "I would never have hurt her," he said bitingly.

"I believe you."

"I can't believe she's dead. It seems so..."

"Senseless," I offered.

He nodded.

"I can't even imagine how you feel, Tanner. All I know is that you and everyone who loved Pauline deserves to know the truth about her death. Will you answer a few of my questions?"

He shrugged. I continued, "You were going to meet her at the Retro around six, right?"

"Yeah."

"You were the first one on the scene. Did you notice anything unusual about the place when you got there?"

He inhaled deeply and looked downward. "No, everything seemed normal until I got to the office."

"How'd you get in?"

"I used my key."

That's right. I forgot that Tanner worked for Shep, also. "Did Pauline have any enemies?"

"No. Absolutely not. Everyone liked her."

"I'm wondering if she mentioned anything to you about an envelope she found in one of the books at the shop."

He looked up suddenly. "Why? Do you think it had something to do with her death?"

"I don't know, maybe. What was it? Did she tell you about it?"

"I called her earlier that day and she said she'd found an envelope with some sort of legal document in an old book."

"What type of legal document?" I could hardly contain myself.

"I don't know for sure. She started to tell me, but the she had to take care of a customer."

My hopes fell. "What did she say exactly, Tanner? Think. It could be really important."

"Not much. I had just called her to see if we were still on for dinner that night. Like I said, she was busy. We didn't talk long."

"Did she say anything else about the document? Anything at all?"

"Well, she must have thought it was important. She said she'd tried to call the owner."

"Did she say who that was?" I pressed.

"No, like I said, she had to go. I just figured she'd tell me about it at dinner."

"What time was it when you talked to her?"

"Around four-thirty or so. She told me she'd be there until six finishing up some paperwork."

That jived with what Owen said about Shep calling and asking her to work late.

I shook my head. I had too many open ends to tie up. It seemed the more I found out, the more I didn't understand.

On the way home, I mulled over the facts. Every conclusion I came to pointed at one of the Farrells as the killer. My best guess was James Farrell. Any guy that keeps a mistress for over twenty years, let's her die alone, and doesn't even take responsibility for his own son ... well, that's the murdering type. No doubt about it. He was the first suspect on my list.

By the time I reached my apartment, I was brain dead. Deciding to give the case a rest, I got busy checking my on-line payment accounts. I had several auctions that were due to finish and I was anxious to see how high the bids had gone. I was giddy with excitement when I found one of my children's clothing lots went for thirty-eight bucks. To top things off, the buyer was an instant payer. Yay for me!

I decided to celebrate by stirring up a batch of brownies. While they were baking, I sent out the rest of my invoices and started photographing next week's sales—which were looking bleak. I needed to get ahold of some more merchandise, but since I'd volunteered my time at the garage sale, my scavenging time would be limited this week.

Twenty minutes later, I pulled the brownies out of the oven. They were still a little soft in the middle, which was just the way I liked them. I spooned some out of the pan, popped the steamy goo into my mouth, and relished the chocolate bliss.

Shep would love some of these, I thought, wrapping tinfoil over the pan and grabbing a couple of clean spoons. If I hurried, they'd still be warm by the time I reached the hospital.

On the way out, I grabbed my bag and an extra warm hoodie, then stopped dead in my tracks. Sarah Maloney was standing just outside my door.

Chapter 13

"Phillipena," she purred. "I was just coming to visit with you. Is this a bad time?" Before I could reply, she pushed past me and made her way into my apartment. She seemed like a woman on a mission.

"I won't be here long," she said, brushing an invisible speck of dirt off her coat and looking around my apartment with an unmistakable look of disgust.

As usual, we were a vision of contrasts. She, a walking billboard of popular fashion, was wearing an expensive quilted, knee-length jacket and a pricey pair of leather boots. I, on the other hand, was wearing sweat pants and fleece hoodie that I had pulled off the floor this morning.

"Actually, Sarah," I began, "I have an appointment, so can we make this some other time?"

She wheeled around and faced me. Her expression darkened and her voice dropped its sweet cantor. "We need to talk."

"About what?"

"Sean."

"What about him?"

"I want you to stay away from him."

Was she serious? Certainly she realized how immature this conversation sounded. She was acting like a high school girl.

"Did you hear me? I said, stay away from Sean!" As if to emphasize her point, she moved closer to me. In fact, she was close enough for me to see the tiny clumps of mascara at the ends of her lashes. She really needed to switch mascaras. I'd used the pink and green tube for years and rarely had trouble with clumps.

"Look, Sarah," I said, placing my hand on her chest in an attempt to keep her at bay. "I don't know what you think is going on, but—"

"I know what's going on. Do you honestly think you can compete with me? You ... you ...," she was looking me up and down as she searched for the right word, "you slut!"

I broke into hysterical laughter. "Slut?" I asked. "Slut? You've got to be kidding!"

I'd been called a lot of things before but never a slut. Little did this woman know, but I was currently enduring a dry spell that was ... well, very dry.

Before I could even come up with a good retort, she was in my face, her bloodshot, clumpy-lash framed eyes boring into mine. "Stay away from him or you'll be sorry," she hissed.

And with that she stomped out, her heavily booted feet causing my rickety steps to groan in protest.

I stood motionless for a few seconds thinking back to my conversation with Officer Wagoner a few days ago. She warned me that Sarah Maloney had become obsessed with Sean. Who would think it? On the outside, Sarah had everything, but on the inside she was one messed-up woman.

I took a deep breath, shrugged it off and moved along. Sure, Sarah was a psycho witch, but I had bigger things to worry about. Namely, tending to my sick friend. I was anxious to see Shep. I wanted to catch him up on my progress, or lack thereof. I also wanted to make up for my weak behavior the other day. This time, I vowed, I'd be rock strong. Shep needed my support and I intended to be there for him.

*

I walked into his room as his parents were leaving. They nodded politely, but didn't stop to introduce themselves or even speak to me. Probably for the best; they weren't high on my favorite people list.

Although Shep didn't look any worse than he did a few days ago, his appearance still took my breath away; but I sucked it up and put on a happy face.

He brightened when he saw me. "Hey there, come on over," he said patting the edge of his bed.

I sat next to him, opening the brownies and handing him a spoon. "Want some?"

His eyes lit up. "Sure do, doll. You know, I haven't had much appetite, but these look good."

We savored a few chocolaty spoonfuls before he got down to business. "So, tell me what you've learned about Pauline."

Trying not to dwell on the weakness of his voice, I plunged ahead, telling him what I'd found, which didn't amount to much.

"So you really think one of the Farrells has something to do with all this?" he asked, after I told him my suspicions.

"I'm certain of it. I'm starting with James Farrell. Did you know Pauline found a document in one of the books from the Sokolov estate?"

"A document? What type of document?"

"I don't know yet. I'm not even sure if it's the reason she was killed."

"Did you ask around about it?"

"I talked to Tanner and Owen. They didn't seem to know much about it."

"So, what's next?" He was pulling himself up and reaching for the water cup on the nearby table.

"I'll get that." I refilled the cup and held it below his mouth, bending the straw to make drinking easier. "I'm working with Morgan Farrell this week at the St. Joan's garage sale. She's James Jr.'s wife. I'm hoping to get closer with the family and maybe pick up some more information."

Shep nodded and then smiled at someone over my shoulder. I turned and saw Sean standing in the doorway.

I stood up, surprised. "Sean. What are you doing here?"

He looked just as surprised as me. An awkward feeling settled over the room.

"Come in, Detective."

"I'm here to ask Shep a few more questions," Sean answered.

"Is this necessary? Can't you see he's not feeling up to it?"

Shep grabbed my hand and gave it a little squeeze. "Take an easy, hon. There's a few things I need to talk to him about too."

I searched Shep's face. "Like what?" I asked, suddenly feeling defensive. I knew what was going on. Shep didn't think I was capable of finding the truth about Pauline's murderer so he was calling in the big guns.

I glared at Sean who was still hovering in the doorway.

"It's not what you think, doll. So, don't go getting all mad and upset. Now, if you don't mind, I need to speak to Sean in private. Will you come back soon?"

I bent down and kissed him on the cheek. "Of course," I said soothingly, before heading toward the door. My plan was to breeze past Sean without giving him the time of day; but he grabbed me as I was passing. "Wait for me down the hall. I'll only be a few minutes. I need to talk to you," he pleaded. I couldn't bring myself to say no.

A few minutes later, he found me just as I was about to retrieve a candy bar from a vending machine.

"Are you hungry? We could go for pizza."

My heart did a little pitter-patter. On the surface, there were several reasons going out with Sean sounded like a great idea. One, I was at a dead end in my fact searching and he hopefully had information I could use. Two, it was already past my usual dinner time; and thanks to Doris's magic fingers, I no longer needed to worry about extra calories. The obnoxious pumpkin colored dress was fitting fine. Three, I would love to stick it to Sarah. Her little warning about staying away from Sean didn't sit well with me. It seemed like a challenge and being the competitive woman I was, a dinner out with Sean would be one more point for my team. And last, but not at all least, seeing him still gave me a tingly feeling, as wrong as it was to feel that way about a practically married man.

However, despite all these reasons, I was determined to take the high road.

"What exactly do we need to discuss? Something about the case or something about us?" I asked, in my most mature voice.

"Both."

Hmm. "Do you think going out for dinner is a good idea, considering?"

"Considering what?"

"Your fiancé?"

He shifted uncomfortably from foot to foot. I have to admit, I was starting to feel a little disgusted with the whole Sean situation. He was toying with me, again. Three years of dating and he never could commit to anything serious. Then he broke off our quasi-relationship because I went out a few times with another guy? Here he was doing the same thing; only *he* was supposed to be engaged.

I drew in a deep breath waiting for him to come up with a good answer but he just kept shifting. As disgusted as I was, reason one and four won out. I needed information and well...that tingly feeling *was* hard to ignore.

"You know what," I started. "I *am* a little hungry, why don't you just follow me to the cafeteria. I'm going to grab a quick bite and we can discuss things down there." I smiled inwardly at my suggestion which, in my opinion, sounded very levelheaded. Plus, dinner in a hospital cafeteria could hardly be called a date.

One awkward elevator ride later, we were in the hospital's basement cafeteria, foraging through our dinner selection which we'd carried on plastic trays to our white-top table. Hospital cafeterias reminded me of my grade school cafeteria. And that was a good thing; lunch was always my favorite period of the day.

As a tribute to my grade school's cafeteria, I bypassed the soft drink dispenser and chose two small cartons of milk—one white, and one chocolate. Just like old times, I skipped the straws and drank straight from the rough cardboard opening.

Sean started talking about his visit with Shep. "Cancer is such a horrible disease," he said, unwrapping a ham and cheese on whole wheat. "I know how close you and Shep are, Pippi. I'm sorry that this is happening to him."

"Thanks. He's much braver than I would be. He seems to have come to terms with everything." I paused to unwrap my own sandwich. "Why did he want to see you?" I asked, wanting to change the subject before I got too emotional.

"He wanted an update on Pauline's case among other things."

"Like what?"

"We had a long talk about you. Seems he wants me to keep you safe."

"You don't need to babysit me, Sean. I can take care of myself."

He smirked and shoved in another bite of his sandwich before moving on to his fruit salad.

"Did you find out if the Westmont police found anything on Shep's laptop?" I asked, loading a fry with ketchup.

"Yup. There was an inventory list from the Sokolov estate. They purchased several items from A to Z a couple days prior to Pauline's death," he replied, stealing a fry from my plate.

"I told you there's a connection."

He shook his head and reached over to swipe some of my ketchup. "It may prove a connection to A to Z Estate Sales, but not to the Farrells. We're taking another look at the auction house."

"What about books? What books were inventoried? Russian books?"

"The inventory list was general. Books were listed, but nothing specific. No descriptions and no mention of foreign books."

I paused, considering this new information. If only Pauline had been more specific. I needed a connection between the book in JimDog's den and the books at both The Classy Closet and the Retro Metro. I briefly considered telling Sean about the envelope Pauline found, but I knew while to me it was sure-fire evidence; to him it wouldn't sound like much.

"Will you let me know if you find anything else at A to Z?" I finally asked.

"If I can. Shep said that Pauline's funeral is tomorrow morning," he commented, quickly changing the subject. "Are you going?"

I squirmed with guilt. I should go. She was a friend. "I don't think so. I had a prior commitment."

"What type of commitment?"

"I'm helping at the St. Joan's garage sale. We're sorting and marking tomorrow."

"St. Joan's? Why? That's not your parish."

"Uh, I'm helping my sister, Mary Frances." I didn't mention that I was working with Morgan Farrell and intended on using her to get closer to the Farrell clan. Sean probably wouldn't approve.

"Oh. I see." Then he suddenly smiled. "Guess that means you'll be too busy to do much more checking around this week, huh?"

I smiled back. "Right. So, you shouldn't worry about babysitting me. I'll be safe and sound at the parish."

That seemed to satisfy him.

We ate in silence for a few minutes, before he spoke up. "Actually, I don't mind babysitting you."

It was a flirtatious remark and for some reason it really ticked me off.

"You know, Sean, I'm tired of this. We dated for a long time and you said you loved me, but you never made any serious commitments. Then, mostly just to make you jealous, I went out on a couple of dates with some guy—"

"A murderer."

"True. But the point is that you completely dumped me over it. You felt betrayed. Then you started going out with Sarah, who, by the way, you had been secretly friends with while we were dating. Now you two are engaged." Glancing around, I noticed I was drawing an audience and lowered my voice. "And, now you're flirting with me?"

"You're right," he said, looking pitifully sad, but I kept on ranting.

"You're getting ready to marry Sarah. Why are you doing this?"

"No, I'm not."

My jaw dropped.

He leaned in closer. "I broke it off."

"What?"

"It's over."

"Oh. I'm sorry." No I wasn't. I sat back in my chair, trying to control the smile that was threatening to break out on my face. I wanted to jump into his arms and kiss him all over.

At least now I could understand Sarah's little tirade at my apartment. She was a scorned woman, desperate to hang on to her man any way she could. Poor thing.

"Why? What happened?" I asked. I just couldn't help smirking a little.

"It just wasn't right between us."

I leaned forward, waiting for him to expand on his explanation. I knew what was coming. He couldn't stay with Sarah because he was still in love with me; he had finally figured out I was the only woman for him; or, my heart thudded, he'd proposed to the wrong woman and was about to tell me I was the one he wanted to marry.

Instead, he stood abruptly, his chair screeching against the linoleum floor, and threw his crumpled napkin onto the tray. "I have to go, but I'll be in touch," he said.

And that was it. He turned and walked out, leaving me hanging once again.

I was torn. Maybe I should feel happy. After all, Sean had dumped Sarah. Then again, maybe I should feel depressed. He was free to run back to me, but he wasn't. One way or the other, more chocolate was in order. I made my way back into the cafeteria and picked up a slice of Boston cream pie and another carton of chocolate milk. By the time I licked the final gob of creamy custard from my fork and took the last drag from the carton, it didn't matter whether I was elated or depressed; I was simply sick. I glanced around. Luckily the cafeteria was almost completely empty. After another double check, I loosened the drawstring on my sweatpants, making way for my expanding belly, and discretely belched into my napkin. My stomach was rolling. It was time to call it a day.

Chapter 14

I didn't even bother with jeans the next day; instead, I stepped right back into the previous day's sweats. A good thing, I thought, after walking into the parish hall and seeing what I'd be sorting through. Before me was more junk than I'd ever seen crammed into a single room. My eyes danced about, taking it all in. I could hardly wait to get started.

I caught sight of Mary Frances across the room. She too was wearing sweats and had her hair pulled into a high pony-tail which swung back and forth as she weaved her way through stacks of bags.

"Hey, Sis. A lot of donations, huh?"

She waved me over, smiling. "Isn't it wonderful? We'll bring in a ton of money this year. Just think of all the supplies it'll afford for the shelter." That was my sister; always thinking of others.

Just as I reached her, we heard a loud thump followed by a high-pitched clanking noise coming from the back entrance. "That would be Mrs. Connely's piano," she explained. "Her son apparently quit lessons years ago and she's sick of dusting it. What a generous donation, huh?"

I agreed, but I wasn't too sure about the two guys who were struggling to fit it through the back door. Cuss words were flying, most of them including a vain usage of God's name. Even I, who could swear with the best of them, knew that was completely inappropriate for a church setting.

I was about to say something too, but was interrupted by Morgan Farrell's grand entrance. "Hi all!" she called out, making her way over. I could smell her cologne before she reached us. I used to wear that same expensive scent in my previous life, when I could easily afford to smell like a hundred and twenty-eight an ounce. Nowadays, if I wanted to smell extra special, I'd peruse the department store cosmetic counters until some heavily made-up brunette wearing a white lab coat sprayed me down. If I were lucky, she'd swipe a little free eye shadow across my lids too.

I did a quick survey of Morgan's outfit. Definitely not sweat pants. She was looking quite svelte in her work attire: designer jeans, dark washed and fitted to a tee; brown leather pointy-toed loafers peeking out from under the boot-cut jeans; and a button-down, crisply ironed shirt, rolled up at the sleeves. Her gold jewelry was understated and instead of wearing dangly earrings she sported diamond studs; flashy, but still practical for working. The entire ensemble, while casual, still cost more than I earned in an entire month or two.

"Where should we start?" Morgan asked, sounding quite enthusiastic and looking toward Mary Frances for leadership.

We decided to divide and conquer. Mary Frances and Morgan paired off, working through small household items, sorting and marking as they went along. I helped the foul-mouthed, piano moving men carry in and set up a dozen long white tables.

After that was accomplished, I started sorting through bags marked 'kid's clothes.' My goal was to get all the children's items separated into sizes and arranged on tables. I practically drooled as I worked. Almost everything I sorted through was brand name. A girl like me could make a fortune selling this stuff on-line.

While sorting through bags was fun, I still had a mission to accomplish. Whenever I could, I tried to engage Morgan in conversation. It wasn't that easy, though. Surprisingly enough, she was a hard worker and didn't waste much time chitchatting.

I kept trying. "So, Morgan, how did you say you and J.J. met? I think people's love stories are so interesting, don't you, Mary Frances?" I looked at my sister for support.

"Uh, huh," she mumbled, trying to fit together the pieces of a dozen or so children's puzzles that had tipped over and become one huge, but colorful, mess.

Morgan popped out from behind a box of blankets. "Oh ... it was a crazy thing, really," she giggled. "Well, a friend of mine belonged to the same country club as his family did. Actually," she giggled again, "she was dating J.J. at the time. Anyway, J.J. is quite the tennis player, and as it happened, he and my girlfriend were signed up to play doubles in a charity tournament when she suddenly took ill. She asked me to fill in for her and I just couldn't help myself. It was love at first sight."

"I bet." I eyed the cute little smirk she wore and glanced down at her long manicured nails. Meeeow ... what a cat. Well, she'd sunk those claws into a rich one. "And here you are now: happily married and getting ready to buy a new home. I bet you're anxious to get out of your in-law's house," I commented.

"Oh, I don't know. It's not so bad living there. Isn't it a beautiful home? I told J.J. that I want ours to be as nice. He's working so hard at the company, why shouldn't he have something just as nice? Besides, it'll be his company soon."

I tried not to show any reaction to her audacity. Mary Frances must have been attempting to do the same. I'd never seen someone work so diligently on putting together a chunky wooden puzzle. "Really? Is Mr. Farrell going to retire soon?" I asked.

"Well, he's not getting any younger, you know."

I couldn't decide if she was being flippant, or simply avoiding the answer. "Well, he sure has built a successful business. What a great thing to be able to hand down to his sons."

"Sons?"

"Oh, I mean son. That's right. J.J. is an only child, isn't he?"

"Yes." She eyed me curiously. Mary Frances was also eyeing me.

I went directly into babble mode. "Well, of course he's the only son. I don't know what I was thinking. I mean, how crazy would it be if all of the sudden someone just popped out of nowhere and said they were a long lost son of Mr. Farrell?"

Mary Frances cleared her throat.

I had Morgan's full attention, but I couldn't quite read her expression.

"That's a weird thought, huh?" I asked, trying to elicit a response.

"Very weird," Morgan replied. Her voice was even toned. She seemed cool although she was staring hard at me. Of course that could be because I was rambling like an idiot. Nonetheless, if she was fazed by my "dual-heir" innuendo, she was good at hiding it.

"Well, it's already past noon, girls," Mary Frances said. "I think we've accomplished a lot for this morning. We should have no trouble getting this set up before the sale on Saturday. Mrs. Kelley's group is coming in later this afternoon to do some marking. How about we call it a day and meet back here at nine tomorrow?"

Morgan stood and brushed her hands. "Sounds good to me. I'm starved. J.J is at the Naperville location today. I thought I'd head over there and try to catch him for lunch. Do you girls want to join us?"

"Um ... I'm not—" Mary Frances started.

"Sure. We'd love to!" I chimed in. What luck! J.J. was the one Farrell I hadn't met. "I mean, I love JimDogs. I'd eat there every day if I could!"

Mary Frances raised her brows. "Actually, you girls go ahead," she said. "I've got to get back to St. Benedict."

Morgan smiled sweetly. "Well, maybe next time, Sister." Then turning to me she said, "Do you want to ride with me or follow? It's just down the road, so it wouldn't be any trouble for me to bring you back this way."

"Well, okay then. I'll ride with you." Any opportunity I can get to learn more about your murderous family, I thought.

Once we were buckled in and cruising comfortably down the road in Morgan's luxury sedan, she asked, "I'm glad you're able to join me for lunch. So, you love JimDogs, huh?"

"I sure do. I eat there all the time. I usually get the Junior J-dog combo meal with root beer. I love the frosty mugs. I also *especially* love the CubbyPup. I take it with extra mustard and onions. Yum, yum. And the bun..." I rolled my eyes in mocked pleasure. "I sure wish I had the recipe for your hotdog rolls."

Morgan laughed. "Do you know how many people have tried to get that recipe from me? Not that I even know it. It's a well-guarded secret, you know."

I laughed with her. We were just two happy, giggly friends riding along in a fifty-thousand dollar vehicle, going out to eat hot dogs together.

"Not even J.J. knows the recipe," she added.

"Really?" I was a bit surprised by that.

"I know. Isn't it crazy? James has all the buns made here locally, under tight security. Then they're shipped to the other locations."

"Wow. He goes to a lot of trouble to keep the recipe guarded."

She shrugged. "It's what's made him millions."

I nodded in agreement, trying to comprehend all that must go into keeping such a secret. "Does J.J. work at this location every day?" I asked, as we pulled into the lot.

"Oh, no. He usually works at the corporate office. I'm not really sure why he's here today. Some sort of boring work stuff, I'm sure." She put the car in park and was peering in the rearview mirror touching up her lipstick—some sort of daring shade of red probably called Red Desire, or Wicked Red. With my coloring, I could never get away with such passionate shades. I was forever doomed to more subdued names such as Taupe, Everyday Beige, or Barely Pink.

She snapped the mirror shut and flashed a freshly colored smile my way. "After lunch, J.J. and I are going to meet with our contractor and start plans for our new house," she gushed.

I stole a quick look at my own appearance. My sweatshirt was dusty and stained from working all morning so I slipped it off, deciding to sacrifice warmth for fashion. Luckily, I'd worn a descent shirt underneath.

"J.J. is giving me free rein on the house design," Morgan continued. "I never knew how much went into building a place. It's so exciting. Come on, let's go and grab a seat. I'll tell you all about my ideas."

Oh yippee, I thought, following Morgan past the crowd at the front counter and straight to the cashier who was wearing the standard JimDog uniform: white pants, red shirt, and a red and white striped baseball cap.

"Hello, Mrs. Farrell," he said, giving Morgan a lustful once over that would get him fired if he wasn't careful.

"Hi there," she replied in a way that made me think she couldn't remember the guy's name. It was probably difficult to remember all the little people. "I'm meeting my husband for lunch. Please tell him I'm here and would you bring out my usual, and uh ... a CubbyPup with mustard and onions?"

I nodded, impressed she remembered.

"And a couple of diet sodas," she added, glancing my way.

"Diet soda's fine," I indicated with a smile, although I never really drank diet anything. I would have preferred a regular pop or a frosty mug of root beer.

It must be great to be Morgan, I thought. We'd just bypassed twenty minutes of waiting in line and our food was going to be brought out to us. I was liking this set-up. Who knew eating weenies could be so fun? Maybe I *could* tolerate listening to house plans for an hour or so.

As "what's-his-name" filled our order we made ourselves comfortable in a booth. A few minutes later, he brought our food. Morgan indicated that we should go ahead and start eating. "J.J. should be out at any moment," she said.

Apparently, she was wrong. I was half-way through my CubbyPup when Morgan started to become impatient. "I wonder what's taking J.J. so long?" she whined, her face suddenly turning pouty.

I shrugged and kept eating. We both looked up as 'what's-his-name' approached our booth again. This time, he looked a little forlorn. "Uh ... Mrs. Farrell. J.J. sent me to tell you that ... well ... he's sorry, but he got called out on some sort of emergency and returned to corporate headquarters."

"What!" She accentuated her exclamation by slamming her drink down on the table, sending plumes of sugar-free fizz all over my shirt. She whipped out her cell and pushed a single button. Apparently J.J. was on speed dial. Boy, was he in for it, I thought, as I wiped droplets off my front.

"Hi sweetie. Where are you?" I did a double take. A second ago her voice was low and cursing, now it was high-pitched and sweet. This girl would be a natural for a children's film voice-over. Or, maybe psycho enough to pull off two homicides.

What's-his-name started slowly backing away as Morgan continued speaking in her sugary tone. "Of course I understand, but what about our appointment with the contractor? We were supposed to meet right after lunch." Her voice was sweet, but her expression was bitter. "That's fine. I'll see you at home tonight. Love—"

Uh, oh. He hung up on the love you part. Not good.

I watched as she turned off her phone and placed it back in her purse, her movements calm and controlled. Then in one sudden jerk she stood up, and with the force of a major league pitcher, launched the rest of her diet soda across the restaurant. Patrons scrambled to get out of the way as it exploded against the far wall.

I looked around. What's-his-name was nowhere to be found. I scanned the front counter and surprisingly enough, no one seemed to even notice Morgan's little outburst. If it wasn't for the guy across the room with the soda-stained shirt flashing a rude hand gesture, I might doubt it had happened at all.

I looked back just in time to see Morgan high-tailing it out the side door. "Wait!" I grabbed what was left of my CubbyPup and ran after her. By the time I got to the lot, she was roaring away, tires squealing like a dozen hungry pigs.

I stood, staring after her, finishing off the last bit of my hotdog. Well, that didn't go as I'd planned. Not only did I not get to meet J.J., but now I was stuck without a ride back to St. Joan's. I could call a cab, but geez, it would cost more than I wanted to spend. To top it off, my sweatshirt was still in her car.

Luckily, out of the corner of my eye, I caught sight of a red and white uniform. "Hey, hey!" I yelled, running to where what's-his-name was opening the door to a dented hatch-back.

"What's wrong? She leave you stranded?"

"Yeah." I threw myself at his mercy. "Can you give me a lift to St. Joan's? My car is parked in the church lot."

"Sure, hop in."

It was a quick ride, but long enough for me to ascertain a few things. First, what's-his-name was Aiden Parker, a college student who happened to be working his way through college one hot dog at a time. Second, according to Aiden, Morgan's fits were nothing new to JimDog employees. Apparently she'd chucked quite a few fountain drinks since she and J.J. tied the knot. Third, Aiden thought perhaps Morgan was quite spoiled. No news there. But, he also confided that he couldn't blame Morgan for flipping out every once in a while. James Junior was a real jerk.

When I asked him to clarify that statement, he simply winked and said, "Well, like father like son."

That piqued my interest. I wanted to ask him more, but we were pulling into the lot at St. Joan's and he was anxious to get home and change for his three o'clock class. I did manage to ask Aiden the whereabouts of JimDog headquarters. It was located not too far away, off of Corporate West Drive in Lisle.

I briefly considered taking a spin past the corporate office, but changed my mind. I probably wouldn't gain much by looking at the outside of a building; plus, I was beat. I decided to head home.

Unfortunately, my first day working with Morgan didn't yield as much useful information as I'd hoped. The only thing I learned, besides Morgan suffered from some sort of personality disorder, was that the elusive J.J. was like his father. What did that mean? Did he have a mistress? That would explain Morgan's fury when she found out he couldn't meet her for lunch. Did she suspect he was sneaking off for a rendezvous with his lover?

If I had a hubby who was cheating, I would do more than throw a soft drink, but that's just me. Some women will put up with anything, especially when it comes to money. After all, Morgan did want that new house badly. Maybe she was willing to tolerate her hubby's indiscretions if it meant she would still get her suburbia dream home.

One thing for sure, if J.J. was the type of man who would cheat on his spouse, then he lacked as many morals as his father. Maybe I did need to take a closer look at him. I knew just how to do it, too.

Since, I couldn't put my plan into motion for a couple more hours, so I decided to pass the time at my workbench. Working on "fixer-uppers" always settled my mind, and I could use a little break from the stress of this case.

The small niche adjacent to my bathroom, designated as my 'trash-to-treasure' area, featured a utilitarian bench made of old sawhorses and a discarded orange laminate countertop that I found alongside a home store dumpster. Underneath it, I stowed several plastic storage units on wheels, the drawers marked with labels such as glues, fasteners, batteries, polishers ...well, in short, every sort of fixer-upper imaginable.

Currently, I was working on one of my latest curbside acquisitions, a blue and white ceramic vase. By itself, the vase wasn't valuable; but as a chic French country style table lamp, it would be fabulous.

I'd done quite a few lamp conversions and found they were popular with my flea market crowd. I could convert just about anything into a lamp—antique bottles, mason jars, teapots. My favorite conversion was a large pink piggybank that I electrified and topped with a pink and white checkered shade. One of my flea market customers paid thirty bucks for it saying it was a 'must-have' for her baby's nursery. It gave me a lot satisfaction to know that homes across the city were lit by my little creations.

As usual, time passed quickly as I sat at my workbench. I was contemplating the best spot to drill a hole for the lamp cord when I noticed it was nearing six o'clock. Time to put my plan into place.

It was twenty minutes before seven when I neared the Farrell's front gate. I'd already formulated a convincing spiel for the gateman. After my encounter with him at the tea, I knew he could be one tough cookie.

"Name," he said, looking down from his white box throne. I decided to ignore the way he turned up his nose at my fifteen-year-old Volvo. Didn't he recognize timeless quality when he saw it?

"Pippi O'Brien. I'm here to see—"

"Do you have an appointment?" he interrupted, glancing through the pages on his clipboard.

A quick glance toward the house told me Morgan's car was in the drive. What luck! My plan was to use my sweater, which I left in her car before the 'diet soda incident', as an excuse to get in and see her. Of course, she'd probably feel horrible about her previous behavior. Plus, since I was showing up at dinner time, she'd more than likely invite me in for a bite to eat and … voila! I'd be back in the Farrell residence. Hard telling what I might find this time.

If only I could get past this pesky gateman.

I pulled back my shoulders and laid it on thick. "No, I don't have an appointment. You see, I accidently left my sweater in Morgan's car when we were lunching this afternoon and I thought I would stop by and get it. I'm sure if you just phoned the house and explained, she'd be happy to see me. We are very close friends, after all," I added.

For some reason he looked confused. He stammered a little, then picked up the phone and started to dial. Just then, I noticed Morgan coming out the front door of the estate and starting for her car. Well, crud! There went my plan.

I wondered where Morgan was off to. Out for dinner with J.J.? Maybe he was trying to make up for standing her up at lunch time.

"Wait!" I yelled at the gateman. "Oh silly me. I just remembered, I didn't leave my sweater in Morgan's car. Why there it is!" I pointed aimlessly to the back of my vehicle. "So sorry." I slammed the car in reverse. "Gotta run!"

I backed out quickly and pulled down the street, ducking under the steering wheel so Morgan wouldn't see me as she passed. More than likely she wouldn't pay attention to my car. I don't think she'd even seen it at the parish parking lot and probably wouldn't recognize that it was it mine. While I hated to abandon my original plan, I was a little curious about what Morgan Farrell did in her spare time. Besides, if she was going to meet J.J., maybe I could 'just happen' to bump into them.

As soon as I was sure she'd passed, I sat up and eased my foot onto the gas pedal. My adrenaline kicked in and I struggled to maintain enough distance between our cars to avoid suspicion. Whenever the opportunity arose, I made a casual lane change and dropped back another two cars. I continued this procedure for approximately three and half miles when Morgan made a right hand turn onto College Street.

Traffic was light; so I increased my distance to four car lengths. I continued following, undetected, as College turned into Yackley Avenue and we crossed under Highway 88. Morgan had no idea I was tailing her.

Soon, I began to recognize our location. We were in Lisle, driving parallel to the highway on Corporate West Drive. I remembered Aiden telling me JimDog's corporate offices were located on this road. Was Morgan heading to the office to meat J.J.? Good. She was probably going to pick him up for their dinner.

Then suddenly, Morgan surprised me by pulling into the Huntley Hotel parking lot. Gripping the wheel a little tighter, I cautiously pulled in after her, still maintaining a safe distance.

She, of course, found a parking space immediately. I hung back a row and watched her exit from her car, sling her bag over her shoulder, and walk with purpose toward the hotel. I noted that she was wearing some sort of sleek black dress, cut way low in the back and heels that would send me into immediate traction.

My heart sank a bit. She was dressed to the nines. Probably meeting hubby for dinner at the Huntley dining room. There was no way I could just 'show up' there dressed in my three-day-old sweat pants. Although, it wouldn't hurt to follow her anyway, just in case.

As soon as she was a safe distance away, I began roaming the lot. Just my luck, Morgan seemed to have found the last available space. Not wanting to lose precious time, I took a chance and made my own parking space at the end of a row of cars, and high-tailed it into the lobby.

Things were hopping at the Huntley. The lobby was packed and by the time I caught sight of Morgan, I was surprised to see she was heading for the elevators, not the restaurant off the back of the lobby.

Well, there was no way to follow her now. My only option was to hang out until she came down. Knowing I was in for a long wait, I settled into a club chair and picked up a rumpled copy of the *Chicago Sun Times*. I kept one eyed peeled while I halfway hid my face behind the newspaper.

I wondered what Morgan was doing dressed so nicely and heading to a hotel room. I doubted she had a rendezvous planned with her hubby. I mean, why would she go to the trouble of getting a room when they lived together already? An affair? That sort of made since. If J.J. was dabbling on the side, why shouldn't she? Only, why here, right next to his office? So, she could rub it in? Maybe.

Or ... oh my goodness! I knew what Morgan was doing. I practically laughed out loud. I mean, it was so obvious. I'd hate to be J.J right now. I could see how this was going down. *J.J., like his father, has a mistress and the Huntley, being so close to the office, is a convenient rendezvous spot. Morgan has suspected his infidelity for a long time, which was obvious by her reaction at JimDogs earlier in the day. She probably hired a private investigator. Yeah, that's it ... the private investigator tipped her off to J.J.'s whereabouts and she's here to make the big bust.* I can just see the room of the door flying open and Morgan standing in the doorway looking dangerously beautiful in her low-cut black dress and pointing an accusing finger at her husband and his mistress. If she's smart, and I'm not sure she really is, she'll use her cell phone to snap a picture of the raunchy rendezvous so she can use it later in court to sue the cheater for everything he's worth. *That way, she'll still have enough money to build her house in Schaumberg.*

I was just starting to really enjoy my little reverie when out of the corner of my eye, I caught sight of a familiar furry face. It was Alex Sokolov, walking very purposefully toward the elevator. He was wearing an overcoat and one of those Russian fur hats. Not a good fashion choice for such a hairy man. From my vintage point, it was difficult to see where the fur of the hat ended and the fur on his face started. The overall effect was one huge hairy blob attached to a blah-gray overcoat.

Seeing him, though, made me think I had it all wrong. This was too much of a coincidence. Morgan wasn't here to catch her cheating hubby in the act. She was here to meet with Mr. Fur Face. But why? Certainly they weren't involved. Or were they? I had to know.

Thinking quickly, I reached into my bag and extracted my Prudence Overton glasses. Good thing I still had them with me. I shoved them on my face and ran across the lobby at breakneck speed. "Hold the elevator please!" I yelled.

Alex looked perturbed, but held the door while I slipped aboard. As the door closed, he reached over and pushed number nine. "What floor?" he asked.

"Nine," I replied, then exclaimed, "Is that you Mr. Sokolov?"

Alex looked surprised.

"It's me, Prudence Overton." I pushed the glasses up my nose. "We met the other day at your mother's house. Wow, I can't believe I've run into you here. I didn't think you'd still be in town. Please excuse the way I'm dressed." I waved a hand toward my sweatpants. "I just finished working out in the hotel gym," I said, hoping they did indeed have a gym. "Anyway, why are you here?"

The door opened and he was starting down the hallway. I followed, waiting for his reply.

"I'm meeting a friend," he replied. "Nice to see you again, Ms. Overton." He stopped at number 947 and was keying in with a key card. Was Morgan in there waiting for him with open arms? I had to know.

I continued down the hallway, pretending to head toward my own room. "You too, Mr. Sokolov," I replied cheerfully over my shoulder. As soon as I heard his door click shut, I trotted back. As I neared his room, I got down on my hands and knees and crawled, just in case he was peering through the peep-hole.

I remained on my knees as I listened at the door. I have to say, the Huntley had invested their money in quality construction. The room was virtually soundproof. I couldn't hear a darn thing.

I had just pressed my ear fully to the door when I felt a tap on my shoulder. I jumped up and stood nose to nose with a maroon and yellow-capped bellboy.

"Can I help you ma'am?" He was giving me a hard look.

"Oh, no thanks. I thought I dropped something, but I guess not." I was whispering, hoping that Alex wouldn't hear the commotion and come to the door.

"That's not what it looked like to me, ma'am."

Man, this bellboy was a sharp one. I signaled for him to be quiet and began rooting in my purse for a little persuasion. Unfortunately, Chuck had taken all my persuasion earlier in the week.

Just then the door opened. "Is there a problem out here?"

"Oh, hi again Mr. Sokolov ... um ... no there's no problem. I just dropped something that's all. This nice young man is helping me look for it.

Alex was standing, with both hands on the door frame. I shifted this way and that, trying to get a glimpse around him. He shifted also. Getting angrier by the moment.

"Is there something you want, Ms. Overton?" he asked curtly.

While his bulky physique took up most of the doorway, I did manage to catch a glimpse inside the room. In it I saw, over by the small table in the corner of the room, the lower half of a pair of woman's legs, neatly crossed and wearing to-die-for red stilettos.

"No, I was just on my way out."

"You bet you are," injected the bellboy, placing a firm hand on the small of my back and ushering me to the elevator. He stuck with me down to the lobby and out the front door.

Damn.

Now I may never know what was going on in that room. Could those legs have possibly belonged to Morgan Farrell? Geez, why didn't I take a closer look at what shoes she was wearing? If those were Morgan's legs, what was she doing with her husband's illegitimate brother? Certainly not an affair? Or, maybe Morgan was more than just a ditzy spoiled housewife. Maybe she was the mastermind behind both of the murders and had teamed up with Fur Face to pull them off. Could she have been the lady that paid Chuck a thousand bucks for the

Sokolov file? No, that wouldn't make sense. If she was involved with Alex, she could have whatever she wanted from Calina Sokolov's estate.

I was so frustrated, I wanted to bang my head against the wall and scream. I needed to calm down and think rationally. I was jumping to conclusions. I didn't know for sure that Morgan even came up to the ninth floor. It was a huge hotel. She could have gone anywhere. I didn't even think she was wearing red shoes. I only saw her for a second before she entered the hotel, but I would have noticed red. Wouldn't I?

Feeling like a failure, I made my way back to my car, which luckily hadn't been towed, and moved it so I had a prime view of Morgan's vehicle. The least I could do was wait for her to leave and check the color of her shoes.

I waited, and waited, and waited.

Then, I woke up.

Wiping drool from my cheek, I squinted against the early morning sunlight searching for Morgan's car. It was gone. My heart sank. I'd fallen asleep and missed her exit from the hotel.

Shivering from the cold, I opened my cell to check the time. After seven already. I stretched and reached over to crank the engine, only it wouldn't start. It must have been running when I fell asleep. It was out of gas. Now my teeth were chattering and my stomach rumbling. I flipped open my cell again and dialed in desperation.

"Hello, Sis, I've got a problem. Can you meet me with a can of gas, a sweatshirt, and some hot coffee at the Huntley in Lisle?"

I paused as she flooded the line with questions.

"Actually, can I explain it to you later? I'm stranded in the lot right outside the main door. Hurry. I'm freezing."

About forty-five minutes later, my trusty sister showed up with the requested items, plus an extra bonus of a half-dozen chocolate glazed donuts. Once the gas was in the tank, we sat in the front seat gobbling donuts, slurping coffee, and basking in the full blast of hot air coming from the car vents.

"It must have been some other woman. I can't believe Morgan Farrell was the woman in Alex Sokolov's room," my sister was saying. "She doesn't seem like the type that would cheat on her husband. You've heard her talk about him. She seems so in love."

"Well, maybe it's a case of affair revenge. Obviously, she suspects her husband of having a mistress. Maybe she's engaged in a retaliatory affair. Could you blame her?"

My sister shot me a dark look.

"Oh, give me a break, Sis. Don't you ever get tired of the old double standard? Men just get to do whatever, while women stay at home and accept it?"

"I'm not condoning any sort of extra-marital affair. First of all, you don't even have proof that James Junior has a mistress. All you're going on is idle gossip from one of his employees. Second, all you saw was a leg. A completely dressed leg. It could have belonged to anyone. You can't be sure it was Morgan Farrell's leg."

She had a point. I really didn't have any sort of evidence at all. "You're right. I've been spinning my wheels. I'm not any closer to figuring out who killed Pauline. Maybe Sean's right; maybe the Farrells have nothing to do with this. Just because they're a dysfunctional family, doesn't mean they're murderers." I put down my donut. I wasn't hungry any more. "I don't know. I've hit a dead end." Another day was gone and I was no closer to finding Pauline's murderer. All I had done was screw things up. I was failing Shep.

Mary Frances put a hand on my shoulder. "Well, you could always pray about it."

I cringed. The last time I sincerely talked to God, I had a gun pointed at my temple. At the time, I was bartering for my life. I actually promised God that if he spared me, I'd never get involved in another case again.

I shivered. Hopefully, God wasn't going to renege on his end of the deal because I couldn't keep a promise. "It's almost nine. We better head for St. Joan's," I said, completely avoiding the whole topic.

Chapter 15

Morgan didn't walk into the parish hall until after ten. In fact, I was surprised to see her as I figured she might be too tired from her late night rendezvous at the Huntley.

"Hi all! Sorry I'm late. I'll work extra hard to make up for it." Her voice held no trace of outrage I'd seen the day before at JimDogs. She seemed happy and quite composed in her skinny jeans, multi-layered shirts, and mid-calf boots. The outfit, while it did look good on her, was a bit over-the-top for working a garage sale. I wondered if she had other plans for later in the day.

Morgan plopped a brightly colored, over-sized quilted bag onto the table and extracted my sweatshirt. "Here you go, Phillipena. I think you left this in my car yesterday."

She handed it over with no hint of an apology for leaving me stranded in the JimDog parking lot. I decided to approach the topic anyway. "So, Morgan. Is everything alright? I mean, when you left me at JimDogs yesterday, you seemed really upset."

Morgan shrugged. "Oh sure, everything's fine." She started sorting and stacking paperback books by category. I had been avoiding the books, unsure of what to do with some of the romance novels that were donated. They didn't seem appropriate for a church garage sale.

Morgan, on the other hand, didn't seem bothered at all. "The afternoon crew sure got a lot done yesterday, huh?" she commented, while absent-mindedly leafing through a novel with a busty woman. It was titled *Sins of the Master*. I blushed just thinking about what those sins might be. Morgan, on the other hand, read the back cover, smiled to herself, skimmed a few pages, smiled some more, and tossed the book into her bag.

She glanced up and caught me watching her. "We couldn't possibly sell that type of book at this sale. I'll take it home and dispose of it," she said.

I glanced over at a large garbage can filled to the brim with broken, unsellable items and then back at her purse; but she made no move to pitch the book. Obviously she wanted to save the garbage for herself. Maybe she wanted to share it later with Alex. Ugh ... I shook off the image. Yuck and double yuck.

I grabbed a bottle of cleaner and some paper towels and moved on to cleaning the donated toys. Mary Frances was nearby untangling the laces on a pair of rollerblades. "Hey," she said to Morgan. "Were you at the Huntley last night?"

"Excuse me?" Morgan replied, stopping what she was doing and staring at my sister.

Mary Frances paused and looked directly at Morgan. "The Huntley in Lisle."

I was all ears.

"Were you there, Sister?" Morgan asked.

The air sizzled with tenseness. I was watching Morgan closely.

Mary Frances went back to work on the laces as if she didn't have a care in the world. "That hotel has the best restaurant. I do enjoy going with Sister Bernadette and Sister Teresa from time to time," she said, not quite telling a lie.

Morgan made some sort of small guttural noise, but didn't respond. She seemed uncomfortable. As far as I was concerned, she was looking guiltier every second. Maybe not of murder, but infidelity for sure.

"Were you there with your brother, perhaps?" Mary Frances prodded. I think she was enjoying herself. She had a wicked little smirk on her face.

Morgan attempted a chuckle; it came out like a snort. "No Sister, I wasn't at the Huntley last night. You must have mistaken me for someone else." She picked up her purse and began rifling through it. "I'm so sorry girls, but I just remembered I have an appointment. I'll be back tomorrow to help out some more."

She was quickly making her way to the door with me in hot pursuit. I wasn't about to let her get away without an explanation.

Just as her hand reached the doorknob, I reached out and got a hold of her arm and spun her around. "Can you wait up a minute, please? I'd like to talk to you about something."

She jerked out of my grasp, turned back, flung open the door and ran right into Patricia Farrell.

"Hi ladies. How's it going here?" Patricia asked, curiously studying Morgan's flushed face. "Are you leaving already, Morgan?"

Mary Frances crossed the room. "Hello, Patty," she said, looping her arm through Patricia's and directing her away from Morgan and me. "I'm glad you're here. Come on in and see how much progress has been made. I think this is going to be the best sale ever. I'm so excited about the possibilities for the woman's shelter. Plus, with your gracious offer to match our earnings this year, we should be able to do something wonderful for them."

"Of course, Sister. James and I are happy to help in any way we can," Patricia replied scowling at us over her shoulder. "Wait for me Morgan, while I talk to Sister," she added firmly. "I need to discuss something with you."

"What is your problem?" Morgan asked in a low, throaty whisper. We were still huddled by the exit.

"My problem? You're the one acting weird. First you throw a fit and chuck a drink across the room, then you leave me stranded at JimDogs, and now ... what? Sneaking around the Huntley with strange men?"

"Mind your own business," she hissed.

So, it *was* her leg I'd seen. "How do you know Alex Sokolov?" I was grasping for straws, but what did I have to lose? I wasted too many days bumbling without any solid information.

"Alex Sokolov?"

"Quit acting dumb, Morgan. Two women are dead and one of them was my friend. If you're involved in this, you'd better come clean."

"Dead?" She seemed to go pale all of the sudden. Her eyes were darting from me to Patricia. She seemed on the edge.

"Yes, all over something that was hidden in a book. A Russian book," I volleyed back.

I was waiting for her reply, when Patricia walked back over. "Well girls, I can see that you've been working hard down here. You all deserve a break. I'm calling ahead to the house to have Anna fix something nice for lunch. Why don't you lock up here and come by in what … maybe a half-hour?" She flipped open her phone, shot another disapproving glance at Morgan who seemed to be shrinking next to me.

"Oh, we wouldn't want to impose," Mary Frances, the ever polite one, called after her.

Patricia glanced back. "No imposition at all. In fact, I insist," she replied in a tone that really did seem insistent. Her eyes settled again on Morgan and they exchanged a look I didn't quite understand.

Then, suddenly Morgan flinched and scurried out the door, not even bothering to say goodbye.

"Wait!" Patricia yelled out, giving us a quick wave before taking after Morgan.

That was strange. No problem, though. I'd catch up with Morgan after lunch and finish our conversation. I couldn't help but smile. This was the break I needed. Only problem was, I felt gross. I hadn't showered, brushed, or changed since yesterday morning. In fact, now that I was thinking about it, I had been wearing the same sweats for several days. They could practically stand up on their own.

I glanced around. Out of desperation, I started searching through the *Women's Size Medium* table. It only took a couple of passes before I happened upon a pair of khaki pants and a long sleeve black top. Perfect.

I caught Mary Frances's attention. "Hey, I'm going to make an early purchase. They're already marked. I'll throw a couple bucks into the cash box when we open, okay?"

Not waiting for her reply, I headed off to freshen up. About twenty minutes later, we were on the road. I was feeling pretty good about my appearance. I'd splashed, rinsed, tied back my hair, and shimmied into my new outfit, which, by the way, fit pretty well. That's the thing with used clothing—no need to break it in; it's comfortable from the get-go.

Mary Frances and I decided to drive separately. Once again, as we passed the gateman and started down the winding drive, I was in awe of the beauty of the Farrell estate. Today, its massive brick and stone façade stood out crisply against the bright, cloudless sky. Mature oaks and maples provided a colorful canopy framing the house and surrounding gardens. Behind the house, I could see the stable hands had turned out the horses. Several handsome thoroughbreds grazed inside the white fenced pastures.

Patricia greeted us inside the foyer and escorted us toward the back of the house. I assumed we were heading to the conservatory again, but instead we ended up in the dining room. I had to admit, Patricia had a great decorating style. Everything about this home was a statement in refined elegance.

"I thought we'd take lunch in here today. There's more table space and the guys will be joining us," Patricia said.

"Where'd Morgan go?" my sister asked, looking around.

Patricia motioned for the maid as we settled into our seats. "I'm sure she'll be along shortly."

We'd just sat down when a clattering came from down the hall. Patricia left the table and went to intercept the men. I strained my ears, but couldn't hear much. I assumed she was warning hubby and Junior about their unexpected lunch guests.

"Fine. But I won't be here long. I need to change clothes before heading over to the site," I heard JimDog say as he made his way down the hall. "I met with the inspector this morning," he continued, walking into the room. "Looks like we'll have it all done by the grand opening. We just need to take care of a few ..." He hesitated for a split second, nodding at us before positioning himself at the head of the table. His expression turned slightly sour as his eyes scrutinizing me. It was obvious that he hated me. "Have you been feeling better?" he asked, without a hint of sincerity in his voice.

"Yes. Much better, thank you," I answered, raising my glass and taking a huge gulp of water. Suddenly, I felt like I was at Sunday dinner with the mob and JimDog was the Godfather.

"You're opening a new JimDogs?" I asked, trying to break the ice.

"Yes, in Skokie."

I hesitated, waiting for him to add more. He didn't.

"Where's Morgan?" J.J asked, sitting down.

"She should be here any minute," Patricia answered. "Let me introduce you to the O'Brien girls. Sister Mary Frances, and Phillipena."

I shook his outstretched hand, which was a limp as a wet noodle, and tried hard not to stare at his head. I couldn't help thinking it looked just like a flesh colored bowling ball resting on his narrow shoulders. His round eyes were positioned closely together above a long narrow nose which led right down to a round mouth that looked to be just the right size for an eight-pound ball's thumb-hole. Looking at his head, it seemed that I could poke my fingers in and go for a strike, or at least a spare.

After a little more small talk, we settled in and waited for lunch. I was having a difficult time focusing on the conversation as I couldn't get past J.J.'s appearance. He was the exact opposite of Alex Sokolov. How could that be with the same father? It was a cruel twist of genetic fate that the same man would produce two sons so physically different from one another. If Alex the Sasquatch and this bowling ball man could combine genes, they'd end up with about the right amount of hair.

"Pippi?" My sister was saying. "Patricia was just asking you about your business?"

I refocused and noticed that all eyes were on me. "My business?"

"Yes," Patricia said, smiling up at Anna who had brought in a tray with plates of salad. "I think it's fascinating that you left a job in finance to become an on-line retailer. It must have been a huge decision for you. How could it not have been with the different life-style choices you must have had to make?"

I sighed, and dug into my salad. How could I explain to this woman a decision to leave a prestigious, six figure salary to take on a career digging through garbage? I couldn't. So, I decided change the subject in a big way.

I took a deep breath and smiled sweetly at Patricia. "Actually, my life is a lot different than it used to be when I worked as a trader, but it's still very exciting. And, I meet the most interesting people. Why just the other day, I was tracking down merchandise that was sold off in an estate sale and I met the most charming man from Russia." I paused for a couple of seconds to make sure I had everyone's full attention. I definitely had JimDog's.

"His name was Alex Sokolov." I let the name drop like an atomic bomb.

The air was suddenly sucked out of the room. Jaws dropped, forks dropped, curse words dropped.

"What did you say?" James Farrell said, the look on his face and the way he was angrily clutching his fork, sending spasms of fear up my spine.

I immediately wished I could take back my words. Unsure of how to proceed, I got busy with my salad, hoping to divert any additional conflict. Unfortunately, a leafy piece of arugula stuck in my throat sending me into a spontaneous coughing fit. I gulped some water trying to force it down, but it had stubbornly lodged itself somewhere between the back of my tongue and my tonsils.

I coughed and sputtered.

Mary Frances looked concerned. Everyone else at the table just looked angry. In fact, the way they were looking at me, I was sure they were hoping I *would* choke to death.

I gulped some more. It was definitely stuck.

"Are you okay?" my sister asked, concern turning to alarm.

I couldn't respond. I started to see dots. No air. I moved my hands to my throat; the universal signal for choking to death.

None of the Farrells made a move to help.

Thank goodness for my sister. In an instant she was positioned behind me. With amazing strength and virulence, she placed her fists around my mid-section and hoisted inward and upward.

The green leafy glob shot across the table and landed right next to JimDog's plate.

I plopped back in my chair, gasping for air. After a few seconds of deep breathing, my vision started to clear. Looking about, I could see that everyone but J.J. and Mary Frances had left the room.

"Where'd everyone go?" I sputtered.

J.J. regarded me strangely and broke into laughter. "Did you really expect them to stick around after you mentioned the name Sokolov?" He laughed some more. His round little mouth stretching wide enough for me to see he had two gold fillings in his back molars. "That Russian woman has plagued this family for years. Really, as smart as my father is in business, he's stupid when it comes to women. Calina Sokolov was the biggest mistake he ever made."

"You know that she passed away recently. Cancer," I inserted.

J.J.'s joviality dimmed for a split second. "No, I didn't know. But, I'm not sorry to hear it. I'm glad to have her out of our lives."

"It must have been hard on your mother to know that there was another woman in your father's life," Mary Frances said.

An unrecognizable emotion flashed across J.J.'s face. He recomposed quickly and shrugged. "I guess she thought it was worth putting up with his little side activity in order to keep her lifestyle."

"How'd that make you feel?" my sister asked. She was slipping into psychiatrist mode.

J.J. was fidgeting with his fork, turning it over and over. I was actually beginning to feel sorry for the guy. "I got used to it," he said. "It didn't really make much difference to me."

"Still, I'm sure it must have been difficult to know your father was unfaithful." My sister was speaking in her soothing, Sisterly voice.

I, on the other hand, was growing impatient with her line of questioning. I was here for information, not a discussion and support group.

"Did you know that Calina had a son and that he may be your half-brother?" I threw out.

J.J. turned to me, his eyes full of rage. Once again, I should have stayed quiet. I just couldn't help myself. Mary Frances was soothing while I was as tactless as ... well ... at this moment I felt like one of those wacky day-time talk hosts revealing the results of a paternity test to one promiscuous woman and ten wanna-be daddies.

J.J. slammed his fork against the table. "What? A child? He had a child with her?"

Hum ... guess he didn't know.

He picked up his fork again and began jabbing it in my direction. "I don't believe that for one second. What proof do you have?"

"Uh." I looked toward Mary Frances for help. She seemed busy folding and refolding her napkin. "Well, actually, I don't have any substantial proof. It's really just a rumor."

J.J. stood abruptly, sending his chair tumbling to the floor. "Why don't you mind your own business?" With that, he flung the fork onto the middle of the table and stomped out of the room.

Mary Frances raised her brows. "That went well."

"Yeah, well ..." I looked around at the empty room. "Guess we'd better be going, huh?"

We headed for the door finding Anna waiting in the foyer with our coats. As I reached for mine, I tried making eye contact with her. Maybe she'd be sympathetic to my plight and offer information that would be pertinent to the case. However, my hopes were dashed when she raised her chin and shot me a disapproving look down her nose. Old pinch-face wasn't going to open up to me. She knew on which side her bread was buttered.

Once outside, I took a deep cleansing breath. The chilly fall air was a welcomed relief to the heavy tenseness inside the house.

Before Mary Frances got into her car, I offered an apology. "Hey, Sis, I'm sorry if I'm creating problems between you and the Farrells. I know they're benefactors, and after all this they may withdraw their offer to match the funds raised at the sale."

She smiled. "Are you serious? Don't apologize for trying to get to the truth. Besides, this week has been the most exciting week I've had in months."

I sighed with relief. "Still, I'm sure she'll renege on her promise to match the funds."

Mary Frances thought for a second. "I doubt it. She made that announcement in front of all her friends. I don't think she'd back out. How could she? How would she explain it? Anyway, don't worry about it. Just be careful. You've made some very powerful people angry. If they are murderers, then they may make you their next target."

She was right. I thought about my parents and all the worry I caused them last time I got involved with dangerous people. I should back off this case and let the professionals do their job. Problem was, I made a promise to Shep and I couldn't let him down.

I squinted toward the house just in time to see the shuffling of one of the window blinds on the second floor. I trembled involuntarily. "I'll see you in the morning, Sis."

She gave me a quick hug. "You better be there, because after practically accusing her of having an affair and then insulting her family, I don't think Morgan is going to be too eager to help us."

That was a shame, I thought, wondering why she didn't show for lunch. Despite the fact that she was an adulteress and possibly a cold-blooded murderer, Morgan was good at sorting and marking.

My stomach started rumbling before I made it to the freeway. Foraging through my ashtray, I was able to scrape together two seventy-five, enough for two items off the dollar menu.

I ordered through the drive through and then pulled over and ate my sandwich in the parking lot. Afterwards, I decided to head back to my apartment and put in a couple of hours of work. I'd have to be more careful about my work, or I'd be doomed to eating off the dollar menu for the rest of the month. When I finally pulled into the alley, I was surprised to find it blocked by two police cars.

Chapter 16

"What's going on here?" I asked, finding my parents by the garage, talking to a uniformed officer.

They turned to me, their faces showing relief. My mother hugged me. "Thank goodness you're okay," she said.

"Yes, we thought maybe you had been abducted," my dad added.

"Abducted?"

My mother still had her arms wrapped around me. "Where have you been? We were trying to call you."

"I didn't get any calls," I said, flipping my phone open. Oops, it was dead. "What's going on?"

The officer, who had been silent up to now, jumped in. "It seems that someone has ransacked your residence."

"My apartment?"

"That's right," Mom interjected. "I came up to get the dress. The wedding is only a few days away, remember? I figured you probably haven't had time to get it pressed. I was going to take care of it for you."

She was right. I hadn't thought to press it. In fact, the last time I saw that dress was when I inadvertently wore it to the hospital to visit Shep. I wasn't quite sure what I had done with it after that; but, there was a good chance that I hadn't bothered to hang it up neatly.

"And," she continued. "When I opened your door, I saw someone had torn the place up. I called the police immediately."

I shook my head. "Uh, oh." I smiled apologetically at the officer. "This is all a misunderstanding. Really. You see, I've had this incredibly hectic week and I haven't had much time to keep things picked up." I indicated toward my mother. "Naturally, she would think it looked like someone had ransacked the place. My mom is really a neat freak and—"

"Pippi, come up here." I looked up to see Sean at the top of my stairs.

I scurried up the steps and stopped short inside my doorway. I stood, unable to process what was before me.

Sean placed a hand on my shoulder. "I'm sorry, Pippi."

My entire apartment was destroyed: Clothing bins were emptied; paperwork torn and scattered, my computer and television smashed, DVD's out of their cases and broken. In the kitchen, every item was opened and dumped out. Flour dusted almost every surface. My walls looked like some deranged contemporary artist had created one of those dark, disturbing modern renditions with ketchup, mustard, and chocolate syrup. To top it all off, a couple of two liters of soda were emptied onto my countertops.

I wanted to scream or cry ... or something, but all I could do was stand and stare. Who would have done this?

"Any idea who would have done this?" Sean asked, mirroring my own thoughts.

I knew it had to be one of the Farrells. They must have been so ticked off after lunch that they came over to my place and trashed it. They worked fast, that's for sure.

I was considering how much to tell Sean. "I may have made one of the Farrells mad."

"Angry enough to trash your place?" he asked.

"Oh, yeah. Definitely."

"Tell me about it," he said, motioning for me to sit down on my couch, which had been repeatedly slashed. Stuffing popped out of every torn crevice. It was starting to dawn on me just how much time and money it was going to take to get this cleaned up. It made me so angry that I decided to spill everything I knew, including the bit about working at the garage sale to get closer to the Farrells. He could laugh at my theories if he wanted, but I needed someone to know all the details in case the lunatic that destroyed my house decided to come after me personally.

"As you know, I've been checking on a few things for Shep," I started. He leaned back and was regarding me with a perturbed look. "Anyway, I already told you I was convinced that James Farrell was somehow involved, or at least one of his family members. Well, part of my cover is this garage sale for St. Joan's Parish."

"Cover?"

"Yes, I'm on the sorting and marking committee with Morgan Farrell. She's married to James Junior, but we call him J.J. So, oh … I need to back up a bit. I think the books that were sold in the Sokolov estate are the reason Jane Reynolds and Pauline were murdered, but I guess I already told you that. What I didn't tell you was Owen, he works for Shep, was on shift with Pauline the day she was killed and he saw Pauline find something in one of the books. An envelope. Although, Pauline's boyfriend, Tanner, thought Pauline had said it contained a legal document of some sort, or at least something really important. She may have tried to locate the owner of the envelope from the names on the document. I'm not sure. But, I *am* sure Tanner didn't have anything to do with Pauline's murder. He really loved her, I can tell. Anyway, I followed Morgan to the Huntley last night and I think she met Alex Sokolov, that's Calina's illegitimate son fathered by James Farrell. Remember when I told you they had been having an affair for over twenty years? At any rate, when I was at the Huntley, I caught a glimpse into Alex's room and saw a pair of legs and I believe they belonged to Morgan. Then, today at the parish hall, I mentioned it to her and she became really angry."

"Hold on," Sean said, raising a hand and shaking his head. "So you think Morgan Farrell did this? Why didn't you tell me about this envelope before?"

"I wasn't sure it was important." Or, really, that he'd take it seriously. "But as far as Morgan being the killer … well maybe

... but it could have been any of the Farrells. You see, today at lunch, they all became angry when I mentioned Alex Sokolov's name. Except Morgan. She wasn't there. But, JimDog became especially angry. Maybe angry enough to come over and do this. Then, I told J.J. that he may have an illegitimate brother, which inspired him to throw a fork."

"At you?"

"No. Just at the table. Quite frankly, I think the whole family is messed up. Although, now that I'm thinking about it, it probably wasn't J.J. because he wouldn't have had enough time. Patricia and James left the table early though, right as I was choking to death, but I'm fine now. However, after leaving the Farrell's I was still hungry, so I stopped by and picked up a little something before heading back here. So, in theory, either one of them, maybe even J.J., would've had time to drive over here and trash the place."

Sean didn't comment. He simply sat staring at me with a strange look on his face. All around us, police technicians gathered evidence and dusted for prints.

My parents came in. My dad had a cell phone in his hand. "I just called insurance. I think that our homeowners will cover most of this. They're sending an estimator over this afternoon." He patted my shoulder. "Don't worry, honey, we'll get this taken care of."

"Oh my goodness," my mother commented. "Here's the dress! Look, it's not damaged at all!" She smiled broadly and held up the dress for all to see. Sure enough, it was completely undamaged. Just my luck.

Sean spoke up. "Mr. and Mrs. O'Brien, I need to take your daughter to my office to make a statement. I'll bring her back here in a few hours. The techs should be done by then, so we can start putting everything back in order."

I noticed he said 'we'. I guess that meant he was going to help with the cleaning. Mom and Dad must have heard the same thing. They shook his hand gratefully. "We'll order pizza.

I'm sure we can trust that you'll make it your priority to find out who did this," my Dad added.

"Absolutely," Sean replied.

"Do you think the techs will turn up something?" I asked, a few minutes later when we were in his car.

"I doubt it. Even if we did get prints, they would have to be in the system for us to make a match. Plus, the officers checked around your neighborhood and no one saw anything unusual. It doesn't help that the garage and the entrance to your apartment are so secluded. Have your parents ever considered cutting down that privet hedge or a few of the trees in their backyard?"

I shrugged. Up until now, I'd always liked the fact that my parents couldn't see what I was up to in my apartment.

He continued, "To think I thought you'd be too busy with the St. Joan's sale to get into trouble."

I didn't comment.

"I guess I should have known better. It seems you've been getting quite involved with the Farrells. Do you have any specific evidence connecting them to either of these murders? That is, besides the leg you saw or the fact that James Farrell has a Russian book in his den?"

I squinted at him. For some reason I didn't like his tone. What was with his condescending attitude? "No, but I will eventually. Why, do you have any leads on the investigation? Any other suspects? Any evidence?" I threw it right back at him.

He closed his mouth and refocused on the road, causing me to think he hadn't found any new leads either.

A couple of minutes later we pulled into his parking space. We didn't really talk again until we were positioned at an oblong wooden table in a very non-descript room. Another officer, a pretty young female cop, joined us. She'd brought a recorder and a laptop and introduced herself as Officer Garcia.

For the next hour and half, I answered all of Sean's questions while Officer Garcia typed notes on her computer.

As it turned out, the interview had less to do with my apartment break-in as it did with my current investigation. Sean questioned me about every possible detail concerning Pauline's death, including the lunch I had with the Farrells. This led me to believe that he must have thought I was onto something. Although, it was hard to tell. Sean wasn't always the most open person.

By six-thirty, we were heading back to my apartment. The mood between us had lightened and it almost seemed like the 'old' days when we used to spend our evenings hanging out together.

When we reached the apartment, I was surprised to find a whole crew working on cleaning up the place. Mom had rallied the troops. Mary Frances was there, along with two of my other sisters, Anne and Kathleen, who both lived about a half hour away. I was touched they'd dropped everything and driven over to help. They even brought a couple bags of groceries to restock my fridge. I had a great family.

Once some order was restored, I started accessing the damage. It would take a few days to get my inventory reorganized and ready to sell, but luckily, the few items I was preparing to ship were untouched.

The worse thing was my computer. Without it, I couldn't run my business. Hopefully I could find a replacement and restore my files from the damaged machine. This was going to set me back a couple of weeks. However, what really got me was the fact that my space had been violated. It would be a while before I'd feel completely safe again. My parents must have been thinking along the same lines. When the job was done and everyone dispersed, my Dad pulled me aside. "Your mother and I think it would be best if you moved back into the house for a while. We're not sure who did this and what their intent is. What if you would have been here when they ransacked the place? They might have hurt you."

I struggled for an answer. On one hand, I didn't want to remain in my apartment alone, but giving up my privacy and moving back in with my parents seemed like a little much. I was stammering for a reply when Sean intervened. "I've already made arrangements for an officer to be posted in the back alley at night. During the day, I'll have someone drive by periodically to check on things."

That seemed to satisfy my parents. They were relieved to know someone would be watching out for me. I silently wondered how Sean's department was going to justify the extra man-power it would take to embark on a twenty-four hour watch of my place.

*

The next morning, I got my answer. I skipped down my steps bright and early to find Sean asleep in his car. I tapped on his window.

"What are you doing?" I asked.

"Uh oh, what time is it?" he questioned, sitting up and rubbing his face. I glanced passed him into the car. A thermos and several crumpled Styrofoam cups littered the passenger side.

"You slept out here all night?"

"Obviously. I have to get going though. I've got to be in by roll call at 9:00," he said, starting the car and putting it into gear. He didn't offer any more explanation before pulling out of my alley.

I stared after him. Maybe he really did love me. I wanted to believe his actions demonstrated his feelings for me. Although, with Sean, I could never be sure. Quite honestly, I didn't have time to worry about all that now. I had way too much to do.

As we suspected, Morgan was a no-show at the parish hall. However, even without her help, Mary Frances and I made quick work of sorting and marking. The morning passed quickly. After leaving the church, I decided to run a few personal errands, the first being shopping for a new computer. And, what better place to start my search than the Mega Electronic Mart in Skokie, which, as I had learned at lunch yesterday, just happened to be the site of the new JimDog restaurant.

For the next hour and fifteen minutes I maneuvered my way slowly northeast. Traffic was stop and go for the first half-hour. According to the traffic report, a delivery truck plowed into the I-294 toll plaza. Guess the guy didn't want to pay his toll. I could relate to that.

I wasn't all that familiar with Skokie, so it took a while for me to find the Mega Electronic Mart. As it turned out, it was the anchor store in a sprawling strip mall surrounded by other popular stores like Pet-O-Rama and Books Unlimited. In the front part of the lot, facing south, stood the new JimDogs restaurant, its bright yellow and brown exterior standing as a beacon of fast food bliss.

I parked across the lot and watched for a while. A small line was formed outside the front door where an orange 'now hiring' sign flapped in the breeze. I could see what was probably J.J's vehicle parked at the side of the building.

As I watched the line dwindle down, I formulated a plan of action. All I needed was one great disguise. Then, once I was on their inside track, it would be easy to see what the Ferrells were really up to. What could be a better cover than that of a hot dog turning, bun-stuffing, JimDog employee? I needed to act fast, though. According to the sign, interviews were only being held until four o'clock.

Twenty minutes later, I was in the restroom at Value Mart, transforming myself into a future JimDog employee. A quick pass through the aisles and a whopping eighty-four dollar charge to my Visa had netted me the perfect disguise. Luckily, Halloween was just a couple of weeks away, so it was no problem finding a wig to cover my red curls. Of course, since I didn't think JimDogs would be hiring a Mistress of the Dark, I had to tweak the wig a bit; but a few twists and several well placed hair pins had me looking more like a dark haired version of Aunt Bee than a sexy vampiress. I topped off the disguise with an extra coat of dark foundation to hide my freckles and a pair of black rimmed reading glasses perched low on my nose. By chance, I found a great black knit wrap dress on clearance. I paired it with some low black flats I'd scored for a mere fifteen bucks.

I nodded at my reflection in the mirror. Gone was any trace of my wild red hair and freckles. Before me stood the newly transformed, efficient-looking, fast food diva extraordinaire. Perfect.

I parked on the other side of the lot and hoofed it to JimDogs just in case J.J. might recognize my vehicle. By the time I reached the door, the line had dwindled down to only a few people.

I waited my turn patiently while eavesdropping on a bouncy teen girl who said her name was Ashley. She claimed she'd make a great employee due to her three years of babysitting experience for Mr. and Mrs. Fitzpatrick's two rowdy boys, but would absolutely need Mondays, Wednesdays, and most weekends off because of her prior commitment to the Wolves cheerleading squad; and, by the way, could only work as a cashier because kitchen grease makes her skin break out.

Geez, today's youth had no work ethic. I scoffed and tuned her out. Scanning the place, I searched for signs of JimDog Junior. He was nowhere to be seen.

The restaurant looked ready to go, except for the restrooms and kitchen, which were still receiving a few final touches. Frequently, men filed past me carrying buckets, trowels, and heavy boxes of floor tiles. In the back, a makeshift table with several tools and what looked to be a large saw was set up.

I continued to wait patiently in line, trying to ignore the small Hispanic man in front of me who kept turning around and smiling. He was saying something in Spanish, but I had no idea what. Maybe with the wig and extra dark makeup, I reminded him of someone he knew. Whatever the case, he was driving me nuts. All I wanted to do was get the gig, so I could get in close with J.J. and see what he was up to. Plus, the way I had been neglecting my business, it wouldn't hurt to make a few extra bucks.

"Mr. Ortiz," the woman conducting the interview called out. The Hispanic man turned and gave me one more grin before making his way toward the back booth. I caught a whiff of flowery cologne as Ashley sashayed by me with a smug look. She apparently felt confident that she had landed a job.

I briefly wondered how the woman conducting the interview had known Mr. Ortiz's name. Hopefully there wasn't some sort of sign-up sheet I'd missed.

I was about to ask, when J.J. burst out of the kitchen area. "She can't do this now!" he yelled into his cell. "Where is she?"

I pulled out my own cell and pretended to be engrossed in texting someone all the while keeping a sharp ear on J.J.

"Find her and tell her to get herself home. I don't need this now. I've got enough stress without having to worry about her crap."

He paused and listened. What he heard made him angrier. He snapped his cell shut and stomped out the door. I could see him heading for his car. I was about to head out to follow him when I heard a voice behind me.

"Are you the woman I spoke to earlier on the phone?" It was the interview lady.

I opened my mouth to reply, but she didn't give me a chance. Shaking my hand firmly, she continued, "I've been waiting for you. I'm Devon Ashcroft. I lost the paper I wrote your name on and couldn't contact you, so I'm so glad you stopped by. I was afraid I wouldn't get this position filled in time." I didn't know what to say, so I simply nodded in agreement.

She smiled. "Well, I have your paperwork and itinerary ready for you," she said, handing me a large vanilla envelope. "All you have to do is show up at ten and be ready to work. Fill out and bring the paperwork back with you, okay?"

I started to correct her, but she continued talking as she gently guided me toward the door. "Mr. Farrell was just called out on a family emergency, or I would have introduced you to him. You'll be working next to him all day on Saturday," she added.

Oh, that sounded good. Just the opportunity I was looking for. "Uh, what time did you say I'd be finishing?" I asked. Cherry's wedding was on Saturday, and there's no way I could miss it. My mother would kill me.

"Oh, you'll easily be out of here by four."

I smiled, clenched my envelope, and gave her a final wave as I left.

That was the easiest interview I had ever had. Although, I did feel slightly irritated that I didn't get a chance to follow J.J. His phone conversation was intriguing. From what I heard, I assumed Morgan was giving him trouble.

I continued to ponder the Farrell family dynamics as I shopped around for a new computer. I finally settled on a mid-range machine, but splurged on a larger, flat screened monitor. Why not? I just hoped my insurance money came through soon. My Visa couldn't take much more action.

Chapter 17

On the way home, I grabbed a large pizza and took a detour by the hospital to see how Shep was doing. I found him sitting up in bed watching a decorating show. To my surprise, he had more color than last time I had seen him.

"Hi, doll. Come on in. Oh my, is that pizza?"

I flipped open the lid. "Yup. Pepperoni and mushroom."

"Oh, my favorite." He scooted over and patted a spot on the bed next to him and pointed at the television. "I usually love this show, but really ... the designer isn't doing this room any justice. Check out that chaise. Gaudy, don't you think?"

I looked at the screen and shrugged. I actually thought it looked pretty good, but I kept my comments to myself. My knowledge of interior design was no match for Shep's skills.

I wiggled under his IV tube and made myself comfortable next to him on the bed. I opened the pizza box across our laps and we dug in.

"My parents just left to go home and get some rest for a couple of days," Shep said as he slowly nibbled on some pizza. "I'm glad, too. Not that I don't like to have them here, but they're driving me crazy. They're constantly fussing."

Making up for lost time, I thought; but I didn't say anything. I could never be as forgiving as Shep. His parents had thrown him out of the house when he was just a teen. What kind of parents did that? Wasn't a parent supposed to love their child unconditionally?

"You're looking better today," I finally said, but inside I was praying that this wasn't the rise before the fall.

"Yeah, well you're looking pretty good yourself. That's not your usual choice of dresses. Is it new?"

I glanced down and chuckled. "Yup. Just bought it today. It really looked good paired with a long black wig."

"A disguise? What were you up to?"

I relayed the day's events and updated him on the Farrells. "I'm moving away from JimDog senior and focusing on J.J. and his wife Morgan for a while. I'm about a hundred percent sure that she's having an affair with Alex Sokolov," I said, telling him about the leg. "Today at the restaurant, I overheard J.J. talking on the phone to someone. He was distraught. I'm thinking Morgan may have left him. They haven't been getting along at all."

"Could be," Shep agreed. "But what's that have to do with Pauline?"

"I'm not sure yet. I was just thinking the envelope Pauline found might have had something in it that Alex needs. Maybe something that assures he'll inherit part of the Farrell fortune." I shrugged. "I don't know. It could be he and Morgan are in it together. There was the lady who paid a thousand dollars at A to Z Estate Sales and the man and woman shopping at the Retro when Pauline found the envelope. Maybe it was them."

Shep didn't look so sure.

I went on, trying to convince him. "It has to be something with the envelope, Shep. Pauline found it in an old book. Owen said he'd shelved books from the Sokolov estate and that there was a lady in the Retro Metro looking at them. Then there were the books in the garbage at The Classy Closet, plus the book I saw in JimDog's den. It was written in Russian, too. So, someone was searching for the book with the envelope."

Shep was strangely quiet.

"I know it seems like I'm spinning my wheels, but something is sure to break soon. I know, Shep, that it involves the Farrells. I need to stay close to the family until I discover something."

He sighed, a shallow labored sigh. "Sure, doll. You'll get it. It makes me sad to think Pauline was killed over something she found inside a book. What a waste. Tanner didn't have any better idea as to what she had found?"

"No, just that it was some sort of legal looking document. Pauline was going to show it to him at dinner, but ...."

"But, she never had the chance," Shep finished. His mood was quickly deteriorating, and I was starting to feel guilty about dumping all this in his lap. The last thing he needed was to become depressed. I vowed to have more answers for him next time.

I gave him a hug and quick peck on the cheek. "Hate to eat and run, Shep, but I've got a lot of work to do tonight. I bought a new computer and I need to set it up," I explained, not mentioning that someone broke in and destroyed my old machine. No need to worry him further.

I left, promising to be back in a couple of days.

I returned home to find Mom and Sean in my kitchen. They were sitting at my bar, laughing over a couple of cans of soda. It was times like these that I missed my old brownstone downtown. At least there, I never came home to find uninvited people in my kitchen.

"Hi, Mom. Hey Sean, glad you're here," I lied. I plopped the computer box down on the cabinet and opened the fridge. I bent over and squinted and then scowled at my mother.

"Sorry dear, there were only a couple left. Sean's had a long day at work, you know. He needed something cool to drink."

Unbelievable. They drank my last soda. "That's fine," I mumbled. "Water would be better for me anyway." I grabbed a glass off the counter and filled it from the tap. "What's up, guys?" I asked.

"Well, I stopped over to tell you something and found Sean sitting in the drive. I thought I'd invite him up for a cool drink. He is doing us a favor, after all. And we're so fortunate to have him here after yesterday's break-in, don't you agree, dear?"

"Uh, huh," I said, sipping water and waiting for the other shoe to drop. I knew my mother. There was more to this than simple hospitality.

"I was just telling Sean about your current dilemma," she added, not missing a beat.

Oh, boy. Here it came. "What dilemma?"

"Cherry's wedding."

"Cherry's wedding?" I asked. I was afraid of where this was leading.

"Oh for Pete's sake, Phillipena! You need an escort for your cousins wedding this weekend and did you ever go to the single's meeting at church? No," she answered for me. "Well, I went for you."

"You what?"

"I went for you. Let me tell you, there wasn't a single good prospect there."

Sean chuckled.

"Mom, I'm not a piece of real-estate. You don't need to scope out a buyer for me."

She threw up her hands. "Well, then, what am I supposed to do? Knowing you, I doubt you thought to ask someone and it's imperative that you not go alone. I mean, how would that look? My sister's daughter, who happens to be much younger than you by the way, is marrying a wonderful man this weekend and you're going to embarrass me by showing up unattended. Like my own daughter can't find a suitable man to take her to the wedding. It's bad enough you haven't settled down yet, but at least you can be decent enough to at least act as if you have a perspective—"

I held up my hand. "Oh, please stop, Mom. That's none of your business ... please," I pleaded.

Sean continued watching the whole scene with interest as he sipped away at my soda.

She dismissed my pleas with a wave of her hand which she lovingly placed on Sean's shoulder. "Don't worry, dear. I've taken care of it. Sean is going to take you to the wedding. I might add," she said, patting his arm and smiling at him admirably, "that this young man is so wonderful. Why, your father and I owe him for all that he's done for us lately."

I grimaced. Owed him? Like she needed to pay someone to take care of me?

"You know, why don't you let us repay you for your trouble?" she said rising from her chair and making her way to the door. "I've got to go now. Phillip and I are meeting friends in a few minutes, but I insist that you come over soon for dinner, Sean. I bet a bachelor like you doesn't get many home cooked meals. I'll have Phil cook one of his specialties. Just let Phillipena know when it would work in your schedule," she added, wiggling her fingers and tossing him one last loving smile.

I let out a huge sigh as soon as the door shut. "I'm so sorry, Sean."

He smirked at me over the rim of the can. "Don't be. I didn't have any plans for this Saturday. The wedding might be fun. I like your outfit, by the way."

I looked down at my spur of the moment purchase. A pang of panic hit as I realized with a jolt that, in just a couple of days, he was going to see me in the hideous orange bride's maid dress.

"It's cute, but not really your normal style," he added.

"I needed it for an interview."

He raised a brow. "An interview?"

"Yup. You're looking at a new JimDog employee."

He ran his hand through his hair. "Oh, no. What have you been up to?"

"Well, I got a job at the new JimDogs opening in Skokie. I start Saturday, but don't worry; I'll be done in time for you to take me to the wedding."

"Is this some sort of ploy to get closer to the Farrells?"

"Yes it is," I said, matter-of-factly.

"How are you going to do that? The Farrells already know what you look like."

"I have a disguise."

"Oh, that explains the weird coloring on your face." I wet a dishtowel and began rubbing off the dark makeup. "It's these freckles. They give me away."

He nodded. "What exactly is your new job description?"

"Uh, well, I'm not exactly sure. It's all right here, though." I retrieved the manila envelope from my bag and opened it. "I don't understand," I said glancing over the paperwork.

Sean took the papers from me and read them over. He broke out laughing. "This is a contract for independent work. Apparently you've agreed to four hours of public relations and marketing." He was still laughing.

"Well that doesn't sound so bad," I inserted, not getting the joke.

"As a giant wiener!" He was practically rolling on the ground now. "You're going to be a giant wiener! Didn't you read this before agreeing to do the job? It's all here. There's even an attachment to the contract that says you'll take financial responsibility if the costume is damaged or lost. You didn't read it, did you?" He was clutching his gut and waving the papers in the air, still laughing. I was glad I was providing so much comic relief for him.

"Well, that's a perfect cover if you ask me. There's no way JimDog Junior or any other Farrell will recognize me in a giant hotdog suit. I can follow them around all day and listen to their conversations."

That took a little wind out of his sails. He stopped laughing long enough to give me a stern warning. "Giant hotdog or not, you be careful." Then, he rolled the paperwork and pointed it at me, another grin slowly breaking out on his face. "I would hate for you to get your buns cooked … or leak ketchup everywhere … or worse yet get eaten alive by one of those goons."

I punched him in the arm and joined his laughter. We were having so much fun, I was about to ask him if he wanted to go out for a drink or something, when suddenly the sound of breaking glass and squealing tires interrupted our joviality.

Sean leapt into action, practically pushing me aside on his way to the door. He was down the steps with his gun drawn, before I even made it out of my apartment.

I looked down at my drive where he was standing, already talking on his cell. "Get back inside," he yelled.

I obeyed, pacing back and forth inside my tiny apartment until he came back a couple of minutes later.

"Someone shot out your car windows," he said, positioning himself in front of the window overlooking the alley and drive.

"What!"

"They must have done it while driving by. They got the back and the two driver's side windows. From what I can tell it wasn't done with a heavy firearm. Probably a .22 caliber. I'll know more when my team arrives."

I swallowed hard. "A .22 caliber? Is that big enough to kill someone?"

"Yes," he said, still watching through the window.

I shivered. "My parents must have left before this happened, or they would have been over immediately," I commented.

Sean shook his head in agreement. "Actually, it's possible that whoever did this was watching the house and waited for them to leave."

That gave me a weird feeling. I didn't like the possibility of some weirdo watching my parents.

He backed away from the window. "The guys are here. I'm sure it's safe if you want to come down and check out the damage."

I have to admit, I looked over my shoulder more than a few times as we stood in my back alley surveying the damage to my car. Who had done this and why? I had no doubt someone was sending me a warning to back off the case. That could only mean one thing; I was getting closer to the truth.

I surveyed the damage. This sucked. All this investigating had taken me away from my business so I was almost completely broke. Plus, I hated to turn in another claim to insurance; my rates would hit the roof. I'd just have to make do for a while. I had a nasty vision of cardboard and duct tape. My beloved Volvo was starting to look like a gangster-mobile.

A sudden thought occurred to me. I left Sean to do his work, while I skipped back upstairs to check out the contract again. I wondered how much money a giant wiener got paid. Hopefully enough to replace a few car windows.

Chapter 18

I woke up the next morning tired and cranky.

Two days and counting until Cherry's wedding which was sure to be the worst catastrophe of my life. I could have killed my mother for talking Sean into being my date. One look at me in that pukey orange dress and he'd run right back into Sarah's arms.

I tried to shrug off the thought. I had more pressing matters at hand. For one, I was bone tired. I don't think I'd slept more than a couple of hours. It was a busy night filling out police paperwork, cleaning glass out of my car, hooking up my computer and catching up on my on-line auctions. I didn't even have a single caffeinated soda to chase away the morning fuzz and I was due at the parish hall in ten minutes. Considering that it was at least a half-hour drive, I was off to a bad start.

I carefully glanced out my front window and peered down at my alley. Sean's car was gone, but there was a police cruiser positioned about ten feet from my Volvo. At least I didn't have to worry about getting gunned down on my back step.

My caffeine depleted brain was thumping by the time I walked into the parish hall. The thumping worsened to a howling scream inside my head when I found Patricia Farrell waiting for me. She seemed to be in hysterics. Mary Frances was trying to console her.

I approached them, a little ashamed that the woman was so upset and all I could think about was how I would do just about anything for a little caffeine and fizz.

"There you are," my sister said. "We've been waiting for you."

"Why? What's going on?"

"It's Morgan," Patricia began, her voice cracking. "My daughter-in-law has disappeared. Something terrible has happened, I know it."

Uh, oh. Now I was in a predicament. I knew, more than likely, nothing terrible had happened to Morgan, unless you count having an extra-marital affair as horrible. Which I did, so maybe Patricia's hysterics were justified.

Patricia addressed me directly, "I need your help. I'm willing to pay anything."

Oh, goodness. Suddenly I was wide awake. "What do you think I can do?" I asked tentatively.

"Find Morgan!" she practically screamed.

I paced a few times, trying to figure out how to approach the topic. "I know this may be difficult to think about, but is it possible Morgan has gone off with another man?"

I was trying to break the idea to her gently. I never expected to hear what she said next.

"Another man? Do you think? That would be wonderful!" Her face brightened. Her voice rose with excitement. "If only we could prove it! No judge would ever grant her alimony if she was having an affair."

Mary Frances and I did a double take.

Then, Patricia dropped her smile and choked out a couple more sobs, switching back into devastation mode so quickly it made me think she might have a severe bipolar disorder.

She started to trembled, her blabbering almost impossible to understand. "I'm afraid of what he's done ..." Tears started to spill.

Mary Frances offered some tissues she'd pulled from her pocket. I was confused. Who was 'he'? And was Patricia really hoping Morgan had a lover? What about her poor son?

"My husband," Patricia continued, "is not at all what he seems to be. He can be so controlling," she finished.

No doubt.

She blew her nose and went on. "I think he might have done something to her. I'm really afraid."

"You're afraid your husband did something to her? What about J.J.? He seems to be the one that has the most to be angry about," I said, still thinking about Alex and the leg I saw in his hotel room.

"No, you don't understand. You see, Morgan and J.J. haven't been getting along for some time. They're practically living two separate lives."

"Really? I thought they were building a house together."

"That house. That damn house!" Patricia had moved beyond crying; now she was just angry. "That's all that girl cares about. I told J.J. she wasn't the girl for him. Why, she came from nothing. Nothing! Her father was a plumber, of all things. She just dug her little claws into my son for his money and all she cares about is that stupid house. Like a house is going to make her someone. She'll never be anyone."

Ugh. Patricia was showing her true colors and they weren't pretty. Even Mary Frances stepped back and was regarding her with disdain.

"He even married her without a prenuptial agreement. He was so stupid. His father and I told him this would happen. In fact, J.J. lied to us and told us he had a prenuptial when he never actually had her sign one. He was so in love and thought it would never end. Well, here we are ...." she waved her hands dramatically. "The little snip approached James last week and told him she was going to file for a divorce. She had hired some private investigator to follow J.J. and had proof of an affair. She threatened to sue him for a bundle, unless James settled with her. She wanted him to pay a huge cash settlement, including shares in the company, plus have that darn house built."

Huh, I thought. Morgan wasn't that stupid after all. If she received the money up front she'd be free to live her life however she chose. Whereas, alimony could be revoked if she chose to remarry. Plus, she'd have a great house to live in—all paid for.

"James was furious. I've never seen him so angry before. He couldn't believe that little tripe was trying to work him over."

Of course, I reasoned, James must have thought Morgan should put up with J.J. having a woman on the side. After all, he had done that sort of thing for almost his entire married life and it seemed to work great for him.

"What is it you expect me to do?" I asked. I was losing patience with these people, but if she was willing to pay me to find Morgan ... well ... I could overlook a lot of their nutty antics.

"Well," Patricia regarded me with deer-like eyes. "I don't expect you to want to help me, but I was hoping you could look for Morgan. Your sister says you're good at that type of thing."

I looked up at Mary Frances. She smiled encouragingly.

Patricia looked at me hopefully. "Maybe you could find her before something terrible happens."

"Why not call the police?"

"Because, if James has done something, I don't want them involved."

"What about J.J.? What makes you think that your son isn't involved in her disappearance? I mean, wouldn't he be upset that she wanted a divorce?" I thought I'd throw that out, although after overhearing J.J.'s phone conversation the day before, I doubted he knew anything about Morgan's whereabouts.

Patricia practically snorted. "James Junior? He's not the type. You've met him. He's gentle and kind. Not at all like his father."

Yeah, I had met the guy. Hairless, puny, and foul mouthed, but gentle? Who knew? Maybe he had more of his father in him than Patricia realized.

"Of course," Patricia added. "I'd pay you whatever you want. Just name it. Whatever."

I was a bit taken back by that. I paused, visions of zeros dancing through my head. Hmm ... just how much should I charge?

"I'm just trying to stop something horrible from happening," Patricia interjected. "I'm trying to help Morgan. If you find her, I'll pay for her to disappear. I'll give her enough money to get out of my son's life forever. All you have to do is find her. Please."

I considered the situation for a minute before replying, "I'll look for her. However, if I find out your husband has done something to her, I won't hesitate to tell the cops. It'll cost you a thousand bucks for my time. Plus, I want the money now, upfront." What I was really thinking was that James Farrell had just moved up to the number one spot on my suspect list. If he was capable of hurting someone like Morgan, then he would have no problem killing Jane and Pauline.

"Fine," Patricia agreed, not even blinking at my fee. I should have asked for more.

As long as I had her attention, I decided to pull out the big guns and try to get some of my own information. "Speaking of your husband and his control issues, what did Calina Sokolov have on your husband that he'd kill for?"

Mary Frances gasped. Patricia, however, didn't. In fact, except for a slight narrowing of her eyes, her expression barely changed.

"What are you talking about?" Patricia seemed more indignant over the mention of her husband's deceased lover than the fact that he might have murdered someone.

"Let's not play games here, okay Patricia? Everyone knows Calina Sokolov was your husband's mistress. When she died her estate was sold off in auction. Several antique dealers purchased pieces of her estate and two of them were killed. One of them was a friend of mine. I can't help but think your husband is somehow involved. Especially, now that you've told me how 'controlling' he can be."

Patricia regarded me coldly. "I don't know anything about Ms. Sokolov's estate and I can assure you my husband wouldn't bother killing an antique dealer. If there was something he wanted, he would have paid for it. Price wouldn't be an issue."

"Are you aware that James fathered a child with Calina? A son. Alex Sokolov."

"I don't know anything about that."

She was lying, I could tell. "Sure you do. He's twenty some years old. Are you really going to tell me you didn't know about him?"

"That's enough, Pippi," Mary Frances said, moving between Patricia and me. I was a little surprised that my sister felt protective over this cold, heartless woman, but whatever. I wasn't going to get anything out of Patricia Farrell anyway. I'd have to prove James' guilt on my own.

"Where's Morgan's family?" I asked, getting back to the task at hand.

Patricia snorted again. "Her family? Her mother died a couple of years back. Auto accident, I think. Her father has been in and out of rehab ever since. He's a drunk. Last I heard he was spending six weeks at The Knolls, trying to dry up."

"The Knolls? That's expensive, isn't it?"

"Yeah, well, Morgan spends my son's hard earned money on more than just designer outfits and expensive handbags."

"I see. Where else would she go for help? Any other family? Friends?"

"She didn't have any other family that I know of and I really didn't bother to get to know her friends."

I'm sure she didn't. I wasn't going to have much to go on.

Patricia handed me a piece of paper. "Here's her cell number. I thought maybe you could put a tracer on it or something."

Who did she think I was? Some sort of CIA operative?

Patricia scribbled out a check and took out another piece of paper from her purse. "Here's your check and I'm jotting down my numbers. Call me as soon as you know something.

Anything." With that said, she tossed down her used up tissues and left.

After she'd gone, Mary Frances turned to me. "I pray that Morgan is alright. That poor girl. How would you like to be married into that horrible family? All these years and I never realized just how sick they are."

"Well, don't feel bad, Sis. I think they've got a lot of people fooled."

"Do you think you'll be able to find her?" she asked.

"I have no idea. I don't have a lot to go on. She could be anywhere."

My sister nodded. She looked around the room. No doubt she felt as overwhelmed as I. "Listen," she said. "You have better things to do than hang around here. I'll call some of the sisters to come over and help. Between all of us, we'll be able to easily finish and be ready for the sale on Saturday."

I did a mental slap. I had overbooked my Saturday—garage sale, Weenie-gig, and Cherry's wedding. Ugh! "About Saturday," I began, "I probably won't be able to stay and help for long. I sort of have another job I promised I'd do."

"No problem. There'll be plenty of people here. I'll meet you at the wedding. You get out of here now and look for Morgan. I'll be praying for you."

At the time, I had no idea how much I was going to need those prayers.

Chapter 19

I'd barely made it to my car when my cell rang. It was Cherry.

"Phillipena. I've been trying to reach you."

"You have?"

"I wanted to remind you to be at the pumpkin patch by 5:30 tomorrow night."

"The pumpkin patch?"

"Yes, for the rehearsal, silly."

"You're getting married at a pumpkin patch?"

"Where have you been? Yes, we're getting married at Stumpy's Pumpkin Patch. You knew that!"

"I did?"

"It's a fall wedding. Where else would we get married?"

Where else indeed? Oh, no. I was going to blend in with all those giant pumpkins. What would Sean think?

"Just be there at 5:30 sharp. No excuses. We're going to have chili and sandwiches afterwards. Bring a sweater, it's supposed to be a little cool," she added before hanging up.

I sat in my car, trying to block the wedding from my mind and concentrate on my own situation. While I truly hoped nothing bad had happened to Morgan, she wasn't my main priority. My real focus was still on finding Pauline's murderer. Besides, Morgan was probably hiding somewhere with Alex.

Alex. Alex was the one person that might be able to clear up a few of my questions. Maybe he had an idea to what type of document his mother would keep inside an old book. I just knew the envelope Pauline found was the key to all this.

I patted the check in my pocket. Easy money. I already had an idea of where I could find Morgan.

*

I was headed for Calina Sokolov's house. My best guess was that if something terrible hadn't already happened, Morgan was hiding out there with Alex. I needed to warn her. I also needed to find out what Alex knew about the envelope.

Under any other circumstances, I would have enjoyed the walk through the Ukrainian Village. The air was crisp and the colorful foliage stood out against the cloudless blue sky, but as it was, all I could think about was how complicated my life had become. My best friend was sick, my finances were a wreck, my car and my love life ... they were all a mess. Not to mention the impending pumpkin disaster. The only consolation, I rationalized, was that my life wasn't as messed up as Morgan Farrell's. She was married to a two-timing, bald, son of a psychotic murderer. That is, if she was still alive.

In the week since I had been there, not much had changed on the outside of Calina Sokolov's house, although now it had a feeling of emptiness. It was as if her spirit had finally faded from the confines of the walls. As I approached the front door, I found myself wondering about the person who spent so many years living in this home as a kept woman. Was she happy with her circumstances or did she always hold onto the dream that James would marry her? How tragic that she died alone without her lover or son by her side.

I knocked several times but received no response. Stepping down off the porch, I made my way around the side of the house and pried open the back gate. A quick peek told me there was no one in the back yard. I made my way around the other side of the house and crawled through some bushes and stretched onto my tippy toes to look through the side window.

Suddenly I heard a cracking sound from behind. I turned and found myself staring down the barrel of a shot gun. On the other end was a not-too-steady Mrs. Stansilov, Stanislav, or whatever, dressed in an overly bright flowered house coat with her wiry gray hair whooshed back from her face. She looked a little like a half-crazed, cross-dressing version of Albert Einstein. I shuddered with fear.

"Go ahead, make my day," she said, her large knuckled, arthritic finger dangerously close to the trigger.

Oh great. She was a Clint Eastwood fan. I was doomed. Why couldn't she have just stuck to the daytime game shows?

"Hello, Mrs. Stanislav. Do you remember me? We visited the other day," I said softly, trying to ease the situation.

"Yeah, I remember you. You're that stupid insurance investigator that accused Calina of being a Russian mobster."

Suddenly it occurred to me that maybe I wasn't so wrong about that theory. I mean, maybe the whole block was some sort of mob compound. Grandma Stanislav here was probably the enforcer.

I stammered for a response. "Uh, well I was mistaken about that. Further investigations have proven my initial theory was all wrong. In fact, I'm here today to follow up on a lead we've received concerning Ms. Sokolov's son, Alex. I'd like to tell you about it, but you'd have to put the gun down."

She transferred the shotgun to one hand and reached down to her crotch with her other hand yanking fervently at her panty hose. A few hose rings disappeared from around her ankles. "What about that no-good son of hers?" she asked, still holding the bobbing barrel at my chest level.

"You were right about him being rotten. It seems he may be involved in kidnapping a woman," I said, making it up as I was talking. I had no idea what to say to this woman to make her put down the gun.

"A woman, you say?"

"Yes. Have you seen a woman here, Mrs. Stanislav?"

"Maybe I have." The old woman was starting to shake again. Her gripped tightened on the gun as she narrowed her eyes on me. "Maybe she didn't look like no kidnapped girl, though. Maybe they seemed to know each other. So, maybe you're just full of crap."

I watched in horror as her finger moved to the trigger. Then, as if she was a seventh grader with ADD, she let go and started working on her hose. The barrel started bobbing again. I cringed. Then, there was a sudden flash of light and a thunderous boom. I ducked as glass behind me shattered. Looking up, I saw that the recoil of the gun had knocked Mrs. Stanislav to the ground in a rumpled heap of housecoat and pantyhose.

I knew an opportunity when I saw one. I took off as fast as I could. I was past Hoyne Avenue when I started hearing the sirens. I slowed down to a normal walking pace and tried to act casual. No need to spend hours at the local precinct answering questions. Good thing that old bat didn't know my real name. The cops could spend days looking for Prudence Overton.

Although, however deranged Mrs. Stanislav was, she had confirmed something I needed to know. She said that the woman at Alex's house looked like she wanted to be there. That could only mean one thing. I was right about Morgan. There was also a good chance she was alive and off somewhere with Alex, or perhaps simply hiding from her murderous father-in-law.

I headed back to Naperville, feeling a little shaky and drained. It occurred to me that with all the adrenaline surges I had probably burned off at least a thousand calories. I could afford to replenish a few at the local drive-thru.

Since it would be impossible to order through windows covered in plastic and duct tape, I had to go inside. I decided to park my conspicuous looking vehicle in the back of the lot by the fenced-in dumpsters.

I chose a sunny, corner booth in which to sit and enjoy my fully loaded burger, large fry, and icy cold soda. I was just about finished when Mary Frances called.

"Hey, any luck finding Morgan?" she asked.

"Are you kidding? It's only been a few hours since we talked to Patricia. Morgan could be anywhere."

"Well, what have you been doing?"

What have I been doing? I chomped down hard on a fry and debated my reply. It's not like I could actually tell her I'd been accosted and shot at by a gun-toting-granny with sagging hose. "Just checking out a few leads," I finally replied, keeping it simple.

"Leads?"

"Well, I went to Calina Sokolov's house, thinking I could find Alex and question him."

"Did he know anything about Morgan?"

"Well, actually he wasn't there. I talked to the neighbor though and she said she'd seen him with a woman. She said they seemed romantic," I said, trying to recall just what it was that Mrs. Stanislav had said. It was hard to remember anything but the double barrels pointed at my chest.

"That's good, isn't it? That means Morgan is with Alex and not dead. Oh this is great news! Did you tell Patricia yet?"

"No."

"Well, call her right away. She seemed crazy with worry this morning. I tell you, Pippi, I'm so glad to hear that Morgan is alright. Say what you want about how weird that family is, but Morgan … well, she doesn't deserve to be hurt. She's young and confused. She'd be better off getting away from that family, don't you think?"

I thought back to my encounters with JimDog and the rest of the Ferrells. "Definitely," I agreed.

I hung up with Mary Frances and placed a quick call to Patricia. She answered on the first ring.

"Did you find Morgan?" she said, bypassing any sort of greeting.

"No, but I did find out that she's okay. She's with Alex Sokolov."

There was a slight pause on the other end. "How do you know that?" Patricia finally asked.

"I went by his mother's house and one of the neighbors told me."

"She said she had seen Morgan with Alex?"

"Well, she said that she had seen him a lot lately with a woman. In fact, she mentioned that she had just seen them together yesterday."

"Yesterday?"

"Yeah. So I'm assuming Morgan and Alex are off somewhere, maybe hiding while your husband cools his jets."

"I see. Well, that's good news. Please call me if she contacts you."

"Sure. Um, speaking of your hot-tempered husband, I'm pretty sure he's not going to be too happy about the fact that you hired me to look into Morgan's disappearance."

"Don't worry. I can handle James. You just make sure to call me if you hear anything else about Morgan."

I hung up, pitched my wrappers, and refilled my soda. I headed for my car feeling much better. Surprising what a little caffeine could do to boost my mood. Or at least that's what I was thinking until I saw my car. I dropped my soda and clasped my hands over my mouth stifling a scream.

I was shaking so badly it took three tries before I successfully punched in Sean's number. In less than five minutes a cop car rolled into the lot. Officer Wagoner was driving. She and the other cop, a young Hispanic man, joined me. We stood looking at the mess before us.

"Is it blood?" I asked, staring at hateful message on the side of my car, *Die Bitch!*

"Have you touched anything?" Officer Wagoner asked.

I shook my head. I couldn't peel my eyes away from the words. For some reason the dripping red letters reminded me of that spooky little kid doing the finger thing and repeating redrum, redrum, in his scratchy little voice. I shuddered.

"Why don't you step back inside, Miss," the Hispanic officer suggested.

Wagoner placed her arm around me and started guiding me back across the lot. "Yeah, let's go sit down and wait for Panelli. He's on his way. He wants to be the one to question you."

I went in and settled back into the corner booth. Ten minutes later Sean walked in.

"It's not blood," he said, sliding across from me. "Just red paint, but you'll need a new paint job. And, one of your tires was slashed."

"It was?" Guess I hadn't noticed much beyond the diabolic message. The thousand that Patricia had signed over wasn't going to go far enough to replace the windows and get a paint job. I resolved to make an insurance claim and suffer higher premiums.

"We've checked with all the employees," he continued. "No one saw it happen. What made you park in such a secluded spot?"

"I was embarrassed by my windows," I muttered, thinking that the windows were nothing compared to having 'Die Bitch' written on my car in hideous red paint. What was my mother going to think?

"I see. Do you think it was one of the Farrells?"

"I don't know. Maybe." I shrugged. "There's been a lot going on. Morgan has disappeared and Patricia is paying me to find her."

Sean sat up straighter. "What? I don't think a report's been filed."

"No, Patricia wanted to keep it quiet until she knew what was going on. Actually, she paid me to investigate because she was afraid James had done something horrible to Morgan. It sounds like the guy is pretty unstable."

"So you think maybe he did this to your car?"

"Could be. I just don't know. Anyway, Patricia claims Morgan was extorting them."

"Extorting them?"

"Yup. For a new house. You see, Morgan is married to their son, J.J, I think I've already told you about him, but anyway, J.J. is cheating on her and she has proof. So, she told James that if he would pay for a new house and give her a boat-load of cash, she wouldn't press for alimony, which I'm thinking, may include a share in the family business. Who knows? I guess James thought J.J. had a prenuptial signed before marrying Morgan, but he didn't. So, now she's in the driver's seat, so to say. Patricia said James was so irate he could have possibly done something to Morgan, so that's why she's hired me. Actually though, I think Morgan is just off with Alex."

Sean's eyeballs were practically rolling with information overload. We sat in silence for a second, while he processed it all. "So, why don't you start over at the beginning and tell me everything that has been going on."

I did and the whole story took over a half hour. By that time, the other officers were finished photographing my car and writing out their report. I signed a few papers and was told I was free to go.

Sean stood with me in the lot as the other officers left. I had called a tow company. "Can you give me a ride to the rental place?" I asked.

"I'll be working late tonight, but I'll be by your place around nine. Will you be there to let me in?" he asked, once we were on our way.

"Let you in?"

"Yeah, I'll be sleeping inside tonight, not out in the drive."

I quivered with excitement. "Inside? There's not much room. Do you want my bed?" *Or do you want me?* I could only hope.

"I'll bring a sleeping bag," he said, rubbing his back. "I can't take one more night in the car."

"Fine," I replied, nodding nonchalantly. I was going to have to play it cool with Sean. If he wanted to rekindle things, it would have to be on my terms this time. No more pseudo-commitments, no more teasing, no more messing around. If he could commit to Sarah Maloney, he could commit to me. I was in it for a ring this time.

Chapter 20

A few hours later, I parked a sub-compact outside my apartment. Thirty-seven dollars a day sure didn't rent much of a car.

I had stopped off and purchased some more things for the fridge and new cleaning supplies. No need for Sean to be grossed out about the hairy blobs living behind my toilet. For the rest of the evening I cleaned, scoured, and scrubbed. By the time I was done, the place was looking pretty nice, despite my slashed-up sofa which kept leaking little puffs of stuffing every time I sat on it.

Sean arrived just as I was putting the final touches on my apartment. I answered the door, noticing first thing, that he was indeed toting a sleeping bag.

"Hi dear, I'm home," he said, grinning.

I laughed. A part of me wishing I could will away the past year and all the things that had come between us. I'd missed him more than I wanted to admit.

I pulled out some wine and a couple of glasses and we sat on the couch where we spent the next couple of hours talking, laughing ... and, unfortunately, not much else. Then around midnight, I pulled out my sofa bed. There was a bit of awkwardness as Sean moved to retrieve his sleeping bag.

He stood with it in hand, looking around the place. With my sofa pulled out, the only open space in my tiny apartment was either in the bathtub, right in front of the door, or in the sofa bed next to me. He chose the spot by the door.

*

The next morning, I awoke to a weird thumping and giggling sound.

I sat straight up. The thumping, as it turned out, was the door banging up against Sean, who was rolled up tightly inside his sleeping bag. The giggling was coming from my precocious seven-year-old niece, Claire.

"Aunt Pippi," she yelled out, forcing her way through the tiny crack in the doorway. She stopped short upon seeing Sean. "Oh, I didn't know you were having a slumber party!"

I rubbed my eyes and tried to focus on the situation. "Where'd you come from?" I asked, not sounding quite like the super aunt I really was.

"We're all here. Mom, Dad, and Sam. Everyone else is coming today, too. You know, for Cousin Cherry's wedding. Didn't you know that I get to be one of the flower girls? My dress is beautiful!"

Well, at least that makes one of us, I thought.

"Papa told me to come up and get you for breakfast. He's making cinnamon rolls, but I'll go tell him that you're busy with your slumber party."

"No!" I yelled, but she was out the door before I could stop her. "Oh, no," I said, scrambling out of bed and searching for my sweatpants.

Sean was hobbling around the room, one foot still in the bag, gathering up his clothing. "I've gotta run. I'm going to be late for work."

"Oh, thanks. Just leave me with the fallout, why don't you?"

"Hey, sorry, but I've already been late twice this week," he said, making his way toward the door. "I'll be back tonight. Stay clear of James Farrell, stay in public at all times, and call me if anything happens."

I followed him out, making my way around the hedge and through the back door of my parent's house. As usual, everyone was gathered in the kitchen where my dad was pulling out a pan of cinnamon rolls. I grabbed a plate and bellied up to the counter.

My sister, Maggie breezed in, dragging her youngest, Sam, who had mud-caked hands. "Hey, Pippi." She gave me an air-hug while maintaining her hold on Sam's hands. "Wash your hands in the sink," she ordered. "Sorry, Dad. He got a hold of the hose and has been making mud pies in your planters out back. He's probably drowned at least three of your geraniums."

"Ah, don't worry about it. They're at the end of their season anyway," my dad winked at Sam. Dad, always the essence of patience, was great with kids. He had, after all, survived raising five girls. Not that Mom didn't help, but she was the bread winner. Dad, with his position at the library, had the most flexible hours. He was the one at home with us after school, the one to drive on our fieldtrips and volunteer at school, and the one who managed the household on a daily basis.

I finished off my first roll and reached for another. My mother raised her brows over the rim of her coffee mug. She, of course, would never indulge in a cinnamon roll, or two. Ever the professional, she didn't want to jeopardize the fit of her designer suits. "Claire was telling me that you had a slumber party last night," she said.

Maggie giggled. "Where's your father?" she asked her son.

"In the front yard with Claire. They're drawing on the sidewalk."

She handed him a roll. "Here take this and go outside and join them. No more playing with the hose," she scolded. I checked my sister out. She was looking great, as usual. I'd heard through the family grape-vine that she and her hubby, Chris, were going to marriage counseling. It must be working. She looked happier than I'd seen her in years. She grabbed a cup of coffee, skipping a roll I noticed, and sat down next to me at the breakfast bar. "A slumber party, huh? Why wasn't I invited?" she teased.

"It was just Sean and, for your information, he was sleeping on the floor."

"Oh, I'm sorry," she replied facetiously.

"Hey!" My Dad cut in, shooting us a dirty look.

My mother passed me a cup of coffee and moved the pan of rolls out of my reach. "Has he found out who broke into your place?"

"No, he's still working on it."

"Well, at least he's keeping you safe. It takes a big load off our minds to know he's watching out for you," she said.

As if on cue, my brother-in-law came in with the kids. Chris was looking pretty relaxed in a faded jeans and a t-shirt. "Keeping her safe from what? What have I missed?" he asked, as Maggie placed a steaming cup of coffee on the counter next to him. He looked my way. "Have you been into trouble again?"

"I told you that Pippi's place was broken into the other day. Sean's been keeping an eye on things, that's all," Maggie explained.

Chris looked confused. "Yeah, but I didn't think she was in any personal danger. Why's Panelli babysitting her?"

My father jumped in, "I for one am glad that Sean is taking this so seriously. I consider it a personal favor that he's watching out for you, Phillipena. Especially after what happened last time."

Ugh. There it was again. Couldn't people just let the I-was-sucked-in-by-a-crazed-murderer incident go?

The room grew silent as the allusion to my last escapade hung in the air like the odoriferous scent of the VFW after a ham and bean dinner.

Finally my mother broke the silence. "I can't wait to see Claire in her flower girl dress and Sam in his suit," she said, changing the subject.

"Oh mom," Maggie started. "You should see how darling...." I sat back, snuck another roll, and listened to the family banter for another half-hour. After breakfast, we all parted ways, agreeing to meet again at the rehearsal dinner.

Chris and Maggie were planning on taking the kids to Brookfield Zoo for the day, while Mom and Dad were going to stock the fridge and change sheets in anticipation of the rest of the family's arrival later that afternoon. With my other three sisters and their families, plus Mary Frances, we'd have a full house. I smiled at the thought. I was blessed to have such a big, wonderful family. I pitied people like James Farrell. His family was such a mess.

Mary Frances was right. No one could really blame Morgan for wanting to escape from that family. Heck, I'd only known the people for a few days and I could hardly stand to be around them anymore. Which made my own plans for the day all the more difficult.

*

I stopped in front of the Farrell's gateman and whipped out my cell.

"Patricia. This is Pippi. I'm at your front gate. Can you tell the gateman to let me in? I need to speak to you in person ... I'll explain when I'm inside. Oh, James isn't home, is he ... good." I breathed a sigh of relief. James had already left for the office.

Anna opened the door as soon as I approached. Patricia was standing behind her, waiting for me. She practically pounced on me. "So, what is it? Did you find Morgan? Where is she?"

I was taken back. Patricia was not only acting neurotic, she looked neurotic. Her hair was disheveled, eyes glazed, hands shaking. She was still dressed in her bathrobe and slippers. Anna was hovering about like a protective mother hen.

"Patricia, I need to speak to you in private," I said, giving Anna the eye. She shot me one right back—hers said screw-you in an orderly, efficient way that only a housekeeper of her status could pull off. I just couldn't figure out what I ever did to get on that woman's bad side.

"What have you found out?" Patricia said after Anna finally disappeared down the hall.

"Nothing new since last time we talked," I reported.

She deflated, causing her to look even more pitiful.

"Did James come down hard on you for hiring me?" I asked, wondering if he had found out that Patricia asked me to look for Morgan. What was I thinking getting involved with these people? Poor Patricia. After learning she'd crossed him, James had probably what... Threatened her? Beaten her? Was he angry enough about it to spray paint that ugly message on my car?

"Yes, he was upset."

"Do you want me to keep investigating?"

"Of course. I need to find Morgan."

"Then, I want to go through her things to see if I can find a clue to where she and Alex might have gone."

"Her things?"

"Yes. Her clothing, correspondence, bills ... everything."

Patricia considered my request for a few seconds before responding, "Fine. I'll show you where their suite is located."

I stared at the back of her feet as we made our way up the winding oak staircase. She was wearing those fluffy-type of slippers with the feathery stuff on the toes and the open back. I marveled at how smooth the back of her heels looked. How did she do that? My heels were rough enough to refinish an old Amish kitchen table.

"Here we are," she said.

I looked up and surveyed the room. Very nice. It was sort of designer showroom meets Paris flea market all wrapped up with a strong country vibe. I liked it.

"It's distasteful, I know," Patricia commented, running her finger alongside a black lacquered shaker dresser. "But how could one expect any sort of taste and style from someone of her background?"

I shrugged. Guess I wouldn't be seeing Patricia at my Third Saturday Flea Market booth.

"Well, I'd better get busy," I said. "Looks like I have a lot to go through. I'll let you know if I find anything." I headed straight for a small secretary's desk nestled near a wall of windows which afforded a spectacular view of the back acreage and stables.

Patricia turned back on her way out, "Phillipena, my husband was furious when he found out that I implicated him in Morgan's disappearance. He can be a dangerous man, so please be careful."

"You're not expecting him back any time soon, are you?"

Patricia absently touched her cheek. "No, he said he wouldn't be home until this evening," she replied, leaving the room.

I felt stricken with guilt. I shouldn't have agreed to get involved in all this. I didn't think through my actions and how they might affect Patricia. I was sure glad Morgan was tucked away somewhere with Alex and out of harm's way. I had no intention of locating her. As far as I was concerned, she could sue J.J. for all he was worth, get her house, and live happily ever after with Alex in her new suburban mansion.

I was looking for different answers. Answers I hoped to find by searching the room that Morgan shared with J.J. Although I was almost completely sure James had murdered Jane and Pauline, I wasn't completely convinced that J.J. wasn't somehow involved. He stood to lose a lot if Alex came forward and claimed his birthright.

I started with the bills. Lots and lots of bills—all the major department stores plus a few from some hipster Wicker Park stores like Landis, Belmontos, and Psycho Babes. Cool. Morgan and I frequented some of the same stores. Although, by the looks of these bills, she wasn't perusing the last-stop sales racks looking for good buys to resell for profit on-line.

I got down on the floor, pulled the middle drawer all the way out and looked underneath. Nothing. I opened the laptop and turned it on, hoping to find it logged onto email. No such luck. Instead, a password prompt blinked at me from a blank screen.

Next, I moved on to the dresser drawers. I pulled out all of them, but paid extra attention to J.J's drawers. The only information I garnered was that he was a brief man—basic whites with blue elastic trim. Boring.

The nightstands proved fruitless, too. I wasn't surprised to find a stack of smutty romances inside Morgan's stand. The one she pilfered from the garage sale, was right on top.

I checked under the mattress, under the bed, all around the closets, and behind the artwork before moving to the bathroom where I searched every drawer, behind the towels, and even in the toilet tank. Nothing.

I stood in the middle of the bathroom with my hands on my hips. If I didn't know better, I'd sworn the place had been picked clean. There wasn't anything personal anywhere. No personal correspondence, address books, or even photos. J.J. and Morgan led a very impersonal, sterile life. Weird.

Perhaps the weirdest thing of all was the fact that all of Morgan's stuff was still there, including her cosmetics. There was no way she'd planned her escape. A girl like her would never leave without her full makeup ensemble.

Of course, she could just buy more. That's what I would do. I mean, if she wanted to disappear quickly, it wouldn't do to drag a thirty pound bag of cosmetics out the front door.

Finally, I admitted defeat and left. I found Patricia waiting for me in the front room. She was drinking some sort of clear liquid on ice in a crystal glass. She raised it and jingled the ice in my direction.

"No thanks, it's a little early for me." *Although, it probably wouldn't be if I was married to the weenie boss.*

"What did you find?" she asked, sipping away. She still hadn't bothered to clean herself up.

"Absolutely nothing."

She didn't seem surprised.

"You said that Morgan had hired a private investigator. Do you know who?"

"No idea."

"Do you know if she has an attorney?"

"Probably, but I wouldn't know who."

That was a dead end. There were only about ten thousand divorce attorneys in the Chicago area.

"It does seem like Morgan didn't plan her escape. She didn't pack anything. Not even her cosmetics."

Patricia gasped and placed a hand over her mouth. "Oh, no. That means that…. Do you think she's de—"

I held up a hand. "Don't jump to conclusions. Like I said, I'm pretty sure she's off with Alex Sokolov. I have the neighbor's story to verify that."

She narrowed her eyes and slammed back the rest of her drink. "You have to understand how important it is that you find Morgan before she does something to ruin my son's reputation or provoke my husband into doing something violent."

"Quite frankly, Patricia, I don't think your husband needs much provocation. He seems to have a short temper."

"James is just being protective of his son."

"His son or his money. I mean, that's what we're really talking about, isn't it? If Morgan sues J.J. in divorce court, she may get half of J.J's company shares. Especially if they were acquired after he and Morgan were married. Most divorce courts consider anything acquired after marriage as marital property and it's subject to equal distribution." I knew my stuff. I had handled the portfolios of many divorcees in my professional days. I kept going, "That means any growth of the business can be attributed to spousal support. JimDogs has really grown since J.J. became CFO, hasn't it? I mean, look at the new store they're opening in Skokie. How many other stores have opened since J.J. came on board? Wouldn't Morgan be entitled to her share of that growth?"

"I bet it really sticks in James' crawl that Morgan will get shares in JimDogs," I continued. "Especially since he thought all along that J.J. had signed a prenuptial agreement before the marriage."

"Yes, James was careless. He never should have taken J.J. at his word. J.J. was young, stupid, in love. He let that girl trick him."

"And now what? You think your husband has killed her?"

"I don't know what to think. That's what I'm paying you for. Find out. I need to know."

I watched her extract a Gin bottle from the liquor cabinet and pour another glassful. She topped it off with a splash of tonic water—no lime. Geez, one gin and tonic like that and I'd be flopping on the floor.

I thought maybe I was starting to understand where Patricia was coming from and why it was important to her that I find Morgan alive. Patricia had lived under James' control all these years, put up with his infidelity and who knows what else. She was no dummy. She could see that history was repeating itself. Just like his father, J.J. was rising in the weenie business and he'd taken a mistress. Maybe she wanted to save Morgan from the pain she'd endured in her own marriage.

"Why have you stayed with him all these years, Patricia? Why did you put up with him having an affair? Why didn't you just leave?"

She moved to the windows. The bright sun made her robed silhouette appear small and shapeless. I watched her tip back her head and drain yet another glass of gin. There was a long pause before she answered, her speech slightly slurred, "What options did I have?"

With that said, she moved back toward the liquor cabinet for a refill. I showed myself out. I'd seen enough.

Chapter 21

Shep was sitting up in bed staring blankly at the television when I walked into his room carrying two bags of Korean takeout. I'd brought the food to ease my guilt over not visiting for a couple days.

"Look," I said, holding up the large white bag marked Seochi's BBQ. I knew it was one of Shep's favorite places. "I brought all your favorites: kimchi, tofu soup, and kalbi." I crossed the room and opened the curtain, allowing some light to stream in. Shep looked tired and pale.

"Oh, yummy," he said, with less enthusiasm than I'd hoped for. I set his bedside table with Styrofoam containers and helped him open the plastic package of silverware.

"I haven't seen you for a couple of days. I was hoping to hear that you made progress on finding Pauline's killer."

I chuckled. Not because something was funny. It was more of a nervous type of chuckle. Shep's mood seemed sour. I didn't want to add to it by telling him I hadn't made much progress.

He was too shaky to balance a spoonful of liquid, so I moved the tofu soup and pushed some kalbi chicken his way.

He started fiddling with the remote attached to the side of his bed. I turned sideways so I could see the TV and still manage to talk to him. He flipped to channel three. The noon news was on. He dug into his food, eating slowly, but seeming to enjoy the chicken. At least he still had a good appetite.

The scene switched from the weather man back to the anchorwoman who was announcing the local stories of the day: the mayor was giving a statement on gang violence; there was a mid-town robbery; and uh oh … a murder in the Ukrainian Village. The anchorwoman referred to a field reporter who was live at the scene.

This is Lindsey Barnes live at the scene of the brutal murder of Alex Sokolov, a young graduate of Princeton University, who has just recently suffered the loss of his mother to cancer. Police are paying particularly close attention to this murder which they believe occurred sometime yesterday morning.

Alex Sokolov? I was all ears as the camera flashed back to the anchorwoman in studio. "Do the police have any leads?" she asked the reporter.

Yes. A witness has come forward and given a detailed description of a possible suspect who was seen prowling around the house prior to the discovery of Alex's death.

I cringed as the screen filled with, a crude, but pretty close likeness of me. Thank goodness the old bitty suffered from cataracts, no telling how much more detail she would have been able to give the police artists. As it was, the artists had completely missed the mark on my hair. On the screen it looked like a fluffy cone of bright orange cotton candy. He'd definitely made my eyes too close together and drawn my nose too wide. No one would think that was me, would they?

I glanced sideways at Shep. He was busy with his food and not paying attention to the television.

Lindsey Barnes was back on the screen. She was standing in front of Calina Sokolov's house with a mic in her hand.

If you've seen this person or have any information concerning this case, please call this number immediately.

A number ticked across the bottom of the screen. I was trying to remain casual, not wanting to alarm Shep, but the tremble in my hand caused me to spill soup down my front. I dabbed at it with a napkin, my mind racing. Alex Sokolov was murdered. When did that happen? Was he in his house dead when I was there? Where's Morgan? Was anyone I knew calling that number right now and turning me in?

The anchorwoman came back on and wrapped up the segment with an emotional plea. *Please don't hesitate to get involved. Call the police if you have any information. This close neighborhood of Russian immigrants has seen its share of sadness lately. Please help the authorities solve this crime.*

I looked back at Shep who had given up on the food and flopped back onto his pillows. He must not have heard the television anchorwoman mention Alex Sokolov's name, or he would have recognized it. I reached over and flipped to a different channel. "Are you in pain today, Shep? You seem really..."

"What? Like I'm in a bad mood? I'm sick of being in here."

I backed up a little, unsure of how to handle the shift in his demeanor. "Things must be getting better. You're not wheezing as much. I bet they'll let you out soon."

He sighed, making a half-attempt at a smile. "Yeah. Sorry, today's just a down day."

"Don't apologize, Shep."

Except for the whirl of machinery and the constant beeping of his monitors, the room grew uncomfortably silent. I started straightening his blankets, trying to make him more comfortable.

He placed his hand over mine. "You know, doll. I think I need some time alone today. Could you come back sometime this weekend?"

My eyes stung. "Sure, I understand," I said, struggling to keep my voice steady. "I'll come back on Sunday." I leaned in and gave him a hug, hanging on longer than necessary.

I barely made it back to my parked car before I broke down. Once my sobs started, they wouldn't stop. Like a crazed idiot, I sat there, my head against the steering wheel, my body shaking uncontrollably. Things were spinning out of control—Shep's illness, this thing with the Farrells, the wedding. I was tempted to drive straight home, finish off a bottle of wine, and take a long nap. Deep down, however, I knew I needed to find some answers. It was the best thing I could do to help Shep.

I checked my review mirror and wiped under my swollen eyes. One thing for sure, there was no way I was going to be able to get much done with my picture plastered all over the news. There was only one thing to do. Drastic, sure. But necessary.

*

After a quick trip to the neighborhood pharmacy, I was back in my apartment, drinking a glass of wine and setting the timer for twenty minutes. The directions said to do a test run on a small portion of hair, but I didn't have time for that. I needed to be at Stumpy's pumpkin patch in two hours.

As soon as timer went off, I hopped in the shower, shampooed and rinsed. I started feeling nervous. I'd never been a brunette before. I had to admit, dying my hair had sounded like a good idea; but now, as I stood looking in the mirror, I wasn't so sure. It was definitely a transformation ... of some type.

I went through my basic routine: gargle, brush, pit-stick, lipstick and mascara, and lots of goop to hold in the frizzes. When I was done, I stepped back and surveyed the final results. Something was askew. I think it was my freckles. They didn't match the black hair. I looked like a paint-by-number picture gone bad.

Oh, well. Not much I could do about it at the moment. Besides, I was only going to a pumpkin patch. Who would care?

Chapter 22

"What have you done?" It was my mother. She was standing by my Aunt Maeve who was staring wide-eyed at my new hairdo.

Both of them were wearing dark blue bib overalls. My Aunt, however, had paired hers with a flannel shirt and a pair of brown boots, while my mother wore a crisp white button-down shirt and, believe it or not, a small strand of pearls. My mother and her sister were a study in contrast; although at the moment they were both wearing the same shocked expression on their faces.

"What happened to your hair?" My sister, Anne asked, joining my little group of admirers. My other sister Kathleen was right behind her.

"You've gone Goth!" Kathleen exclaimed.

"I have not. I've just changed my hair color, that's all."

"Why?" Anne asked, rubbing her protruding pregnant belly.

"Yeah, what's wrong with red?" Kathleen added.

I looked around, suddenly feeling like the odd one out. Everyone around me sported different shades of red: Mom and Maeve, a beautiful auburn; Kathleen, a head of blondish-red curls, and Anne, long straight fiery red hair.

My hand involuntarily moved to my own hair. "I well ...." I was trying to find a suitable explanation, but what was I going to say? As a red-head, I was a wanted woman. Black was my only choice. "Does it look that awful?"

They all stammered, but no one came up with a reply. That is, except Anne's four year old who pointed at me from afar and yelled, "Look, Aunt Pippi dressed up as a witch."

I practically shriveled with embarrassment. I wanted to run and hide, but I couldn't because in about fifteen minutes I was going to have to practice my part in this whole fiasco. So I did the next best thing.

I walked right up to a scarecrow, stole the straw hat off his head, shoved my hair inside and pulled the drawstring tight. Then I saddled up to the keg and held out my plastic cup for a fill-up.

My Uncle Chuck was manning the tap. "Why hello there, Pippi! You've sure grown since I saw you last."

My Uncle Chuck always said that, even though I was way into adulthood, he couldn't quit commenting about my growth.

"Hi Uncle Chuck. Nice rehearsal party. Where's Cherry?"

"Oh, she'll be coming around the corner any minute," he chuckled and tipped his cowboy hat.

I glanced around and spotted her—the source of over a week's worth of angst, my cousin Cherry. I glared her down as she approached with her future hubby on her arm. Was it wrong for the maid of honor to wish so much evil and hateful things on the bride?

"There you are, Phillipena! Oh, can you believe I'm going to be Mrs. John Garcia tomorrow?"

I practically choked on my beer. I'd only met the guy briefly and forgotten his last name was Garcia. It just hit me. My cousin was going to become one of my favorite ice cream flavors ... Cherry Garcia.

I struggled not to laugh as I shook John's hand and made small talk. He seemed nice enough. Who knew? Maybe ice-cream was the way to go.

I managed a couple more cups of beer before the minister arrived and started the rehearsal. It was easy enough. All I had to do was walk, smile, hold the bridal bouquet, smile, and walk again. No problem.

Afterwards, Stumpy's party caterers brought out large trays of sandwiches and kettles of chili. Everyone sat around discussing the next day's events.

"It will be wonderful," Cherry was gushing. "After we're pronounced man and wife," she looked lovingly into John's eyes when she said that, "we're going to light the bonfire."

I perked up. No one had said anything about a bonfire. I guess that was Cherry's alternative to lighting a wedding candle.

"Then we'll all gather around and hold hands and everyone can give us a life blessing. After the blessing ceremony, we'll pass out the roasting sticks and hotdogs."

I glanced at my mother. I thought she was going to croak. I moved out of earshot and over to the food table. I decided to skip the double stacked sandwiches and instead refilled my beer. Uncle Chuck was nowhere to be seen, so I just stood by the tap and kept refilling. It wasn't the best beer, but at that point, anything would do.

*

The next thing I knew, I was waking up in ... "What happened," I gasped. I shot straight up, wide awake. I took a second, trying to get my bearings, before jumping out of bed. I was still fully dressed.

I walked out to the kitchen. Not my kitchen. Sean's.

He looked up from the skillet where he was scrambling eggs. "I hate your hair."

"Yeah, me too. What am I doing here?" I grabbed for a mug of coffee like it was the only lifejacket on a sinking ship.

"You don't remember?"

I thought back to the night before. I had a slight recollection of waving my hat in the air while riding astride a bail of straw all the while shouting something about Annie Oakley being the true unsung hero of the west. I rubbed my temples and moaned. "Oh, was I that bad?"

"Your sister, Kathleen, said you drank half the keg by yourself. The good news is that Cherry was also two sheets to the wind, so I don't think she noticed your condition."

"I'm not worried about Cherry. It's my mother who's going to kill me."

"You're on your own with her," he said, passing a plate of eggs my way. I took one look at the wet looking yellow mush and almost hurled.

"Eat. It's the best thing for a hangover." He sat down on the stool next to me with his own plate heaped full.

"What, did my parents call you to come rescue me or something?"

"No. I went out to Stumpy's to find you around eleven. I was waiting at your place and you never came home, so I was worried. You were too sick to be on your own, and there was no way I was going to be able to get you up your steps, so I brought you here. Your parents agreed that it was the best alternative. Especially in light of all that's happened lately. They're still worried that someone is after you."

I picked at my eggs.

"Is that why you did that to your hair?" he asked.

"Hmm?"

"Your hair. Did you change the color because you're trying to throw off the person who is after you, or is it because a police sketch of you is all over the news?" He opened a cabinet drawer, pulled out a bottle of aspirin and slid it across to me.

I grimaced. I should have guessed he would already know about that. I took my time opening the aspirin bottle, trying to formulate a good answer. "Okay. I was at Alex Sokolov's house and ran into that old woman, Mrs. Stanislav, who by the way, gave a lousy description of me. I look a lot better than that drawing that was on the news."

I paused, but he didn't offer any comment.

"Well, anyway, all I did was look in the window. I was trying to find Morgan Farrell, which I was hired to do, so I had every right to be there. Mrs. Stanislav is the real criminal. Did you know she tried to kill me? She shot at me with a big gun. I bet she doesn't have a FOID card for it either. You should check into that."

"It's nowhere in my jurisdiction."

"Are you going to turn me in?"

"I feel obligated to. You're a murder suspect." He finished his eggs and drained his coffee. "I'm a cop. Sooner than later, someone is going to figure out it's you, even with your black hair, and then I'm going to be in big trouble. Everyone knows that we ...."

"That we what?"

He shrugged it off. "Probably some of the guys already recognize you; they're just showing me respect by not reporting it yet."

"No one would honestly think that I killed Alex Sokolov."

He stood and moved to the sink with his plate and mug. "No, no one that actually knows you would think that you murdered the guy, Pippi. It's just that you need go in and get this cleared up. You were witnessed at the scene of a crime. If anything, you might have information that could help the investigation."

"Can't you call someone and clear it up for me?"

"I'd be happy to go in with you and help in any way I can; but it's not as simple as making a call. I mean, what do you want me to say? *Hey guys, that's my girlfriend in the police sketch, but it's all a mix up. No need to bother her about it.*"

Girlfriend? Did he just call me his girlfriend? The idea both thrilled me and ticked me off. I thought better to ask him about it though. Instead, I stayed on topic. "Yeah, guess that won't work." It was hard to think all this through with such a fuzzy brain. "I will go in, I promise. First thing tomorrow morning. Just let me get through today. I have that hotdog thing, and then the wedding. Can't it wait until tomorrow?"

"No, I think you ought to go in now. I'll get showered and we'll go together."

"Fine," I replied. "I'll get tidied up a bit, too. Can I use your guest bathroom?"

He came across the kitchen and placed a hand on my shoulder. "Thanks, Pip. And don't worry; it'll all work out okay."

I smiled, but kept my focus down, shifting eggs from one side of the plate to the other. I didn't dare look up. He'd see the guilt written all over my face. Instead, I kept shifting eggs until I heard the shower running full steam. Then I scribbled a quick note, took his keys, and quietly slipped out the door.

Sean was going to freak when he found the note and realized I had left. At least I had the courtesy of letting him know where he'd be able to find his car and keys. I wondered if he would come after me; he pretty much knew my itinerary for the day. Hopefully, he had enough going on that he wouldn't bother chasing me down.

Speaking of which, I only had a couple of hours before I was due at the new JimDog's grand opening. Leaving Sean's car in Stumpy's parking lot with the keys under the mat, I got in my rental and high tailed it back to my apartment for a quick shower and change. Even though my locks had changed color, I still grabbed the black wig with heavy bangs and smeared on some extra heavy makeup to cover my freckles. If anything, I was consistent.

The whole way to Skokie, I kept glancing in my mirror, wondering if Sean would put out an APB on me, or just hunt me down himself. Neither was a good option. Maybe I should have followed his advice and turned myself in.

I arrived in Skokie with no time to spare. The new JimDog store had made quite the transformation in the last few days. The building was completed and included a new giant weenie, JimDog's trademark, on the roof. A large banner and a giant, forty-foot high balloon marked the occasion.

Things were already bustling by the time I walked inside. I caught a glimpse of Ms. Ashcroft across the room. She was standing by the kitchen with J.J. and another woman.

I readjusted my wig and approached cautiously, hoping my disguise would fool them.

They all turned in my direction as I approached. "There you are," Ms. Ashcroft said. "I have your costume ready. It's hanging in the restroom. Did you sign the paperwork?"

I handed over the envelope noticing that the secretary and J.J. were standing awfully close to each other. The type of close that suggested intimacy.

At first glance, they made an unlikely couple. He was dressed in a classic cut suit which would have looked great if his head didn't look like it belonged on the eight pound rack at the Ten Pin. The woman next to him was also dressed classically—like a classic bimbo, that is. Short skirt, tight shirt, and heels high enough to challenge a stilt walker.

I nodded and uttered a quick thank you, not wanting to chance it that J.J. might recognize my voice. As it was, he'd barely glanced my way so far. His eyes were pretty much stuck on the short-skirted woman.

I headed for the back of the restaurant to change.

Once inside the restroom, I stepped into the six foot weenie and zipped up. The costume came complete with a long sleeve white tunic, leggings, gloves, and foot covers. The polyfoam body zipped right up to my neck and then attached to a large matching head complete with eyes, a toothy smile and a mustard streak up the middle. I looked very yummy.

Out in the restaurant, the doors were opening and the meat-loving crowds pouring in. My job was to circulate, hand out stickers and balloons to kids, and be available for photo opportunities. I got the hang of it pretty fast. Actually, I was good at being a giant hotdog. The kids loved me.

I was getting into a groove when, over the happy shrieks and giggles, I heard JimDog's booming voice. "Welcome to JimDog's," he was saying to a young family hunkered down in one of the booths.

I lumbered over in his direction, but stopped short as I saw J.J. approach. JimDog didn't look happy to see him. He grabbed his arm and pulled him over by the back kitchen entrance. I followed, but hovered around the corner and tried to stay out of sight as best I could in the giant hot dog suit. I strained to catch their conversation.

"I see you brought *her* with you," JimDog said.

"Yeah, so. You think you're the only one entitled to a little fun on the side?"

"I never paraded mine out in public. What are you thinking? Not too smart, especially now that your wife is missing."

"She's just off somewhere. She'll get over it and come home."

"Yeah, well she'd better show up. There's too much at stake for her to be running around on the loose. You need to get her under control."

"I'll take care of it. I told you I would." J.J.'s voice was faltering.

"You'd better, or I will."

"Like you took care of Alex Sokolov? I guess his death solves a lot of problems, doesn't it? Really, Dad, your own son? He *was* your son, wasn't he?"

I heard some movement and a little thud. I assumed James had pushed J.J. against the wall. "Shut up, J.J. You don't know what you're talking…"

"I want a balloon."

I looked down to see a four foot bundle of energy prancing at my feet. "I want a balloon," he whined.

I motioned for him to be quiet, but he persisted. "Balloon, balloon!" He was getting louder and tugging at my bun.

I was trying to shoo him away, when suddenly I felt someone grasp my arm. I looked up to find James's face boring into mine.

"Hey, let go," I pleaded, trying to shake him off, but his grip was tight. He dragged me through the crowd and into the men's room. J.J. was right behind him. Once inside, he backed me against a urinal and yanked off my hotdog head. I reached to try and secure my wig, but was too late. It had faltered and he grabbed ahold of it, too.

It was just like all the ending scenes in Scooby Doo where Velma rips off the villain's disguise and announces his true identity. *Aha…it's not really a hotdog, it's … it's….*

"It's that crazy red haired woman," JimDog announced. Then, momentarily confused by my new brunette coloring, he grabbed a hold of my real hair and yanked again.

"Ouch!" I shrieked. Then, with all my might, I kicked him in the shin.

He doubled over and dropped a few cuss words. Seizing the opportunity, I opened the bathroom door and ran like the dickens. I ran through the restaurant, out the side door, and straight towards my rental, all the while fumbling for my keys inside the hotdog suit. J.J. was right behind me and closing in fast.

Luckily I found my keys and slipped into the car just before he caught up to me. I clicked and double checked the locks. He started banging on my window like a crazed lunatic.

"Take an easy. This is a rental!" I yelled out.

He kept banging.

I jammed the keys into the ignition, peeled out and left J.J. in my exhaust. Right before leaving the lot, I glanced in my mirror and saw him making a rude gesture my way. The Farrell men really lacked class.

*

It wasn't easy driving while wearing half a hotdog costume, but I managed to put some distance between the two JimDogs and myself before my cell started to ring.

I made a quick pull over in a gas station lot and dug my phone out of my bag. I expected it to be Sean, but it was my mother.

"Hi Mom. I'm kind of busy right now, can—"

"Kind of busy? Do you know what time it is?"

"Uh—"

"It's after three o'clock."

I didn't get it. The wedding wasn't going to start until seven. "Okay…"

"Don't you remember that the photographer is going to meet us there at five for pictures?"

I thought back. "No. When did you tell me that?"

"Last night at the rehearsal."

Oh, no wonder I didn't remember; I was probably already half-baked when she told me. "No problem, Mom. I can be there at five. I'll go home and change now."

"You're not being a very good maid of honor. You should be here attending to Cherry. She's a nervous wreck."

She was right, I wasn't being a good maid of honor. Although, technically, I was just the fill-in maid of honor. At least I was better than Willow who had got herself into major trouble with the law. Speaking of which, I hoped Sean didn't catch up to me until the wedding, or I could find myself in the same predicament. That would really upset my mother.

"I'm sorry, Mom. I'm on my way." I snapped my phone shut and headed for home, promising myself that I'd put the case out of my mind for a while. I needed to focus on Cherry and her big day. I was going to be the best maid of honor ever, despite the ugly dress.

Chapter 23

Who knew a cheap rent-a-wreck could do over eighty-five so smoothly? Not bad for thirty-seven a day, plus tax. The little rental wonder got me back to Naperville in a forty-five minutes flat. Of course, I got a few weird looks along the way. Guess people weren't used to seeing half a hotdog zipping down the freeway in a tiny compact.

I ripped into my drive, pausing for a moment to check for signs of possible police surveillance. I couldn't believe that Sean had let me get by with taking off that morning. He must have figured he'd catch me at the wedding. Hopefully, he didn't plan to remove me from the festivities in shackles.

I shot up my steps, stripped off the hotdog costume, and hit the shower for a quick rinse. The steam made my curls turn to frizz, but no problem. I simply twisted and secured them with a clip. A quick smear of mascara and lip gloss and I was wedding-ready.

I grabbed the dress and started to pull it over my hips. Uh, oh. It was kind of tight. How did that happen? It fit a couple of days ago. It must be PMS. That would explain a lot of things.

I danced around, bending and squatting, trying to get the material to stretch; but the pumpkin-colored polyester proved resistant to my efforts. So, out of desperation, I stripped back down and ran to my inventory boxes. I ripped and tore through clothing until I found it—a Lipo-In-A-Box Girdle. I'd picked it up for a steal at the Salvation Army. I had seen it featured on an episode of a daytime talk show's favorite picks not too long ago and ... well ... if anyone needed lipo in a box, it was me.

Somehow, I managed to hike the flesh-colored-spandex instrument of torture up over my behind and onto my torso. Then, I tried the dress again. Perfect, except for the fat rolls under my pits and well ... I didn't even dare turn around in fear of seeing back fat. At least I got it to zip. Everything was great, unless I needed to eat, drink, or take a deep breath. The price of beauty.

I put on the matching pumpkin died shoes and trotted right over to the house. The whole gang was there, minus the guys, who were banished from the area. Aunt Maeve was busy fussing over Cherry, who was decked out in a cowgirl wedding dress, complete with white accessories—a fringed jacket, cowgirl hat, and rhinestone accented boots.

"There you are," she gushed as I approached. "Oh, you look great in that color, especially with your new hair. I just love it."

I didn't think her compliment was valid, especially coming from a girl who was going to her wedding looking like she'd just stepped off the set of *Gunsmoke*—before they added Technicolor. I'd be going back to red real soon, despite the police sketch.

"What do you think," she asked, picking up a piece of tulle and attaching it to the brim of the hat. "Veil or no veil? It just sticks on with Velcro, so I can go either way."

"Uh..." I was speechless. The room grew silent waiting for my reply. I could tell this had been a hot issue before my arrival. I looked at my mother for help. She was wearing a pained expression.

Mary Frances spoke up. "Maybe on for when you walk down the aisle, but off for the reception?"

"Yes. Great idea," I agreed. Cherry smiled. Everyone breathed easier. Leave it to Mary Frances to come up with an amiable solution.

After another few minutes of fussing, we all took off for Stumpy's. I opted to ride with my sister, Kathleen, and her family in their minivan. There was no way I was going to be able to scrunch my lipo-in-a-box body behind the wheel of the subcompact. As it was, I could hardly manage with the whole back bench of the minivan. Worse yet, the stupid thing was squeezing all the liquid right out of me. I had to go to the bathroom before we even got out of the driveway.

Fortunately, Stumpy's had set up a few extra porta-potties just for our family's special occasion. Someone had also set up a flower covered arch and two large baskets of mums where I assumed Cherry and John were going to take their vows. Instead of chairs, straw bales were arranged in long rows, each bail dressed with a large white bow. Off to the side was a huge bonfire, where we'd gather later to roast weenies, chug beer, and ... if I was lucky, put together a few smores. After which, we could all mosey over to the pavilion where a mobile dance floor had been laid out and a couple of fellows were busy testing amplifiers. Although, since the only instruments I could see were a fiddle, a banjo, and a squeeze box, I'm not sure what needed to be amplified.

"Isn't this wonderful," Cherry said, squeezing my arm and leading me toward the flowered arch.

"Wonderful," my mother echoed.

I just nodded and smiled. I kept on smiling right on through the ten million pictures that ensued. Maeve and Chuck must have allocated most of the wedding budget to the photography category. Just my luck. I would be forever archived as a giant, dark-haired pumpkin.

Guests began to arrive, just as the sun was starting to set. I spied Sean right away. He didn't look too happy; but at least he wasn't wielding hand cuffs.

I took my place in line for the procession and waited while the fiddler stepped forward and raised his instrument. The crowd grew quiet. I grimaced, half expecting him to break into a lively rendition of *The Devil Went Down to Georgia*. However, to my surprise, he played a beautiful Canon in D-major.

I must say, the ceremony went much better than I anticipated. Actually, it was quite nice. The sun, dipped under the horizon just as Cherry and John took their first kiss as husband and wife. From there, they walked hand in hand with a giant torch and lit the bonfire in some sort of symbolic gesture that was lost on me. Next, the guests had a choice of getting in a line for pulled pork sandwiches or roasting a weenie on the open fire. No room for vegetarians at this gig.

It was all just crazy enough to be fun. Spirits were high and both sides of the families seemed to mix well. The band had started a lively tune when Sean approached. I couldn't help but notice how good he looked in his dark jeans and button down shirt.

"Hey, looking good, Sean," I said, hoping to lighten the inevitable quarrel that was sure to follow.

He gave me the once over, raised a skeptical brow, but made no comment concerning the dress I was wearing. Instead, he placed a firm hand on my back and guided me out of the food line. "We're going down to the station together as soon as you can break away from here. I can't believe you took off this morning. I trusted you."

"You knew where I was. You could have come after me anytime you wanted," I retorted.

He tensed. "That wasn't the point. You were supposed to show up on your own recognizance. A man was murdered. Doesn't that mean anything to you?"

Sean was getting all worked up. A guy like him didn't like to bend the rules. He was as straight as an arrow. If anyone knew that, I did. I mean, how many times did I try to get him to break various rules? Besides, I already knew who'd murdered Alex Sokolov. I overheard the whole thing at JimDogs. So, as soon as I could get him alone, I'd fill him in on my latest discovery. It was perhaps the biggest break in the case so far. That would sooth his ruffled feathers.

I turned and placed a hand on his shoulder, giving him my most reassuring look. "No problem. I was planning on heading in soon anyway. Just let me eat, and make a little merry, and I'll be on my way."

"No merry. You had enough of that last night."

"Right. Hey what's this?" I asked, turning the collar of his shirt over.

He shrugged away, but it was too late. I knew exactly what it was—a lipstick smear.

I grabbed his collar and yanked him in for a closer inspection. "It's a lipstick stain," I said through a clenched jaw. "It's ..." I'd seen the shade before. I knew exactly who it belonged to—Sarah Maloney.

"Listen, Pippi. This isn't what it seems. She—"

I swallowed a couple of times, willing myself to stay calm. "No wonder you didn't come after me today. You were too busy with Sarah!" I spat out her name and spun on my heels. I didn't get two steps away before he spun me back around. He had his hands on my forearms, pinning them to my sides. Try as I might, there was no way to get off a good face slap. So instead, I kicked. Only the dress was acting like an orange straight jacket around my lower torso. I kicked and kicked and only managed to land a small one on his shin. "I can't believe you've gone back to her!"

"Would you settle down and let me explain."

"Excuse me," a voice interrupted.

I stopped kicking for a second and looked up to see Mary Frances.

"Please tell me this is some sort of new country western dance I'm not familiar with," she said, giving me the 'eye'.

I instantly simmered down. Sean let go of me and greeted my sister. "Hello, Mary Frances."

Mary Frances smiled. "Always good to see you, Sean," she said warmly. "Do you mind if I steal my sister for a few minutes? Something's come up."

I could tell Sean was reluctant to let me go. I'm sure he thought I might make another run for it.

"Sister Eileen just called me," my sister said in a hushed tone once she finally pulled me away from Sean. "Morgan's at St. Benedict."

"St. Benedict?" I almost laughed out loud. Morgan at a convent?

"Yes, Sister says she's in hysterics. She keeps mumbling something about sanctuary."

"You mean like sanctuary from the law. What did she do?" My mind immediately flashed to Alex. *It had been Morgan all along. How could I have missed it? She was the one with the most motive—that stupid house! She wanted that house more than anything. She'd somehow found out about the document in the book. It must have proven that Alex was entitled to his share of JimDog stock. She'd killed two women, but failed to get her hands on it. Of course, that night at the hotel she was trying to seduce him in order to get ahold of it. It must not have worked, so the only thing left to do was kill Alex. Otherwise the share of the stock holdings she'd gain from divorcing J.J. would be drastically reduced.*

I glanced over to where Sean, the two-timing jerk was waiting, with his eyes glued to me. I should really tell him about this new information but then I preferred to have him feel like a stupid idiot if I single handedly solved three murders.

"Pippi!" My sister was shaking me back to reality. "We should head over to St. Benedict, don't you think?"

"I'm supposed to make a toast—"

"Don't worry. I've already talked to Maggie. She's going to cover for you."

"Yeah, but Sean is watching."

She looked over at Sean and smiled sweetly. "Okay, wait here and act natural. I'll take care of it. Just be ready to make a break for it."

She took off before I could get an explanation. So, I headed back over to the buffet line, grabbed a plate and started loading up. I hadn't even made it to the baked beans before Sean was next to me.

"Have you calmed down yet?" he asked. "I want to talk about this."

I slapped a pile of beans on my plate, sending little brown splatters everywhere. "Look, Sean. I've had it with you," I said, struggling over the racket coming from the pavilion where the band had started playing again. "I give up. You obviously have some sort of problem with commitment. You couldn't commit to me, you couldn't commit to Sarah. One day you're flirting with me, then the next you're kissing Sarah. Well, I'm not going to be played like this."

He reached out for me. I backed up, wound up, and raised my plate. This guy was going to get his dinner the hard way.

"There you are!" It was Maggie. She glommed onto Sean's arm, saving him from a face full of baked beans. "I've been looking for you. My daughter's class is doing a unit on community helpers and she's decided to do her report on police officers. Can she pick your brain for a couple of minutes? I promise I won't keep you two apart for very long."

I lowered my plate and gave Maggie a knowing look. Mary Frances was good.

Sean, of course, obliged Maggie's request. As soon as they were a safe distance away, I made a break for the parking lot. Mary Frances intercepted me. "Come on, my car's over here. I've already called Patricia. She was so happy to hear that Morgan's alive. She'll catch up with us at St. Benedict."

It was a quiet car ride. We both were lost in our own thoughts. I'm not sure what Mary Frances was thinking about, but I was chastising myself for not seeing through Morgan's innocent act. Here I thought that she might be in danger, when all along she was the killer. How'd she do it? She must have been partnered with Alex from the get-go. Once the deeds were done, she eliminated him, too. I was going to get a confession from her then call the police and watch her little designer-clad butt being hauled away.

Okay, maybe my sentiments were a little twisted. The girdle was making me crazy. By the time we turned into the parking lot, my face was turning blue from lack of oxygen.

"Are you feeling okay?" Mary Frances asked, parking in the circular drive in front of the main entrance.

"No. Do me a favor and unzip me, would you?"

She looked at me strangely, but complied.

Once unzipped, I yanked all two yards of pumpkin chiffon up to my neck and started maneuvering like a Cirque du Solei contortionist, which wasn't easy in the front seat of a Volkswagen Bug. Once I had finally freed myself from the torturous contraption, I sat back in the seat, an orange circle of chiffon around my shoulders, and let it all hang out for a few seconds of jubilant liberation.

My sister's eyes were darting back and forth. "Well, this is the first time *this* has ever happened in front seat if my car. Pull your dress down; we need to get to Morgan before she decides to take off again."

I slipped the dress back over my torso and turned for her to rezip me. She fruitlessly tugged for a minute or so, before we decided to abandon the effort and leave the dress half-zipped. No big deal. St. Benedict wasn't full of fashion divas anyway.

As we neared the steps, I heard a rustling sound. "Did you hear that?" I asked.

"No, it's nothing. Come on, catch up."

As soon as we entered the chapel, Sister Eileen scurried over, her face flushed with excitement. "I didn't think you would ever arrive, Sister. I just didn't know what to do. She's inconsolable."

Mary Frances put a hand on the older woman's shoulder. "You did great. Thank you for calling us. We'll take it from here, if you'd like to go back to your room and rest."

Sister Eileen looked relieved to be able to get away from Morgan's hysterics. I assumed it was the most excitement she'd seen for a while. The poor thing was probably worn out.

I looked down at Morgan who looked like a child huddled against the wooden pew. She had her legs drawn to her chest and was rocking in unison with her sobs. The rhythmic sound of her cries mixed with the creaking of the pew made an eerie sound that echoed throughout the chapel, giving it a haunted feeling.

"Morgan, we were worried about you. Where have you been?" my sister asked, reaching out to stop Morgan's swaying. Morgan shrugged away and kept rocking. Mary Frances and I exchanged glances. I decided to give it a try. "Look Morgan, I'm in tight with the local police. I can help you through this. I'm sure killing Alex wasn't premeditated."

She stopped moving and looked at me through puffy eyes. "What are you talking about? I didn't kill Alex."

She seemed so earnest. "Okay," I said, pretending to go along with her. "Then you're here because you're running from your father-in-law. You must be very afraid of him."

"Of James? No. You've got it all wrong. I'm—"

Clicking heels echoed through the chapel, causing us to glance toward the sound. We became frozen in place as we watched Patricia make her way toward us. She was dressed to kill (literally) in black knee-high boots, tight fitting leather pants, and black gloves, which were unfortunately wrapped around the handle of what looked to be a very dangerous gun ... oh my ... why was Patricia carrying a gun?

Morgan scampered behind me, her shaking hands holding me out as a barricade between her and Patricia. "How did she find me?" Her tone was high pitched and frantic.

"I called her. She'd been so worried about you," Mary Frances replied in a faint voice, stepping forward and addressing Patricia who was now standing about two feet away with the gun pointed directly at us. "Put the gun away, Patricia. You don't want to hurt anyone."

Patricia tilted her head back, an ugly laugh escaping through twisted lips as the gun danced in her hands. Suddenly, I had a flashback to the year before when someone I'd trusted turned a gun on me. At the time, I promised God if he got me out alive, I'd never get involved in another murder case. I realized now that I'd broken a bargain with God. That's why this was happening. I deserved to die this time. It was just poetic justice it was going to happen in God's house.

"Hurt someone?" Light from a row of flickering candles cast menacing shadows across Patricia's face as little evil cackles sounded from her lips. "I'm not going to hurt someone. I'm going to *kill* someone, and that someone is you, and you, and you." She pointed the gun at each of us respectively. Sharp little whimpers were coming from behind me where Morgan was crouched ... or maybe they were coming from me. I couldn't tell. I was in a complete state of panic. I should have listened to Mary Frances. I should have been more prayerful ... less lustful ... less dishonest ... less ...

"Why would you want to kill us?" Mary Frances asked. She was so brave.

"Actually, Sister, I don't really want to kill you; you're just in the wrong place at the wrong time. But your sister? I'll kill her just because she's a pain in the butt ... and a horrible dresser," she added.

There was a weird moment when everyone forgot about their impending deaths and turned to look at me. That's when I realized I was going to die in this gawd-awful dress and it wasn't even zipped all the way!

"It's me she wants," Morgan whimpered, still crouching behind me.

"That's right. It's you I want. Come out from behind there, dear, and let me see your face before I blow it off."

I shivered. This woman was absolutely evil.

"Stay where you are, Morgan," Mary Frances calmly ordered. Although I really didn't think Morgan was going to just jump out and face the gun-wielding Patricia.

"Oh, come on now. Don't you want to come out and tell everyone what a naughty girl you've been, Morgan? That's right. Morgan isn't as sweet and innocent as you all think. She's very conniving. Aren't you Morgan?"

"You're the conniving one, Patricia." Morgan said, finding her voice. "You're responsible for three deaths. And why? For money?"

Patricia snarled, "That's easy for you to say. You don't have to put up with J.J.'s philandering; you didn't sign a prenuptial. No, all these years I've had to tolerate James having an affair with that Russian woman. How do you think it's been listening to the whispering behind my back and pity-looks from my friends? But what choice did I have? Without James, I had nothing."

I spoke up. "Well then, why didn't you just murder James? Why Jane and Pauline? They were innocent." That seemed like a reasonable question to me.

"I thought about killing James, but you know how it is. The spouse is always the first suspect. My plan seemed more fun and it was foolproof, until Morgan got involved."

"And what plan was that?" I asked, gaining more nerve by the minute. If I was going to die, I might as well have a few answers first.

"It was all about that stupid bun recipe. All that crap about it being his mother's recipe was a lie. I knew where he got it ... from Calina. She'd given it to him and had been receiving a cut of the company all these years. I knew if I got that recipe, I could barter for anything I wanted. All I had to do was threaten to go public with it. And, why shouldn't I? I was right there with James the whole time the business was being built and I wanted a piece of it."

"I see. What about Jane and Pauline? Why them?"

"Anna, our maid, overheard a phone conversation between Calina and James." Patricia was so wrapped up in telling her clever plan she didn't notice that Mary Frances was moving away from our little group. She went on, "Calina knew she was dying and wanted to wrap up a few details. She told James she'd kept the original copy of the recipe in the second volume of the book. She was too sick to send it, so she asked him to come and get it."

"Oh, that's why he only had the first volume of that book in his office. She had the other."

"Yes, isn't that romantic?" Patricia's voice dripped with venom.

"So you decided to go after the recipe yourself? Beat James to the prize," I asked.

"Yes, but she died quickly. The next thing I knew, Alex, that idiot, came home and sold everything from her estate," she continued, her voice strangely void of emotion. It's like she was on automatic pilot. "I had to get those books back."

"So, you approached Jane Reynolds about buying them."

"Of course, but she'd already promised them to some other buyer. She was so stubborn. I offered her twice what the other buyer was going to pay, but she insisted that she had already committed to someone else. It got nasty between us. I had no choice but to kill her. She wouldn't give me the books."

"But you didn't find the recipe in those books?"

"No. I knew that volume must have gone to a different buyer. So, after I killed the shop owner, I pitched the books to cover my tracks."

I shivered. "And Pauline?"

"Oh, *that* girl. I'd found out about the Retro Metro from the auction house and was there when her boyfriend called. I overheard her telling him about the envelope she'd found. It was almost too easy. Like it was fate that I had been standing there when she called him. I simply waited until she was alone that night and.... You should have seen her beg for her life. Really," she rolled her eyes, "so pathetic."

Every fiber in my body screamed with repulsion. I started shaking. Not with fear; but with anger. "You must have been desperate to get that recipe," I managed to say.

Patricia become more agitated. Not a good thing since she was pointing a gun at me. I snuck a peek at Mary Frances. She was edging toward a statue display by the candles.

I refocused on Patricia whose eyes had taken on a strange, far-away look. "Yes, you could say I was desperate. I got the recipe and arranged to meet Alex at the Huntley. I rented a room so there wouldn't be any risk that someone might see us together."

My eyes were instantly drawn to her leg. How could I have been so wrong? "So you were the one with Alex at the Huntley?" I asked. I was stalling for time. Out of the corner of my eye, I could tell Mary Frances had almost reached the statue. What exactly was she planning on doing?

"Yeah, you were breathing down my back. I knew you suspected those secondhand dealers were killed for something. If I came forward with the recipe all of the sudden, you'd know I was guilty of murder."

"I see. It would make sense for Alex to have the recipe, though. It was his mother's, after all."

"That's right. So I showed it to him and tried to convince him to come forward and use it to claim his shares in JimDog Corporation. With that recipe in hand, he could use it to barter for anything he wanted. I was offering him a lot of money to sell those shares to me," Patricia went on, seemingly eager to reveal her brilliant plan. "He was all for it, too. Then, *she* got in the way." She was indicating toward Morgan.

"What do you mean?"

"Morgan saw us together at the Huntley."

"I thought I was going to catch J.J. with his mistress," Morgan's tiny voice came from behind. "I'd paid the clerk to tip me off when someone checked in under the name Farrell. I rented the room across the hallway and planned on waiting a bit before surprising him in the act.

Patricia chuckled. "She was surprised all right."

Morgan continued. "I didn't even know who that man was. I didn't start to put things together until the next morning at the garage sale when you accused me of being at the Huntley with Alex Sokolov."

"She tracked him down," Patricia jumped back into the conversation. "They must have compared notes because somehow Alex put it together that I'd killed those women. He was freaked out. He wanted out of the deal. He was going to head back to Russia."

"So, you went to his house and killed him too?"

"He was a loose end. I had to kill him. Just like I have to kill all of you."

She closed in on me and straightened her aim. I ducked, closed my eyes and covered my head. Behind me, Morgan started screaming hysterically.

A loud crack echoed through the air.

I jumped, then jumped again at the sound of something hitting the floor. I opened my eyes and immediately looked down. Patricia was lying in a crumpled heap in front of me.

I wasn't shot. I wasn't shot! But what had happened? I looked around and then back down to where a thin stream of blood was draining from Patricia's head. Shards of blue and white ceramic littered the floor. The gun had slipped from her hand and was lying next to her limp body.

We all stared in silence. It was Mary Frances who finally spoke first. "She's not dead, is she? I didn't mean to kill her!"

"What did you do?" I asked.

Mary Frances was visibly shaking. "I hit her with the statue. Is she dead?"

"You should have stayed out of it, Sister," came a voice out of nowhere.

My head snapped around and my jaw dropped as Sarah Maloney stepped out of the shadows. "Now I'll have to finish the job." She stepped in with a gun pointed at me. "Killing you is going to be such a pleasure," she said in a hauntingly low voice.

I held my hands up. "Wait—"

I saw a flash of light and there was a deafening crack by my left ear. My nostrils filled with an acrid smell. I dove into one of the pews, my head spinning, my heart thudding in my head, my throat closing with fear. Suddenly my entire mouth was dry. I was practically paralyzed with fear. *What was happening?*

Another shot sounded next to me sending wood splinters from the pew everywhere.

I started crawling the best I could between the pew and the kneeler, but I could hardly maneuver in the tiny space. I heard footsteps coming closer. She wouldn't miss next time.

Mary Francis screamed my name.

Sarah voice rose above the chaos. "I told you to stay away from him!" I looked over my shoulder. She was standing over me, a gun pointed right at my head. Over the barrel, I could see the insane wildness in her eyes. "No," I whimpered; my voice a tiny whisper in the huge sanctuary.

"You just couldn't leave him alone, could you?" she shrieked. I watched in horror as she tensed her arm, squinted her eyes, and moved her finger over the trigger. I screamed and squeezed as far as I could under the pew.

I felt the impact as the gun's boom resounding in my head and a sharp burning pain started spreading through the back of my leg. There was another loud bang and more screaming. I felt numb, dizzy. My leg felt like it was on fire.

Everything went silent around me except for my short, ragged breaths. Suddenly, I felt someone pulling at me, trying to extract my limp body from its safe haven.

"Oh God, please don't let her be dead. Oh God." It was my sister. I struggled to reach her, but my arms wouldn't work. I started to hear a lot of footsteps and voices. They seemed to be coming from far away. Then there was another pair of hands. Stronger hands. They lifted me onto the top of the pew. The wood felt cold and hard against my back.

My vision was blurry, but I could make out my sister's face. She was talking, telling me something but I couldn't understand the words. Then, I slipped into darkness.

Chapter 24

"You're just lucky she could get your hair back to its original color," Mom was saying as she helped me maneuver my crutches up the porch and into their front door. Watch that step, it's slick," she warned. There was already a thin layer of snow on the ground and the forecast had called for two more inches before the end of the day.

It was hard to believe that only a few weeks had passed since Cherry's wedding. My life had changed as dramatically as the weather. I was now living in my parent's house, recovering from a gunshot wound in the butt. More specifically, to the lower lobe of my gluteus maximus; which, lucky for me, was well padded. All the extra fat absorbed the bullet and prevented it from doing any real damage to my pelvis area. Of course, I would probably always have some pain and it would take a while for the muscles to heal. I'm sure some would say it was ironic that I should endure pain in such a tender area, since I was such a pain in everyone else's butt.

Not only was I recovering physically, but emotionally. While I was still in the hospital, my dear friend Shep passed away. It hurt to know I was unable to be with him in the very end. However, I felt some peace in knowing that he knew the truth about Pauline's murder before succumbing to his illness.

According to his wishes, Shep was cremated and his ashes spread over Lake Michigan. There was no ceremony or funeral service, but my sister told me people had placed candles and flowers outside the Retro Metro in his honor. Shep helped hundreds of runaways and street kids. His memory would forever live on through the lives he had changed.

A couple days after his death, his parents came to my hospital room. We talked for a long time, sharing stories about Shep. To my surprise, they weren't the awful people I thought they were. They were just ordinary parents who had made mistakes. Mistakes they would regret forever. I felt sorry for them.

That same day, an attorney visited me with official papers. Shep had willed me the Retro Metro. The attorney explained that there were no leans against the business and I could chose to dissolve it and sell off the assets; or, after a few details were resolved, take it over and run it as my own. It was a big decision.

*

Mom had no sooner settled me on the TV room's sofa when the doorbell rang. "Could you get that Phil," she said to my father who was reclined in his favorite chair and watching a football game.

He reluctantly obliged, grumbling the whole way. I took the opportunity to grab the remote and switch to the Mystery Channel. Cable was going to be one of the great perks of living with my parents.

Someone cleared their throat and I looked up, surprised to see Sean standing in the doorway. I sat upright, adjusting my wrinkled shirt and running a self-conscious hand through my hair.

"You're back to red. I'm glad," Sean said.

He'd only visited once while I was in the hospital and that visit was limited to official police business. He took a statement, made some small talk about my condition, and left. I heard from Officer Wagoner, that he was pretty messed up in the head. Finding out your fiancé, or ex-fiancé, was a crazed lunatic was a little too much for him.

"Yeah, well since I'm not a murder suspect anymore, I thought I'd go back to my natural color. Brunette wasn't me, anyway."

"How's Mary Frances?"

"She's holding up fine." Actually, Mary Frances was amazing. I'd never known anyone stronger than my sister. In the end, she'd saved my life by grabbing Patricia's gun and killing Sarah before she could finish me off. It couldn't have been easy for Mary Frances to pull that trigger. She'd never hurt anyone in her life. However, when it came down to it, she made a heroic decision and demonstrated an amazing amount of strength.

Sean moved closer and sat next to me on the sofa. "Patricia Farrell is finally talking. It's a pretty twisted tale. I thought you might want to hear it."

I sat up a little straighter. "You bet I do." Fortunately, Mary Frances hadn't killed her when she hit her over the head. There were a lot of loose ends that only Patricia could tie up.

Sean continued, "Between Morgan's testimony and Patricia's confession, I've been able to piece the whole story together. It seems Morgan knew her husband was having an affair with his secretary; in fact, she had hired an investigator who verified her suspicions. The investigator told her that J.J. and his mistress conducted most of their trysts at the Huntley next to the JimDog corporate headquarters. He even had photographs of them together."

"All the proof she needed for a nice divorce settlement?"

"You got it. But she also wanted the self-satisfaction of confronting him in the act. She'd paid the front desk girl to tip her off when a room was registered under the name Farrell."

"So, that day I saw her go to the Huntley, it wasn't to meet Alex, but to catch J.J. with his mistress." I'd heard as much from Morgan already.

"Yes, but I guess you already knew that. Anyway," he continued. "Morgan was surprised to find Patricia there with some man, but she had no idea who he was."

"I gave her that piece of information the next day at the garage sale when I confronted her. I guess in a way, I set the wheels in motion for Alex's murder."

Sean shook his head. "Don't take any blame. It was all Patricia's doing."

I nodded. "Sure. It's just all so horrible."

He nodded. "After you confronted her and gave her Alex's name, Morgan tracked down him down. The two of them figured that Patricia must have killed Jane and Pauline to get the recipe. The rest of it you already know--Alex backed out of the deal and Patricia killed him."

I shook my head. "So, what happens to Morgan now?"

He shrugged. "I don't know. I'm guessing it'll take her a while to recover emotionally; but she's young. She'll get her divorce from J.J. and be awarded a huge alimony settlement. Eventually, she'll probably end up in another equally sick relationship with someone else."

"And Patricia?"

"The case against her looks air tight. I'm sure she'll spend the rest of her life in prison."

I sighed. "What about you, Sean? Everything with Sarah?" I probed, wondering if he was ready to talk about her yet.

He looked down and started wringing his hands, nervously popping a few knuckles. "It's all so ironic. Last year, when you took up with that guy and he turned out to be a killer, I was so hard on you. And, now I've—"

"Stop. There's no way you could have known how sick Sarah was. It's not your fault."

"The signs were all there. She was so possessive."

"I know. I can't believe she trashed my apartment and shot the windows out of my car."

"It looks like she wrote the message on your car, too. A couple cans of red spray paint were found in her apartment. She must have been stalking you all along. She followed you to the church that night and when Patricia failed to kill you, she stepped in to finish the deed. The fact that she even had a gun with her proves that she intended to cause harm. She was out to get you, Pippi." He'd started pacing back and forth. "All this time and I didn't even—"

"Stop Sean. You're not responsible for Sarah's actions. We can put all this behind us and start over."

"No," he said, standing abruptly. "Let's not go there. Not yet. I mean..." he shoved his hands into his pockets and shook his head. "This isn't a good time for me now."

"I understand, but I want to help you."

"That's not what I'm saying. I don't want your help."

His words stung. "I don't get it. We're friends. We should be able to support one another. I just want to be here for you. I need you to be here for me."

"I know. I should be here for you. You just lost Shep. You've been hurt ... you were almost killed." He was starting to get louder as he spoke, his features tightening with stress. He moved to the floor and knelt in front of me.

"I'm so sorry, Pippi," he whispered, his voice low and husky. I reached out to touch his face, he stopped my hand and turned it over, gently kissing my palm. I could feel the moistness of his tears. "I want you to know," he said. "That I was wrong this whole time. I love you. I always have. I always will. I just...." He looked away.

"You just what?" I asked softly.

He pulled away and stood up again. "I've put in for a transfer."

"What?" I couldn't believe what I was hearing.

"As soon it's cleared, I'll be transferring temporarily to Detroit. There's a case I'll be working undercover on. It's big. It'll be good for my career and for me."

I shook my head, unsure of what to say. I wanted to scream. *Why was this happening now? What about us?*

"It's for the best, Pip," he continued. "I need to get away from everything for a while. It's just temporary. I'll be back."

"How long will you be gone?" I whispered, trying to stay under control.

He shrugged. "A while. I don't know."

Something inside of me gave away. I knew there was nothing I could say to change his mind. "Go then," I finally said. A sense of peace washing over me.

He knelt down and pulled me up, bringing me close to him. "When I get back," he whispered, his lips inches from mine, "I'm going to come looking for you."

I wanted to believe him, but I knew better. My mind wandered back over the years of our relationship and the same old issues that had plagued us from the beginning. Even as he moved in closer, whispering promises about our future together, I knew something had changed—not with him, but with me. As I accepted his kisses and listened to his platitudes, my heart grew a little colder. By the time we finally said goodbye, I'd made up my mind. I realized I'd been holding on to an unrealistic hope for a future with Sean and it was never going to happen.

Sometimes, when someone holds onto something too tightly, they close the door to other possibilities. That's what I'd been doing all these years. I'd lost enough time. I was worth more than Sean was obviously willing to give me and I was done waiting for him. I was ready to let go and move on. Surprisingly enough, it didn't even hurt all that badly.

I was also ready to make some other changes.

I decided I was going call the attorney and let him know that I'd be taking over the Retro Metro. My insecurities weren't going to hold me back. Sure, I'd failed miserably at my old job, but for the last couple of years I'd proven that I *could* make a living following my passion. Shep must have believed in me, otherwise he wouldn't have left me the Retro Metro. All I needed to do was combine what I knew about the corporate world with my passion for resale merchandising, and I could grow the Retro Metro beyond everyone's expectations. I was going to make Shep proud of me.

Then there's family. After watching Shep's parents try to make up for the time they'd lost with their own son and seeing the Farrell family's ugly dysfunction up close, I'd learned just how important family is to me. I'd let things go over the years. I'd been caught up in my own life, my own issues, and had taken for granted the people that meant the most to me.

All in all, losing Shep and almost losing my own life had brought everything into sharper focus. I'd come to realize that life was too unpredictable and all I held dear could be taken away in a heartbeat. What's more, I'd wasted a lot of time waiting around for Sean. Well, I was done with all that. From here on out, things were going to be different. I was going to strike out on my own, move forward and live my life so that, one day when my time really did come, I could look back with no regrets.

THE END

ABOUT THE AUTHOR

A former high school language teacher, Susan started working as a freelance translator and writer after leaving the teaching profession. During her writing career, she has worked to compile several literary encyclopedias, text books, and medical reference dictionaries. In addition to her work as an academic writer, she has published several nonfiction articles in national magazines. Recently, she has turned to writing fiction and has published several short mysteries. *Murder for Bid* is her first novel. She lives in the Midwest with her husband and four children. To see more of her work, check out her website at www.sfurlongbolliger.com

Made in the USA
Middletown, DE
10 February 2017